# PUNKS

Robbie Moffat

**PALM TREE PUBLISHING**

**PALM TREE PUBLISHING**
Iver Grove, Iver SL0 0LB
and
W13th St, Wilmington, Delaware 19801

First published NOVEMBER 2022

Simultaneous published in the
United Kingdom and USA

Typeset: Verdana 8pt

ISBN-10: 0 907282830
ISBN-13: 978-0907282839

## **INTRODUCTION**

This novel is about two young punks travelling in South America in 1978. Their views on money, freedom, travelling, the getting away from reality, music, poetry, youth movements, hippies, punks and drugs.

Its what some kids of their age do with their lives, before they get married, mortgaged and chained. Some of them don't make it that far.

Life's hard on the road,
the pennies jingling,
the notes jaded, crumpled and torn:
a back pocket as a wallet,
in a pair of jeans
faded, creased and worn.

## TRINIDAD

Charlie Lampton had dreams of finding emeralds washed down from the mountains and lying in the gravel beds of all the rivers and lakes of South America. But he was only a nineteen-year-old who knew nothing of living hand to mouth. The Lost City of the Incas was Charlie's South America. The slums of Port of Spain held no insight for him, they were not real, they were still part of the dream. To Rob Tennant, his companion, they were the same slums he'd witnessed in Nairobi and Bombay. They were not new to him. They had the worm quality that accompanied poverty.

Finding somewhere to stay in Port of Spain wasn't easy. Trinidad was an overcrowded island, a melting pot of nations, milling it's narrow streets. The first offer they received was a quick hour's tumble in a bordello. They declined. You know how it is. They were tired from the jet lag and the heat. The London they'd left on an April's day had been 7C. Flying into a sticky 33C in Port of Spain, the pleasure of the flesh was far from their minds – pretty though she was. Trudging the streets for an hour, they found a reasonable room on Charlotte Street. At eight dollars it was a heavy price to pay for a bed for one night when they were supposed to be bumming their way around. They concluded that it was oil that was doing it, the black vulture rigs sitting offshore pumping the liquid up and pumping all the prices on the island up as well.

Charlie was happy to have somewhere to put his head down, a pillow to think from. He was amazed that he was in Port of Spain. He was Punk. Yet, he was only a Punk in the sense that he was the right age, of the right generation, and had been in the same hopeless looking dole queues. "Here you are, son," a Department of Employment assistant had said to him. "There is a job in a climbing equipment shop on Grey Street." "How much does it pay?" he had sensibly asked. "Twenty-three pounds a week" had been answered. "God! You can't even buy a pair of decent concert tickets for that," he had exclaimed. "Do you want the job or not?" had been returned. "There are plenty of others interested. After all, you haven't got any 'A' levels, have you?"

So that had been work: putting woollen ski hats on film star looking dummies and attending to snob nose students. It required little more than the ability to rub two skis together to make a sale. Talk of cushy, it bored the mind. Twenty-three quid a week didn't go far, and where in the grimy Newcastle had there been to spend it but at the City Hall or the Polytechnic. Life was all music. The Clash. The Buzzcocks. The Damned. The Jam. The Stranglers. Occasionally he paid to see bands like the skinny old Rolling Stones sweating it out after one number. The Sex Pistols never made it to Newcastle. Therefore to Charlie, Newcastle was the end of the earth.

Charlie was a middle class Punk. His father was a Union leader and lived in swanky Jesmond. When there was no music, all there was to do was drink. Newcastle was famous for its strong beer but Charlie had been sick of it. Without chicks, it would have been unbearable. He had caused friction by taking home girlfriends and playing the Pistols full blast. His parents naturally were unhappy with what he was doing with his life. He blamed them for not sending him to public school and his parents couldn't forgave him for being expelled with a couple of 'O' levels from the local comprehensive.

His father's socialist policies as a Trade Union leader hadn't instilled Charlie with anything but a hate for the establishment and discontent with his job in the climbing equipment shop. The only way he had relieved the boredom was watching re-run movies at the Jesmond Cinema. The past had held as much as the future seemed to hold. But in Port of Spain he was having a good night's sleep, dreaming of his first flight, the memory of light cloud, blue sea. When looking down on the Atlantic finally became boring, he took to reading Rob's *Pears Encyclopedia*, diligently digesting the section '*A Quick Guide to the Brain*'.

Rob's mind had been blank until Charlie mentioned warts. "Says here" Charlie quotes "that concentration on making warts disappear, the con-templation of them, willing them to depart in peace, is the only known cure." "That would suit the pacifists" Rob replied. "The ones who feel the only answer is to meditate, ruminate and leave the violent removal to others when meditation doesn't work." "Eh!" Charlie responded with a jaw-drop look. Rob waved him off with his hand. "Forget it!"

Rob was four and a half years older than Charlie, and as such, very pedantic. He had been raised in a tenement building in Glasgow, an average city slum. In the 60's, Glasgow had become a prime target for re-housing and Rob had watched as the bulldozers pulled down the tenements and pile drivers put the multi-storey flats up. It was his first experience of culture shock. It had been a nice peaceful slum area, now that it was a modern multi-storey flat complex, it became gangland territory. Rob wanted nothing to do with it. Fortunately he had enough brains to make the cut into a senior secondary school. It was a relief. He only had to hold his own against the school bullies once a month instead of every day. Until another government plan turned his school, overnight into a comprehensive. Things got rougher, Rob got tougher and wanted more and more to escape the violence. The area's community pride and spirit had evaporated. With the influx of people from other areas, the feeling that the people were better than their houses changed to the extent that the houses now seemed better than them. The familiarity of the area had gone. In five years, all Rob's memories of his early years were erased. Many of his old playing haunts had been levelled and multi-storey flats had sealed the memories under twenty-one floors of concrete in the name of progress and change. It was a pity. He had been too young to understand the changes. He felt as though he'd moved a hundred miles away, the different streets, the new people the changes had brought. He only understood how rapid the change had become when the building stopped, the influx of new people ceased, and his schooling ended, Although the change had destroyed his childhood background, it had stimulated a need for the constant change to be continued. Change seemed to promise hope, a future better life than that of his parents.

Like thousands of Scots before him, Rob moved to England. After two years, he tired of English life and took the Hippy Trail to India. It was a new horizon, but he and India wore each other out after a year. He strayed back to England. The changes to him out East had been amazing but he needed time to reflect and recover. He settled in Newcastle. Another year passed, the desire for more adventure festered. It took him off on a long trail as he bummed his way from Egypt to South Africa. He returned to Newcastle, his thirst for adventure quenched. He planned one more journey, then he'd give up the road. This time he had wanted to share his experiences of travelling with someone else.

"How are we going to get back?" Charlie asked. "We've got one way tickets to Trinidad, two hundred pounds between us and very little else." "Look" Rob replied "we'll get ourselves round South America and worry about how to get back later. The thing about life is that once you've found the way to somewhere, you always know the way back. Getting there is the problem." Charlie synthesised Rob's reply and felt more at ease. "Okay. According to the map there are thirteen countries. Which ones shall we go to?" Charlie continued. "God! You've got a lot to learn" Rob declared. "All of them of course!" "I thought this was a holiday" Charlie sighed. "Jesus, Charlie! There are thirteen countries. If you start off with a hundred percent, you're starting off with something. If you make fifty percent on that hundred, you'd still be above average. Without expectations, you might as well stay at home. To be the best, you've got to see the most. If you lose the thread of that while travelling, you sink into a world of hotel rooms and cheap restaurants."

Rob had his doubts about Charlie. It would have been better travelling with a woman. Rob's other friends had been too tied up in relationships or studying geography from the safety of an atlas, or like Melvyn Toad, had his money wrapped up in a sports car he was loathe to sell as he couldn't drag himself away from the steering wheel. The mention of South America had been a splendid idea, but once he thought of having to sell his red sports car, excuses issued forth like waterfalls. Nor would William go, his desire to be an ambitious engineer on the shop floor of industry exempted him from throwing it to the heavens. Nor could Alistair, who couldn't even get himself out of bed to find a job to earn the money to buy his air ticket out. So, that left Charlie Lambton, a young directionless kid, with no qualifications, no prospects and no idea of what to do next. He had left his climbing equipment job, in an attempt to leave home. He made several previous attempts, the first an effort to move to Oxford but he soon forgot that idea. The second was a move to Bangor to be close to a friend who had squeezed into university there. That lasted five weeks and he returned home, leaving a trail of debts. The third was a move to London, where he survived five days and returned to Newcastle home-sick. The final attempt had been a move to Northumberland to work for a Farmer Potts, but par for the course, he got bored and moved back to his parents' house. Charlie couldn't understand why his parents were so annoyed every time he returned. To them, their son was going nowhere.

But Charlie had latched on to something new - Rob Tennant. "What are we going to do when we run out of money?" Charlie asked again while they were hatching their plan to travel together. "Don't worry. I'll borrow some money from William, go down to Thomas Cooks, buy some travellers cheques then go back and report them stolen. Cooks will give me another set of traveller's cheques to replace the stolen ones. I'll cash them, give the money to you and you can go to Barclays and do the same thing. Then we'll give the money back to William and each of us will have enough money tied up in the traveller's cheques to see us through South America."

"You mean we'll cash the lost cheques in South America" Charlie said, catching on. "Oh no" Rob replied "its only a precaution. Basically the cheques are for showing at frontiers to satisfy the immigration authorities. It means no matter how broke we are, we can always prove we have sufficient funds. If we do get round to cashing them" Rob explained "the bank would have a hard time proving anything. If we signed each other's cheques, they'd never nail us." Charlie scratched his head. "So we won't cash them? Right?"

Rob still had his doubts about Charlie. He had met him shortly after he had been expelled from secondary school while he was still recovering from his Indian experience. The last thing he wanted was to be buddying up with a school kid. Yet somehow Charlie had managed to hang in there, hovering around the joints, smoking Rob's hashish and grass. After a while, Rob came to enjoy Charlie's brashness and inexperience. He was a fresh breeze after the sultriness of India.

Three years passed, life had its changes, Rob

went to Africa, and came back broke, yet he had set his mind on travelling around South America. When Charlie first suggested going with him, Rob had been wary. He told Charlie if he wished to be on the same flight, he had two months to save the money for an advance-booking to Trinidad. Charlie, with the chance of adventure burning in his veins, wheeled an' dealed, claimed back income tax, saved his dole and took a job on the side with Farmer Potts again. Besides the tractor driving, he fiddled with Farmer Potts while on the diddle. They would buy frozen chickens and rabbits from a Newcastle wholesalers, defrost them overnight and re-sell them at the Bigg Market as fresh farm produce at inflated prices. None were the wiser. A sum of money from his parents, on top of a camera, twenty quid for a leather jacket he sold to a friend and a quick buy-sell deal of a sports car to Melvyn Toad and Charlie had scraped his money together in time to book his ticket to Trinidad. It was then that Rob realised Charlie was actually going.

It was cheaper to fly to Trinidad than the South American mainland, a mere seven miles away. Regular air fares from London to the main Latin cities were cool rip-offs. From Trinidad besieging the South American mainland was an easy and inexpensive task. Or so they thought.

At the British High Commission in Port of Spain, they are shown into the office of Mister Cruickshanks. He looked at at them over his spectacles, his fine crop of eccentric grey hair falling over his brow. "I see" pausing to sweep his hair away from his eyes. "It should be no problem, seeing you have your own yacht." "Oh no, we haven't got a yacht." Rob informed him. Cruickshanks was aghast. "I beg your pardon? The receptionist told me you had a yacht." "Oh no, I wish we had" Charlie proclaimed. "Well" Cruickshanks pondered "that makes it a different matter altogether. Let me just consult my records."

Cruickshanks shuffled over to a filing cabinet. He pulled out a folder and opened it. "Yes, I thought so, for Venezuela you don't require a visa if you fly, but you must have an onward ticket." "What about arriving by boat?" Charlie inquired. "By boat…? Well it says here you need to have a visa issued by the Venezuelan Consulate." "Oh, that's a bummer. What about Guyana?" Rob asked. "Oh, that's no problem!"

Cruickshanks blinks over his spectacles. "It's in the Commonwealth. However, a return ticket is advisable." He takes off his glasses. "In my opinion, Georgetown is not the pleasantest town in the world. Why not fly to Venezuela instead?" Rob ignored the suggestion. "Are there any boats from Port of Spain to Georgetown?" "Difficult" Cruickshanks smiled "but if you try Huggins Shipping Agency maybe they can help." "We'll do that," Rob replied. "Thank you."

The Huggins Shipping Agency was near the port. "To Georgetown?" the representative retorted. "You're joking! Try Alstons Shipping Service." At Alstons Shipping Service, "Georgetown! We never go near the place" their representative declared. "Try Coastal Steamers." At Coastal Steamers, "Sorry, we only sail to Tobago. Try the docks, Juno the Customs and Excise man should know." They hunted for Juno, but when they found him he was in a foul mood. "Come back in ten days time" he cursed. "I've had enough of this" Charlie despaired. "Let's go and see about flights to Georgetown."

Rob was reluctant. On top of Charlie's impatience, they had only $330 (£170) between them, not counting the £700 of lost traveller's cheques, which of course were meant only for showing at frontiers. Enquiring in a travel shop, British Airways, Pan Am and Air France flights were all quoted $90 return. Charlie was for buying the tickets there and then. Rob was hesitant. "That would leave us with $150 between us to see the whole of South America." "So what? We've got to spend it sometime and I'd rather spend it in Georgetown than squander it here in Port of Spain." "I agree, but we've only been here two days." "I don't care," Charlie snapped, "two days is enough. We either take the flight or spend the same amount staying here for another ten days." Rob weighed up the options. "I get it, but I'd rather wait for a boat. You see nothing flying." "As if you see anything on a boat" Charlie sneered. "If we wait for a boat we might never get to South America." "Of course we will, you're just impatient" Rob replied calmly. "Rubbish! You're just too cautious" Charlie countered. Rob looked straight into Charlie's eyes. "And you are rash!. We need to think this through."

On that, the conversation ended and they headed along Charlotte Street towards their hotel. Turning up

Queen Street and taken up in thought, they missed their next turning, crossed George Street and were almost on Piccadilly Street before they realised they had gone too far. They made a right up a side street. Three Rastas were leaning against a wall. "Hey, man, you want smoke" one called out. "Sure" Rob replied. "Come on then, man, over here!" The Rasta led them behind a wall and produced a reefer. "Ah ask only one dollar a smoke." "You're kidding!" Rob exclaimed with pretended surprise to dispel any idea that they were rich tourists. "No man, dat here es one dollar." "Expensive, eh Charlie?" Rob said with a shake of his head. "Confuse me mine, man" the Rasta interceded. "Here man, try." He pushes the reefer Rob's way. Rob takes a couple of drags and passes it to Charlie. It is good weed.

The Rasta proceeded to try and sell them a pound weight for $150. Rob and Charlie, out of it money wise and head wise, feigned a waning interest. "Sure, man, great stuff, but I'm not sure, you know, maybe if we came back, you know, let us think it over like. Trust us." The Rasta nodded "You take your time, man. Ah be here."

Some Dutch bloke had once told Rob that he couldn't trust French or Italian travellers. The British on the other hand were friendly, honest people. Rob had laughed and told him not to take the British as a whole, for amongst the British travellers, lurked irregular types. He had been thinking of himself. He had ripped off two travellers for £240 on a hoax dope deal in Delhi. No one was perfect, flag or no flag, the Queen and all that, even the British were crafty liars at heart.

They made their way back to the hotel. They were well stoned. Charlie taking advantage of it, convinced Rob that they would be better flying out of Georgetown the following day. Ah, the dreaded weed, thought Rob, it's worse than drink for turning a man's head to do something he knows as folly.

Leaving Charlie spaced out on his bed, he went to the hotel lounge to watch television. It was showing an American cartoon he had never seen before. Sharing the settee with him was a man from St Vincent. They fell into conversation. "Well is dat so? Georgetown you go. Well so'd am ah. A have me a ship coming Monday and we sailing Georgetown. You wanta come?" "I have a friend," Rob tells him. "Dats OK, one, two, it no difference. Ah am da cook. You can sleep in ma cabin. It's a big ship, da captain don't mind us taking friends aboard." "That sounds great" Rob declared, still a bit wary at the chance coincidence. "What's you name? Ma is Lawrence." "Robert" he answered. He corrects himself. "Rob, call me Rob." "OK Rob. Ta day's Friday. Come Monday, we all sail Georgetown, OK!"

The cartoon ended, Lawrence lumbered off to his room while Rob slipped back to his. Charlie didn't hear him coming in and was caught masturbating. "Frustrated Charlie" Rob smirked "No! Just indulging in a little escape from this shit hole. I'll be glad when we fly out for Georgetown." "Well we're not," Rob interjected coolly. "We're going by boat." Charlie's face fell as Rob explained the talk with Lawrence. "And what happens if there is no boat!" "Faith, Charlie, let's wait for Monday and see."

Over the weekend they lived on *liver rotis* from the Spring Time Hot Roti Palace across the street. Charlie played a penny whistle in F key and compared his music with fifteenth century free form he'd learned at school. He said it was complicated, but to Rob it was little more than a screech. Occasionally, they saw Lawrence, who reassured them of his coming ship and meanwhile got round to admitting he was gay. Charlie backed off considerably while Rob became aware that Lawrence was making a play for him. Charlie told him to stay with it, if it meant getting on his boat. Rob played safe and began showing a lot of affection towards Charlie. He cut Charlie's hair with a large pair of tailor's scissors that would have been more appropriately employed for cutting off ears than the hair around them. It was hot in Port of Spain and Rob remodelled Charlie from a spiky punk style to a close crop.

Lawrence sat watching with twinkling eyes and the smile of an innocent child as Rob cutting Charlie's hair. His eye whites were red and bloodshot, and the dark brown pupils radiated a blankness that was impossible to penetrate. He was excited by the motion of the scissors and fixed his gaze on them. He openly confessed to his previous affairs with white men. Charlie remarked with "Oh really" or "Is that right?" Rob listened intently until Lawrence dropped the name of someone in the Royal family. They wanted more information but he quickly moved on to talk of his friend in Germany who one day would send for his black lover.

Lawrence continued to watch, as Charlie, satisfied with his new appearance, played cards with Rob. Charlie grew uncomfortable with Lawrence's staring, all to the backdrop of loud body blows coming from the cinema screen next door to their room. The room window caught the flickering of the changing cinema screen. It had been pirates, cowboys or soldiers not that long before. Now the new generation of movies like *Star Wars* and *Close Encounters* were competing with Bruce Lee who was showing in the cinema next door in 'Enter the Dragon'. "All these King Fu films are the same" Charlie muttered as he threw down the two of hearts. Rob picked up two cards. "I wish they'd show something else next door. We've been through the same sound track about twenty times since we arrived." Charlie played the three of hearts and Rob picked up three. "And the interlude music, I wish they could find an alternative to Bob Marley, great though he is." Charlie played another three. Rob cursed and picked up again. Lawrence sat quietly, trying to work out the card game, before finally quitting their company. "Funny old bloke" Rob said. "Doesn't say much does he?"

That evening they gave the Spring Time Hot Roti Palace a miss and ate chicken chow mein from the Champion Movable Food Wagon, down on Independence Square. The wagon owner gave them the spiel. "Heh, man, brother man, this chicken chows the best in town." Clowning around, he did his best to sell the benefits of Trinidadian chow. Rob and Charlie could do little else but laugh and splutter noodles onto the sidewalk.

On the way back to the hotel, Rob encouraged Charlie to buy his first green coconut. Charlie insisted on taking it back to the room and opening it himself with his Swiss army knife. He cut his finger to the bone. The blood splashed everywhere – the floor, his bed, ran down his leg – before he recovered his composure and used a match and Sellotape to splint his finger. "You'll tire of coconuts at this rate" Rob mocked him. "Never!" Charlie snapped, turning over in his bed to gaze at the wall and the map of South America he'd pinned there.

Sunday morning came. Rob awoke at six o'clock to Charlie rambling on about *I Ching*, *Confucius* and *Pyrrhonism*. It was too much for Rob at such an early hour. Since Charlie had got hold of the Pears encyclopedia (to Rob's annoyance), he hadn't let up on reading out aloud. Education and relevant information had gone to his head. Charlie had previously thought the *Guinness Book of Records* was comparable with the *Bible*. Now, the encyclopedia was proving superior reading to both. "Subbud, Transcendental Meditation, Scientology, Vitalism" Charlie mumbled, flicking through the pages. "Charlie! Will you shut the fuck up" Rob chided "or I'll take the book away from you. For the record, I'm a member of Subbud, have grown tired of Transcendental Meditation, have contempt for Scientology and have plenty of notion about Vitalism without being reminded of it. All I want is to sleep in peace." Charlie felt hurt. "I'm going for a shower." He banged the encyclopedia closed. Rob, with his usual arrogant manner and air of superiority had snubbed him again. Charlie felt like beating Rob to death. He was a smug bastard, and certainly knew how to make himself unpopular with his pedantic spouting. Fucking Aries twat.

Later, strolling down Frederick Street, they made up. A taxi driver tried to talk them into taking a cab ride around the island. They were depressed, he said, he could tell by their demeanour, he had experience of tourists. If the sun shone and the tourists frowned, the only thing to cheer them up was a trip around the island. Rob and Charlie looked at each other and laughed, told the cabby to piss off. They would have to be very sad tourists to pay $20 for an hour's taxi ride.

Over a paper cup of non-aerated grapefruit juice in the Calypso Pool Café, Rob read the local paper, the *Sunday Punch*, while Charlie was chatted up by the girls serving the drinks. Rob, in a cheerful mood, asked the girls why they found Charlie so attractive. "Oh" they said, "we like his body, his smile, his blue eyes, the gold ring in his ear." Rob looked Charlie up and down. "I don't know what you see in a lump like him. You wouldn't want to make love to him?" "Oh yes!" screamed the girls, stroking Charlie's hair and trying to remove his gold earring. Charlie seemed lost. "Which one wants to be first?" Rob asked the girls with a laugh. "Me, Me, Me," they all answered. Charlie shot up from his chair, shook off the girls and bolted for the door. Rob's laughter and the girls' giggles followed him out. A couple of minutes later, Rob caught up with him in the street. Little was said and they strolled down to the Mariners Club and had a Carib beer.

"Do you have any sandwiches?" Rob asks the barman. "No, sir. Da cook's still in bed." It was half past eleven, but Rob avoided the temptation to raise an eyebrow. They lounged in armchairs and watched an Indian dancer on television praise the coming of spring. While downing their beers, the Trinidad Tripoli Original Steel Band could be heard practising out back. Otherwise The Mariners Club was deserted and they were hungry, so they left and took a beef chow mein from Hoy Pings wagon on Independence Square. Time was passing slowly. Nothing much was happening in Port of Spain.

Back at the hotel, Lawrence sought them out. "Ma ship arrive tomorrow morning, and we all go five o'clock tomorrow night. Morning we in Georgetown" he grinned. "But ah don't have no money 'til da ship arrives. Maybe you give me ten dollars, an I give you all back tomorrow." Rob and Charlie glanced quickly at one another. "Sure Lawrence" Rob answered, digging ten dollars from his pocket. "Here you are" handing him the money. "Thanks" Lawrence beamed and left the room. "Well, Charlie, what do you think?" "I don't know. That wasn't a very good sign." "No. But if he rips us off, ten dollars is nothing. If he makes off with it, we haven't lost much." "True" Charlie agreed.

The following morning, there was no sign of Lawrence. His room had been vacated and the manager stated that he had checked out at six. Rob went down to the docks and asked if there were any boats leaving for Georgetown that day. As they had suspected, no. Past experience had taught Rob to be sceptical about plans, until they crystallised. Lawrence had cheated them out of ten Trinidad dollars (two pounds fifty pence sterling). Perhaps it would have been more if they had trusted him from the start.

"Well Charlie, it looks as though we're flying after all."

## GUYANA

Rob had longed to visit South America since his days in India. Asia had seemed commonplace and nothing out of the ordinary for young people like himself, travelling around in search of whatever they could find. Talk had often strayed to the romantic images of Latin America and numerous conclusions made that it was the continent to visit. To have been to South America was the ultimate in travelling. Asia had to be shared with millions of others, the elbow room limited and the respect gained from other travellers minimal. Anyone could go to Asia overland, it was no real test of initiative or endurance. It was easy going. Magic Buses plied the roads, hordes of kids clung to one another for safety. Asia was a kindergarten.

South America was something special. It was an isolated continent, approachable only by air. It was rumoured inexpensive, but no one knew much about the continent unless they'd been there. And the travellers Rob had met who'd been there were few and far between. "So this is South America" he told himself as he queued with Charlie at Guyanese immigration control. After all these years! What was his first impression of South America as he queued in the darkness of a clammy tropical evening? What did he feel besides the stickiness making his shirt cling to his back, the suffocating thick air that drew heavily on his lungs, the *kwa-kwa* of the crickets? The immigration officer, poker faced behind his desk, the queue of passengers, white-knuckled, clutching brief cases and wiping brows with handkerchiefs? What made the small airport terminal different from all the other tropical places he'd visited? It was the moths! Large brown moths, dashing themselves against the yellow light bulb above the immigration officer's head. Moths as large as small birds frantically fluttering around the passengers. The fine tropical moths from the interior of the Amazon settling on clothes, moths Rob had associated with Humphrey Bogart movies and Graham Greene books.

The immigration officer stamped their passports with the minimal of questions. As they cleared customs, Rob's attention was re orientated to the excitement of the taxi drivers fluttering around him.

He ignored them. "Excuse me" he asked an attractive Indian woman attended by two porters weighed down under kilos of baggage. "Do you know of anywhere cheap to stay in Georgetown?" The woman smiled. "How long you both stay?" she enquired. "Oh, a day or two" Rob replied, looking to Charlie. "Then there is no problem, you both come and stay with me."

That was how they met Amelia King, a Guyanese Asian touching thirty-five, beautifully radiant and looking no older than twenty. Charlie just couldn't keep his eyes off her. His mind started clicking at the possibility of sex. Rob directed him into the back seat of a taxi and Charlie, slow to understand, went to say something to Amelia, but Rob stopped him short. "My friend's still contemplating the Air France meal we had on the flight" Rob divulged to Amelia. "He lives in another world half the time. He's only nineteen." Amelia, sitting up front, turned her head with a mild expression of understanding. "That would explain it." Immediately all Charlie's hopes were shattered. "What did you tell her that for?" he uttered without Amelia hearing. "To take that look out of your eye and keep life simple" Rob replied. "So forget it."

It was a full half-hour's drive before they came to rest outside a wooden house built on stilts. A teenage girl came to the gate. "My eldest one" Amelia said with a smile. "I have five, all of them girls. Melanie looks after them while I'm away. She's a good girl for thirteen years old. But let's take the luggage inside and we can make ourselves at home."

From the outside, the house appeared large, but it was deceptive. The stilts gave the impression it was a two floored house, which it was not. The stilts served the function of keeping the house above the wet season floods and the occasional bursting of the sea wall a quarter of a mile away. Much of coastal Guyana had at one time been marsh, reclaimed by the Dutch who built extensive retaining walls and irrigation ditches and canals. Flooding was a way of life on the coast strip and as a result, all the houses stood on stilts. On the outskirts of Georgetown where Amelia lived, Lilandaal was beneath sea level. The inhabitants that weren't raised fifteen feet off the ground period-ically were forced to flee, or swim.

Inside Amelia's house at Thirty Three Back Street – a good one by the standards of the neighbourhood.

There were two bedrooms, a lounge, a kitchen area and a toilet with shower. For a Guyanese, Amelia was comfortably housed, even with five children, though it wasn't immediately apparent to Rob or Charlie.

She had begun to unpack her baggage and Charlie excused himself to take a shower. Rob watched as Amelia continued to unpack, producing bottles of shampoo, nail varnish, bobbins of thread, tins of talc, bars of soap, assorted mugs, cups, glasses and plates, packets of hair rollers and bunches of plastic flowers. "I do a little business" she declared with a wink. "Guyana's terrible. No this, no that. You can get nothing here, the government bars everything, the shelves in the shops are empty. I fly to Trinidad twice a month, sell a little Guyanese gold, buy a few things in exchange, bring it back to Guyana and make a little profit. I give the customs at the airport a little something and they don't check my bags. It is good business. A bottle of shampoo in Trinidad costs one dollar fifty. Here I can sell it for six dollars. With no man and five children I must do something to survive. It is always nice to come home. The children miss me."

Her other four kids, ranging from three to eleven, had been showing their faces sporadically since she had returned. "Melanie, put tea on" Amelia shouted to her eldest while giving the youngest a hug. "The things I do for you, baby" she sighed.

Rob and Charlie woke at Amelia's in the morning to a wet day. Charlie briefly couldn't remember where he was, then recalled excitedly that he had spent the night under a mosquito net. The tropics were a new experience for him and mosquitoes a new burden in life with which he was learning to cope. He was already covered in bites, the folly of taking a shower after dark now apparent to him. Carefully in the bright morning sunlight, he dabbed his swollen spots with anti-histamine cream with advice from Rob to refrain from scratching them.

Dressed, they joined Amelia and the children for a breakfast of crab that one of the children had caught in the nearby canal. Charlie was initially agog and Rob slightly amused as they set to with their fingers and sucked on the spindly legs after cracking and crunching the shells. Amelia welcomed them to stay another night so they could have a good look round

Georgetown. With the neighbours constantly calling to sample her Trinidadian wares, Rob and Charlie left her to her business and caught a route taxi into town.

They had taken Cruickshanks' advice and bought a return ticket from Trinidad to Georgetown. However, at the airport the immigration officer had not asked to see their return tickets. As a result they were intent on finding the local Air France office to refund their returns. Their luck was out, it was Tuesday and the Air France office was closed. At a loss, they bought two chicken rissole sandwiches from a market stall and stood eating them in the heavy tropical rain in the hope of deciding what to do next. Two cups of coffee later, they were still standing in the rain idly watching market life and the girls go by. Life in Georgetown was slow. Yet the buildings were beautiful, large rambling wooden houses three or four floors high, rickety old staircases, ambling upwards, painted white or in the pink hue of the setting sun. Cruickshank's description of Georgetown was totally inaccurate.

On Main Street stood St George's Cathedral, the largest wooden building in the world, a veritable paradise for termites, a recurring nightmare for the ever-employed restoration carpenter who had been there longer than any bishop or verger. Every five to six years, he and his workers completely replaced every piece of wood, then started all over again. The Cathedral offered Rob and Charlie shelter from the rain while they continued to contemplate what they should do next. The choirboys were rehearsing and gave the Cathedral a solemn atmosphere occasionally broken by the bang of the carpenter's hammer. Two of the choirboys, late for rehearsals, came cycling furiously down the aisle on their pushbikes. When spotted by the verger, they ashamedly dismounted, lowered their heads and proceeded to the altar wheeling their bicycles. The verger remained frowning then turned away. The two boys broke into fits of giggles but the choirmaster caught sight of them and motioned them to quickly join the other boys. Their voices soon joined the rest, and the cathedral filled with the voices of angels.

"I was a choirboy once" Charlie uttered, lying horizontal on a pew sucking on a mango. "It certainly doesn't show, sucking a mango like that in Church. Where's your respect?" Rob replied. "If you'd been a choirboy, you'd know that the only people who respect the Church are the ones who never go to church" Charlie stated with conviction. "You don't have to tell me that, mate" Rob fired back, prodding the pew in front with his finger. "I went to Church until I was fifteen, and that's where I first learned about the class system. All the way through the Sunday School and Bible Class years, I thought doing good deeds and going to church every Sunday was what it was all about. But then I noticed that I was expected to put a sixpence in the plate like the other kids, instead of three pence which was about all my mother could afford." Charlie is not listening. "Then they began to ask what my father did, did my mother go to church or was there anything really unusual about my family's life. When I told, in all honesty and innocence, that I hadn't been christened and my mother had been married when I was five years old – nice boy though I was – the Church began to close the Bible in my face." Charlie continued sucking his mango. "That is parochial Presbyterianism. It is the breeding ground for the class system. The Church was not the great house of ideas and understanding that I thought it was up 'til then."

Charlie raised his eyes to the ceiling of the largest wooden building in the world. Rob droned on. "I thought it time to stop going to church when the wives of two elders caused a fuss bickering over who should chair the Women's Guild. The congregation including the Minister and the Church Officers were split between the two wives so fanatically that at the Sunday Service many of them refused to speak to one another. I watched the childish display and began to have an insight into their petty struggle for power. The religious side of the Church was secondary to the status and self-esteem gained from thinking oneself a goody-two-shoes. It disillusioned me, so I said goodbye to the Bible Class teacher and left the insanity of the Church for the Big World."

"What do you mean the Big World?" Charlie said, still sucking on his mango. "That sounds a load of crap to me. The Big World! Bullshit! It sounds like the end of a fairy tale." "It was" Rob smiled. "I started going to dances, discos, bars, even started smiling at girls." Charlie stopped sucking his mango. "I wouldn't mind having a go at Amelia" his mind refocused by Rob's mention of girls. "No chance, mate, you're just a wee babbie. She's a woman, you wouldn't know what to do with her." "I bet you I've had more women at my age than you had when you were nineteen" Charlie boasts. "I'll not dispute that, but I bet you can still count them on the one hand?" "And a thumb" Charlie adds in correction. "Let's get out of here before bore me with a whole dung load of childhood memories. You'd think you were an old man the way you crack on."

Amelia had suggested they visit the botanical gardens, Georgetown's most reputed show piece. Rob stopped a passer-by and asked the way, but Charlie was reluctant to go. He wanted to drink Coca-Cola in a bar and stay out of the rain, but he conceded to go along when Rob told him it was next to the Zoo.

They were not in the botanical gardens five minutes when Charlie had seen enough of weird trees and jungle plants and was making for the Zoo. Rob let him go and remained awhile to gaze at the flora. The head of the discarded statue of Queen Victoria poked up from the lily pond. How empires decline. The mighty Empress had been removed from Main Street shortly after Guyanese independence and had been the focal point of great civilian unrest. Guyana's population was almost fifty percent Asian – fifty percent African. The Asians had wanted the Empress to remain on Main Street, but the Africans had instigated her removal on gaining power and had dumped her face-down in the botanical gardens' undergrowth. Some anguished empire die-hard Asians had restored some dignity to the Empress by righting her back on her base. She was the last reminder of British rule and the lilies were taking her over. Yet the Asians pledged she would return to her exalted position on Main Street, if and when they ever wrestled power from the hands of President Burnham and the Africans.

Meanwhile, Charlie was in the zoo talking to a hyacinth macaw. He had already exhausted the salmon-breasted cockatoo and the grey-winged trumpeter and, on seeing him, the green-backed maroodie headed for the back of its cage. He had caught the happy-eagle brooding and a laughing-falcon making faces at a tropical screech-owl. The sun-parakeet was sitting in the shade. A white faced tree-duck was being chased by a channel-billed toucan, not to mention a seven-coloured parrot showing off its splendour to a common black-hawk. The zoo was was fun. Charlie fed the Indian elephant a mango and hissed at a ten foot snake wrapped sleepily round a tree. He found the crocodiles tame and boring, the jaguars and cheetahs lazy and equally as boring. Rob caught up with him by the monkey cages as the rain began again.

They left the Zoo, hitch-hiked back to Amelia's, washed and ate a meal of rice, chapattis and freshly caught fish from the canal. Charlie gave a quick hour's low down of England to three of Amelia's spellbound neighbours and declined too hastily offers of marriage to two of their daughters. It seemed that they considered him a handsome English bachelor and highly eligible in the Guyanese marriage stakes. Personally he was flattered, yet he had hoped they would suggest that he could show their daughters a good-time. Instead they idly chattered on about breeding, financial background and matrimony, their daughters being set up in a semi-detached house in close proximity to London, so that they wouldn't have to travel far from Heathrow Airport when they came to visit. Surely, Charlie thought, that was all in the future, showing their daughters a good time seemed a much more practical consideration.

Rob thought Charlie had been a bit too hasty in declining the offers. The least he should have done would have been to hold out five seconds longer before saying no. His vehement, instantaneous reply had slightly offended Amelia's neighbours, and there was no further mention of marriage. They drank sherry and rum, then showed the neighbours the sixty-odd selection of British postcards they had with them for just such an occasion.

The following morning they were out in the yard, washing themselves and their tee-shirts. Amelia's estranged husband Leon showed up. Going into the house he proceeded to beat the shit out of Amelia who ran hysterically about the house screaming at him to leave her alone. Charlie looked at Rob and signalled that he wanted to intervene, but Rob told him it was best not to interfere in domestic quarrels between man and wife, especially as they were strangers. They carried on with their washing, while the neighbours stood by their windows, listening to Amelia's sobs and

Leon's hands contacting with her body in heavy blows. "If you had made love to Amelia" Rob said to Charlie "he'd be hitting you instead of her."

Leon appeared from the house, politely said goodbye and departed, closing the gate behind him. The two boys gave a good quarter-hour's breathing space before re-entering the house. Amelia was sitting in an armchair, sobbing quietly, trying to pull herself together. "He's no good that man. He lives with another woman and still he won't leave me alone. Whenever he comes here he wants money so he can go trade in marijuana. Whatever money he makes, he spends on his other woman. I tell him come back and we can work something out. But he says his other woman is such a sweet doll he can't leave her. He knows I've just come back from Trinidad and have money. This time I say no, so he beat me. What can I do? I just want to be left alone."

"Melanie, put tea on" Rob called to her daughter. There was little they could suggest bar the obvious that she either move away or found another man to protect her from her husband. They could comfort her no further.

After the tea, and Amelia had calmed down, Rob and Charlie journeyed to the Air France office. Their tickets were refunded in the form of Miscellaneous Charges Orders (MCO) to the value of twelve dollars. All that entitled them to was twelve dollars towards any international flight they cared to make within a year. The tickets were valueless, but the MCO's would be of particular help to them later in their journey.

Returning to Amelia's, they decided to push on to Surinam. Amelia, in a more cheerful mood, offered a few suggestions and tips for the road. Saying their goodbyes, they walked to the main coastal road and caught a bus to Rosignal. Rob read poetry from the encyclopedia while someone up front in conversation with Charlie told him that army life would do him a world of good. They crossed the Berbice River by ferry and jumped on another bus that would take them to the frontier town of Springlands.

They arrived in Springlands mid-afternoon. Rob went to change ten dollars in the Arawak Hotel. It seemed just like any customary border town found in Asian countries, the hordes of money changers swarming round him like flies. Yet for Rob they lacked the sparkle and the twinkle in the eye of the stoned Pakistani or the bonged out Afghan, the shankered Indian or the wrecked Nepali. They all seemed tame or indifferent and content to wait until their next life to make their fortunes. Their money changing profession was one of drinking beer and watching the world pass by until the next deal. And though these guys had their hoodlum looks tattooed on their faces, it didn't stop the odd one from throwing a guarded friendly smile Rob's way.

With a chicken chow mein lunch behind them and the river ferry to Surinam not until next morning, they took a stroll down a small palm fringed track to the river bank. They sat and contemplated the Corentyne flowing seaward. On the far bank, the Surinam rain forest stretched as a ribbon of fungus green, hazy beneath the grey and misty clouds of a tropical rainstorm two miles distant and heading their way.

An old ferryman stopped to chat. A curvy school teacher on afternoon break wriggled past. From out of the trees, a long curly haired Mestizo appeared in rolled up blue jeans, feet shod in a heavy pair of unlaced hobnailed boots. He clumped his way straight towards them. "Hi! Passing through?" he beamed. "Yes" Rob replied. "Got anywhere to sleep tonight?" "No, not really" answered Charlie, quick on the uptake. "It's likely to rain soon, you better come and stay at my place" he grinned.

Juno Declerc was a twenty-year old kid who was unemployed and had no desire to find a job. All that mattered to him was music and playing with his band. Smoking marijuana was part of the music culture and travelling around was part of the romantic scene in which he occasionally involved himself. He'd had a few adventures and experiences with both, and had got as far as thumbing rides in Brazil before the homesick blues and starvation set in. So there he was hanging out in Springlands until something else came along. Everyone else knew that before long that something else would be a woman.

Juno led them to his house, introduced them to his mother. Mrs Declerc was a pleasant maternal woman who invited them in and immediately began preparing a meal as Juno related to Rob his poverty stricken travel adventures in Brazil. His pretty sixteen year old sister Florence cornered Charlie with the family photo albums. Charlie didn't seem to mind much as his eyes wandered from the photographs on to pretty Florence. The portraits of Uncle William, ex Governor of Nigeria, didn't interest him in the slightest, Florence was the prettiest picture in the house. Ironically, in the background, the local radio station was playing Ringo Starr's single 'Photograph'.

Mrs Declerc finished cooking, sat them down at the kitchen table and served them chicken chow mein. It was good chicken chow mein but was chicken chow mein the only food in Springlands? Mrs Declerc poured out the tea. "Terrible second rate tea this. You know, there is no soap in this country. It's these communists. I don't like communists. We've just had a new extension built onto the house. There is no glass for the windows, no bowl for the toilet, there's nothing but wood. It's these communists, they control everything. Look what's happened since they took over. It's these Russians, they are a waste of time! Even the Americans would be better. That Burnham man is playing at being a good Russian and a useless president."

In escape, Juno took them upstairs to the new verandah. Some musical friends in the street shouted up to him. "You coming to jam tonight, Juno?" "No man. I've got company. You got your guitars with you. Why don't you come up?"

The playing of guitars and mellow singing began. The mosquitoes commenced to bite as the peanuts were passed around. All the talk was of music – Charlie wondering if they'd ever heard of New Wave or Punk – Rob mentioning he knew someone who set off from England to play for a reggae band in Jamaica. Juno's band played rock. They reckoned they had a head start if they could pull their music together as they were living in the only English speaking country in South America. But it was hard. Springlands wasn't exactly on the map, and Guyana wasn't renowned for its music, and sitting on a verandah being bitten by mosquitoes didn't improve their playing.

Mrs Declerc brought out the boys a tray of tea and bread smeared in orange butter. "The shortages, you know" she excused. The Tilley lamp was pumped and Juno and his friends continued to entertain with their guitars and songs for another hour. Meanwhile, Mrs Declerc prepared a camp bed for Rob and a mattress for Charlie to sleep on. With the evening growing late, a mosquito coil was lit and they were left to put their heads down for the night. Not long afterwards a naked Florence slid quietly under the sheet and wrapped her arms around a sleeping Charlie, no doubt dreaming of mangos.

## SURINAM

Surinam immigration and customs control proved to be a mere formality, arrival in New Nickerie a simple stepping from the authorities building into the sunshine. Rob and Charlie sought the shade of a large tree and from its cool watched some local workers joke and laugh as they laboured. "Well, looks as though we're in for language difficulties if they speak Dutch here" Rob announced. "Suppose so" Charlie grunted, thinking about food. "Lets change some money, I'm starving."

Rob tried to change Guyanese dollars for guilders with the workers, but they were not willing to help. One pointed to a hotel nearby. They trudged into the hotel bar, dry mouthed and empty bellied. The Friday afternoon pay-day drinkers turned to stare at the two strangers, then broke into a babbling of Dutch. In the crescendo of stuttered greetings, someone offered Rob a swig from a bottle of Black and White whisky. "Ah, man, just like being back in Scotland" he said showing off by downing a large measure. "Typical Scotsman" Charlie scoffed as Rob passed him the bottle. Charlie took a swig and pulled a face as the whisky burnt his throat. "Typical Englishman" Rob laughed.

A drunk motioned them to take a chair at his table. They found themselves sharing drinks with two local workers and two soldiers who by some miracle were kept upright by the table and the backs of their chairs. One of the soldiers still sober enough to order another bottle, had the barman serve a bowlful of cooked chicken legs. No sooner were they on the table than their eager hands were fighting to fill their mouths. They sent the picked-clean bones arcing through the air to feed the dogs drooling by the door.

Finished, one soldier suggested they go to another bar. Rob and Charlie went with the flow. Moving on to the Blue Hawaii Hotel, they straightened themselves up in the street, then staggered into the bar, past a dozen drunks, drunker than themselves. They ordered up more Black and White, and more food. With strong insistence from all sides, Rob was obliged to chew on a turkey's foot while Charlie opted out by wielding a pool cue. He took on the local champion and sent everyone into shrieks of laughter as in his drunkenness he tried to change the rules of the game amidst shouts of protest from the champ.

Someone handed round a bag of cassava crisps and threw Charlie a turkey's foot. Confused by his own new rules, Charlie returned defeated from the pool table and chewed on his snack. Rob passed round the postcards, and somehow in the melee of hands, the one of pregnant Juliet on the balcony calling, "Romeo, Romeo, wherefore art though" disappeared. More whisky was poured, their vision blurred and mono-chrome ensued.

Charlie with his brains sloshing, and Rob, his Scottish blood thinned out, were still coherent enough to understand that the key placed in Rob's hand opened the door to Room No 2. The pair waved farewell amidst the workers' cackles and the jukebox playing '*I Hear the Sound of Distant Drums*'. They crawled up the stairs on their hands and knees. Rob with uncontrollable swaying found the key hole and as the door swung open, a shattered Charlie tumbled onto a bed which collapsed under his weight. He was out of it. A flash of lightning lit up the window and the rain began belting down. Rob, still on his feet, closed the door and opened the window wider to let a rush of wet afternoon breeze waft him sober.

It was evening when Charlie awoke with a sore head, and with a feeling of despair. He wondered what he had done with his life since leaving school, almost three years earlier. Rob gave him an abrupt answer. "Nothing." Charlie thanked Rob for saving him the bother of thinking about it. "It's nice to have friends" he replied sarcastically. Rob laughed, left the room to take some night air on the verandah and felt no guilt at leaving Charlie sweating on his bed, wondering where his last three years had gone.

The mosquitoes were biting, so he rolled down the sleeves of his shirt. Perched on the rail, he thought over the women he had been flirting with before his departure from England. It was little comfort to have left them behind, yet they were hardly the adventurous types. Nice girls but nothing serious. After all there was plenty of time. A friend's father had once told him that there was no point in getting married until his late twenties, for by then all the best women would be divorced, and free again.

His thoughts tapered as he began to doze. He suddenly jolted awake again as he realised he was perched on the verandah rail. He looked down. If he had slid off the wrong side, it was a twenty foot drop to the ground below. A small alert man joined him on the verandah. Quick with the wit and short of praise for life in Guyana, he was a carpenter. The money in Surinam was better than anything he could earn in Guyana. He asked Rob to join him for a walk so that he could show him the pokey little town whose inhabitants had a lot of money to splash but only one thing to sped it on, drink.

Josh Greenheart guided Rob through the Dutch styled streets of New Nickerie, pointing and commenting here and there before temptation lured them into a bar. He bought Rob a beer and asked him about his travelling life. Rob said that didn't amount to much. He'd been to Asia and Africa and done Europe when he was younger than Charlie, yet still he felt he had accomplished nothing. It was all very well to say he had been to Calcutta, Cairo or Cape Town, but he hadn't exactly achieved anything. It seemed to Rob that no matter how much he travelled the world, he'd accomplished nothing. He didn't have a university degree, he hadn't written a book, he hadn't made a fortune, he didn't even have any kids. He hadn't invented anything, he hadn't entered politics, he had not helped mankind in any shape or form. To date all he had done was travel the world and that was hardly any effort at all. There seemed little value in what he had learned and his experience was of little use to anyone else. He couldn't work out if his non-commitment to anything was a strength, or a failing? Yes, he had been to places that other people knew from films and books. His world was more real than the dreams of a bored university graduate or the worker who had to support children. Yes, maybe he undervalued his freedom, his zero responsibilities other than to himself in a world where achievement was not measurable. Perhaps to others, his lack of responsibility was an achievement. He didn't know. His present nothingness was an expression of his frustration, his wish to break from his travelling life and seek a new direction. University and children were options still open to him.

As the Parbo beer slipped down, Rob was returned to the reality of the bar he was in with Josh Greenheart when a motorbike was parked in a corner.

The bar was festooned with posters of Jimi Hendrix, Rasta Man and Make Love Not War. Marley's 'Jamming' played on the juke box. Apart from the fact that nearly everyone was black, it could have been anywhere. They walked back to the hotel saying little, parting outside Rob's room.

Charlie was still awake. "You know, Rob" Charlie said in all seriousness, "I haven't done anything with my life so far." Rob laughed and flopped on his bed. "That's why we're here, Charlie. Get some sleep."

Morning, and they were out in the market place, ready to move on. They crouched over cups of coffee in a rickety shack watching the rain come down. Charlie said his head felt hot, but Rob dismissed it as a hangover. A man offered to take them to Paramaribo at twelve o'clock in his pick-up. The rain was easing and as it was still only nine o'clock, so they decided instead to get out on the road and hitch-hike. An old couple drove them a few kilometres to a place called Paradise. They waited ten minutes before a Chinese man driving a pick-up truck stopped and told them to climb in. He had been to London and spoke a few words of English, enough to communicate that it was a nice day, apart from the rain. There was little else they could find in common with the driver and the conversation grew thin until they reached a shallow river. Crossing a river in a small dug-out while the pick-up went across on a floating wooden platform, Rob flashed the postcards of home to the Chinese driver. Instantly he wanted the postcard of the Household Cavalry on parade at Buckingham Palace as a souvenir of his time in London. Rob gave it to him. Forty-five kilometres further on, he dropped them at a crossroads, and thanked Rob for the postcard. They in turn thanked him warmly for the ride.

Four field workers, idly sitting by the road, acknowledged their presence with a wave. There was little time to return it. A white farmer pulled up and drove them five kilometres further on. Dropping them off, he turned down a track, and had barely disappeared into the bush, than the heavens opened. The downpour forced them to seek shelter in a bus stand.

Rob played his harmonica, while Charlie piped out the *British Grenadiers*, *Good King Wenceslas* and *Auld Lang Syne* on his penny whistle. Charlie said his head felt worse and thought it might be sunstroke. Rob looked at the big black clouds and said it was more than likely caused by his abysmal whistle playing. But to make sure, he pulled out the encyclopedia and turned to the section on medical ailments. Armed with some new information, he asked Charlie to open his mouth so he could look at his tonsils. Charlie told Rob that he was wasting his time as his tonsils had been taken out when he was eight years old.

As the rain eased they waved down another pick-up truck. Going to Paramaribo? They sure were! They jumped in the back. Pressed close up against the back of the cab to keep dry, they had not gone far when the truck stopped. The driver and his friend got out and with a twelve-bore shotgun took aim at a great white stork hovering overhead. He missed. The stork disappeared hastily into the marshes. Several other small birds took to the air in alarm. Rob surmised the wildlife in that normally peaceful swampy environment, devoid of humans, had got complacent. The country was two-thirds the size of the UK with a population of three hundred and fifty thousand. The coastal road through the low lying marshland was the country's only main road. In one direction lay the sea and in the other, the largest jungle in the world, the Amazon rain forest. No one fully knew what mysteries the interior still held, or what tribes inhabited the impenetrable vegetation, and no one really cared. Surinam's wealth was in bauxite, which accounted for almost ninety percent of its export trade. Supplemented with rice, sugar and citrus fruits, the country enjoyed a standard of living that shamed Guyana, yet by European standards was still very low.

Driving on, they filled up at Victoria, then made a detour by turning off the main coastal road. The jungle took over as they bumped along a narrow track that led to a ramshackle, mud, bamboo and corrugated-iron bungalow. Rob and Charlie dismounted from the truck and stood quietly in the small clearing of banana tress, watching as an old man and a young boy loaded three hundred coconuts into the back of the pick-up. The driver kept count while his friend negotiated a fair price with a half naked man holding a machete while pointing at an old wrinkled lady. The driver handed over the cash and agreed to take the machete man's mother back to her homestead. With the loading completed, everyone drained a coconut. Rob and Charlie clambered back into the tail of the truck. They had to move a mountain of coconuts before they could settle down comfortably. The truck started off with the old lady up front.

They trundled back to the coastal road and continued towards Paramaribo. The rain fell again, and by the time they got dropped off in the capital, they were damp, dirty and uncomfortable. They felt out of place. The better dressed locals turned to stare as they wandered wide-eyed along the street. In a music-playing snack bar, they drank fifty-cent coffees to work out their next ploy. They decided that Paramaribo wasn't such a hot place to be hanging around. With only seventy dollars left between them, it was best to keep moving. To pay for an overnight stay seemed unnecessary, but the rain made sleeping out a damp prospect. Charlie was a little dejected and Rob tried his best to remain cheerful.

After a Chinese meal of pork rice and noodle soup, they sat on the ferry stage in the gloom of the evening, their arms wrapped round their legs, their chins resting on their knees. They stared out across the river. Nothing much was said. They watched as the ferry glided towards them from the far bank of the Surinam river, the night lights twinkling, a crest of white-water breaking at the bow. The shifting silhouettes of passengers flirted in front of the deck lights. A hint of smoke snaked upwards from the ferry's funnel into a patch of blue-black sky before dispersing into the overcast clouds. A mosquito bit Charlie and he groaned in annoyance. The smell of rain was again in the air and all the heaviness prior to a tropical downpour weighed on them, pinning them to the view. Rob, in anticipation of the arriving rain, rose quickly and cursed the mosquito biting stillness. He paced up and down the length of the ferry landing while Charlie remained motionless.

The ferry docked. The passengers filed off on foot, or wheeling bicycles. The boarding passengers stepped on. Rob signalled Charlie to pick up his pack. They were leaving. Charlie didn't argue and followed Rob blindly aboard the departing ferry. The landing stage was raised and the ferry glided back out into the dark of the river.

On the far bank they disembarked. The rain began to fall. They took cover in a shelter, and sitting on a makeshift bench they listened to the rain running off the corrugated iron roof. They repelled the attacks of the insistent mosquitoes. They were unbearable. Sharing the bench with them was a seventeen-year old Asian boy also caught by the rain. He spoke a little English, schoolboy English, but it was good enough to get by on. They fell into conversation and answered his youthful questions which half-the-time they knew he didn't understand. He was a pleasant boy, though perhaps a little short of brains. Yet experience had taught Rob that the fewer brains a person had, the nicer the person usually turned out to be. The boy invited Rob and Charlie to spend the night at his parents' home.

When the rain eased, they followed the boy to his home. The house was a cardboard shack with a tin roof. The only furniture was a table and a chair, countless sacks of rice, an oil drum or two and posters of the Swiss Alps on the walls. On the plot of cultivated land out the back, the sunflowers and maize dropped heavily with the rain. A few chickens huddled together in the eaves in protection against the wet. The boy's parents were shy, his father wrinkled by work and the sun, his mother tired and worn looking by years of heavy domestic toil. His sister was a little girl clothed in a dress made from sacking and gazed with beautiful big brown eyes that evoked pure affection. Her eyes made the whole shack shine. The father rolled a cigarette and passed round his tobacco and the mother made mugs of tea. It was a rare social occasion and made them proud that their son could speak English. In their time, they had hardly mastered Dutch. They were third, perhaps, fourth generation descendants of the original workers brought from India to labour on the sugar plantations and cultivate the land. They had no social status within Surinam and respect did not often come their way. They had their piece of land and nothing else seemed to matter much as they grew their own food.

It was a bonus in life that their son was going to be something more than a farmer. That he could speak another language meant so much. The two strangers would never have entered into their life if their son could not have spoken English. It was a measure of their faith in having kept their son at the state school. Life in Surinam promised more, now that they were independent. Before, everything was ruled from Holland, a distant place across countless seas. Now, with Paramaribo as the capital, their son stood a good chance of doing well in the city when he finished school. He wanted to go to Amsterdam, but they were against it. The future was in Surinam. Even the threat of the Brazilians taking over could be forgotten if their son stayed and worked in Paramaribo. Bringing the two foreigners home was success in itself.

Rob and Charlie were tired, and the boy led them to a smaller shack twenty yards away which housed a makeshift double bed. Before he left them for the night, he asked a few more questions about how to travel to Europe the cheapest way and about work once over there and were the girls nice and if they could give him the address of a girl he could write to as a pen friend, he would be happy. Charlie wrote out the address of his seventeen year old sister and told the boy she was very pretty. The boy broke into an embarrassed smile, neatly folded the piece of paper and placed it in the breast pocket of his shirt. He wished them goodnight and skipped off joyfully. It was one of the happiest moments of his life. It was his first step in escaping the boredom of Surinam and going off to Europe to see the world.

Rob and Charlie were out on the road the following morning, hitching. They didn't have to wait long. A saloon car pulled up. The driver was a young man in his thirties accompanied by his wife who appeared to wear the trousers. The wife cradled a young baby in her lap. Rob and Charlie filled the back seat and the car took off. The conversation was polite and was ended when they settled back and listened to the radio. The jungle whizzed past, little shack type villages here and there as blurs in small clearings. Roger Whittaker droned on the radio, then was quickly followed by Nina Simone's 'You Put a Spell On Me'.

They crossed a couple of rivers by ferry and eventually reached the small town of Moengo. The couple dropped them at the crossroads out of town and Rob and Charlie thanked them. But not so fast! The wife insisted that they were owed ten guilders for the ride. Charlie laughed and said "No chance." The wife, demanding her ten guilders, said she would call the police. Rob, equally adamant not to pay, told her to go ahead. The wife turned to her husband and told him to do something, but he shrugged his shoulders.

She made him get out the car. As he looked at them, he didn't fancy taking Rob and Charlie on single-handed. There was nothing else he could do but get back into the car. They argued. They should have made it clear from the beginning that they wanted money. His wife was a smart-arse. One of these days she was going to get him into real trouble. They didn't even need the money he said as they drove off bickering.

Rob and Charlie were left by the roadside. The occasional car whipped past, but none were interested in stopping. The rain began to fall again and they took cover in a shelter. Everywhere they went, there was a shelter close by. They offered shade from the sun as well as the rain. Under this particular shelter sat a man of Indonesian descent. He smiled at them, then continued to watch the rain for the next half-hour. Jumping to his feet, he waved down a mini bus and paid the driver to take him to Albina, the frontier town with French Guiana. He turned back to Rob and Charlie, thought for a moment, then waved to them to board the mini bus, signalling that he would pay for them. On the bus he told them that a white man had saved him from drowning a few years before and he felt indebted. Paying for their bus fares gave him an opportunity to thank the white man again. Rob and Charlie understood and felt touched, and made the best of it by sprawling out over a number of the seats.

They were in Albina by twelve o'clock. The immigration officer had gone for lunch and wouldn't be back until one. "To hell with it" Rob declared, hopping into a dug-out. "Who needs an exit stamp?" "Goodbye Surinam!" Charlie cried out as the dug-out carried them across the brown Maroni River and towards the shore of French Guiana.

## FRENCH GUIANA

Rob and Charlie's dug-out ground to a halt on a sand bank of broken bottles glistening in the sun. It was a hot fifteen minute walk to find the immigration office and a further half hour before they found the immigration officer. The formalities completed, they left the office as it began to rain again.

St Laurent du Maroni was a village plucked out of the heart of France and placed in the heat of the South American jungle. It was French right down to its bread rolls and bicycles. Perhaps the profusion of tropical vegetation and the oppressive heat made it different from the average village in Artois or Lombardy, but that was all. The rest was perfectly French. Beneath the creeping trees and above the crawling plants stood the walls of the old St Laurent Penitentiary. It is sometimes mistaken that all the French criminals transported to Guiana ended up on Devil's Island, but in reality only the life prisoners were sent there, where conditions were considerably more bearable than in St Laurent, where life was hell. Few ever survived St Laurent. Malaria, yellow fever, dysentery, malnutrition and starvation killed most off, and others died at the hands of the brutal guards or fellow prisoners. At St Laurent the prisoners worked for their food. If they were ill, they couldn't work and therefore weren't fed. The weaker got weaker and no one ever got stronger. On Devil's Island, the murderers and traitors were allowed easy tasks if they behaved well. At St Laurent, the petty thieves and criminals were treated with contempt and spat upon. For most, a better fate would have been the guillotine. It would have brought about a quicker, fairer end and final punishment for whatever small crimes they had committed. St Laurent had been the worst deal a man could get from French justice.

It was Sunday and everywhere was closed. Not a soul in sight. All were indoors escaping the rain and having their Sunday lunch – beef steak, salads, bread, wine and everything else French, talking in loud voices which drifted out into the street through the slatted shutters, the odd peal of laughter lifting a sleeping bird from a roof as the rain drowned out everything else. The boys sheltered under the eaves of the local market on the Cayenne Road. Rob read the encyclopedia, while Charlie fell to doodling on a piece of paper. Although wet, the day remained warm as they sat enjoying their rest, little concerned about throwing out a thumb at the rare passing car. A man, dressed in a pair of blue cords with a matching a light weight shirt and an Indian colour band around his neck approached them. With a shock of long grey-streaked hair, a black bushy beard, tanned arms and face, with a heavy pair of boots on his feet, he greeted them with a big smile.

He was Brazilian and sat by them, produced a cigarette and a piece of folded paper containing some weed. He motioned Charlie to roll up, while he and Rob exchanged knowing glances. Charlie liberally laced the tobacco rolly, lit up, and they got stoned. The Brazilian coughed on the tobacco, then commenced to gibber away in Portuguese, Spanish, French, whatever took his fancy. He was from Sao Paulo and had hitch-hiked through the Amazon to Venezuela. Sao Paulo hadn't been good for his head. The city was growing so fast he couldn't keep up with the changes. It was the fastest growing city in the world and it wasn't doing him much good. However, he had to go back, there was nowhere else he enjoyed living so much. He hated Sao Paulo, but he wouldn't live anywhere else. He concluded that he just needed a rest that was all. And before he had fully decided whether he did like Sao Paulo or not, he was up on his feet and saying goodbye. He disappeared into the interior of the village and that was that.

It was growing dark, and the rain came and went in heavy showers. They were hungry and found a small Chinese woman selling kebabs opposite the village cinema. Screening was Clint Eastwood in 'For a Few Dollars More'. They gave it a miss. What they really craved was a cup of tea, but nowhere was open. As the rain started to throw down again, they gave up, removed their shirts and ran through the downpour, back to the shelter of the local market. The night closed in and the rain obliterated the rest of the world as they prepared to sleep. They lullabied themselves into slumber with Charlie's sweet penny whistle playing and Rob's mellow tones on his old tuneless harmonica.

Half past six, they washed in the morning dew. After a wait, they were on the road being whisked towards Cayenne at eighty miles an hour. The driver put on an Abba cassette. It made the jungle and the open road a pleasant dream which made them nod off continuously. Rob awoke to Ritchie Haven's '*Sometimes I Feel Like a Motherless Child*' and the driver telling him that he was turning off. They had gone a hundred and twenty miles in little over an hour and a half. The jungle roads of Guiana couldn't be beaten for speed. They were forty miles from Cayenne and while waiting by the road, Charlie went for a shit in the bush and used a giant jungle leaf to wipe his bum.

A Chinese man stopped and dropped them on the outskirts of Cayenne at the Seven-Up factory. One last ride in a pick-up took them into town. They were hungry. They bought a metal cooking pot, six eggs, bread and a litre of milk. They walked to the beach and set up beneath the trees in the shade of a lovers meeting place. Collecting driftwood, Rob made a fire while Charlie fetched some water from a nearby house. The eggs took an hour to boil. Meanwhile they studied a young couple cavorting around in the sand. Charlie went for a swim and Rob called him in to eat. The meal was simple egg sandwiches, but they enjoyed it because it was their own cuisine.

Rob left Charlie by the fire and wandered along to the town quay to make enquiries. He talked to a man from St Lucia who told him that a boat left for St George d'Oiapogue every two weeks. That would see them to the Brazilian frontier, where they could catch another boat to the city of Belem on the mouth of the Amazon. The downside was that the next boat to St George wouldn't leave for another twelve days. The alternative was to fly from Cayenne to St George. The small plane went most days of the week and cost twenty dollars each way. Rob thanked the man for the information, and stayed a little longer to hear his story about the forty-five kilo fish he had caught the day before.

Rob returned to Charlie and gave him the news. They decided they would go the following day and buy two plane tickets to St George. That would leave them with twenty dollars between them. Tempting thoughts of cashing their lost traveller's cheques occurred, but they reckoned it was best to wait until they ran out of money. They would need time to practice each other's signature.

The day went quickly. Rob played his harmonica, Charlie bought some vegetables from the market and they cooked a passable meal on the fire. Dusk came on and both remembered past times in Newcastle. The fire glowed, the breeze stiffened and Rob found Gemini in the sky. They bedded down and had settled when it rained again. Both swore like hell, grabbed their belongings and dashed for the shelter of a block of flats where they tried to sleep under the tenants' cars. Disturbed after half an hour, they moved to a shelter further up the beach. An uneven narrow wooden bench became their beds.

The sunrise came over the palms. They awoke to the parks department men brushing out the shelter. It was just too French. Breakfasting, Rob sat by the market place while Charlie sought out the airline office. Rob was already thinking of the traveller's cheques and of how dangerous pen and paper were. One could sign one's whole life away, putting his signature on the cheques, he would be signing his own confession. If Charlie booked the tickets, they would be down to maybe ten or fifteen dollars once they got to St George. At least the would be facing the Brazilian frontier. French Guiana was okay, but there were better places in the world.

Cayenne was in every way another small French town, with French customs and French personalities. Pretty but nothing to inspire or to set the passions raging. They may as well have been in Europe, after a breakfast of croissants, bread, cheese and orange juice. Where were the paellas, the hot Latin blood, the revolutions on every corner? This was not South America. It was little France a la Latin. Huh, Rob observed, there goes a blue gendarme wagon full of blue uniformed policemen. I ask you? he asked himself. There has to be more to South America? Guyana, Surinam and French Guiana? Probably countries he would forget about.

Brazil, that provided him with much more exciting thoughts. Portuguese or not, life would be much cheaper and more relaxing than the previous two weeks they had endured. Phew! He craved a *quart du vin*. They'd had no alcohol in Guiana, yet supposedly they were there to have a good time. Well, he would see. Travelling was always up and down. In India he had lived like a king by comparison. One day he would have to return there, life was easy out East. Perhaps time had hazed his bad memories as well. It was so difficult to be sure about the past. Memories deteriorated as fast as the experiences came anew. They say fish is good for the memory. Dope certainly was really bad for its effect on his past. It made his memories stutter and glare back at him through the haze as a lie. It was better to be alive and involved with the immediate. Charlie came into Rob's vision, waving the tickets, a big smile on his face. "We go tomorrow."

The tree-top plane ride in through the corridors of cloud, over the broccoli patch of Amazon green, was a daunting experience as the small plane began its descent to the village below. Engine failure and no-one would ever find them in that jungle. Charlie leaned forward in relief, surveying the quarter mile wide River Oiapoque. He only had bedtime stories to compare it with. It was just like reading a book … the Amazon jungle and its vastness enclosing a tiny village lost to civilisation in the equatorial backwaters of the world.

The description was apt. St George d'Oiapoque was a habitation of some five hundred tribe people and colonial guardians. Law and order was enforced by three gendarmes and three French Foreign Legionnaires who passed their time playing cards or scrabble, and drinking. It was a relaxed settlement, far removed from Cayenne and European influences. The village was inhabited by fishermen in dug-out canoes, women who ran to the shore to buy their fish, children playing and diving into the river from the landing stage as they were watched by old men sitting benches. The rain rolled in from across the river, the dogs lined up to have a turn on the latest bitch on heat, the cockerels fought or chuckled over who had lost. On the far bank lay Brazil, a world of creeping jungle and uncertain sounds with no palm trees to indicate any semblance of human habitation.

Rob and Charlie disembarked from the eight-seater plane. A gendarme asked them if they were going to Brazil. Yes they replied. He stamped them out of the country and wished them well with their onward journey.

There was the sudden realisation by Rob and Charlie that with eleven dollars between them, they didn't have much money to continue their journey into

Brazil. Once again the thought of cashing the traveller's cheques entered their heads, not now as a passing fancy, but as a necessity. They would have a better time if they did so. After all, Charlie wasn't into being made a better man through starvation. Rob wasn't into going hungry either. Not with seven hundred pounds of traveller's cheques just begging to be cashed. Anyway, everyone did it, didn't they? Or was that how criminals convinced themselves that they were right? There was no point in being good honest law abiding self-respecting citizens when the hunger of expectation could be solved by a simple signing along the dotted line. They had come to see South America and even if it meant by foul means, they could secure their dream enjoyably without any enduring misery. They somehow would face the consequences later, but if they lived now, the rest would take care of itself.

Unfortunately, there was nowhere and no one in St George who would cash their traveller's cheques. A muscular Brazilian, kitted out in blue shorts and yellow football shirt in preparation for the upcoming World Cup in Argentina, told them of the bigger Brazilian village of Oiapok further up river. Maybe they would have some luck there. They jumped into a local dug-out and directed the boatman to take them there. They had nothing to lose but the five dollars it cost for the ride to Oiapok.

Forty-five minutes later, they were in Brazil, sitting in the local eating house, drinking excellent coffee, listening to 'Please Don't Let Me Be Misunderstood' with no way out. No-one would cash a traveller's cheque. On top of that, the only way to leave the village was by the river they had come in on. The local boat to Macapa on the Amazon river wouldn't call for another six days. Unable to cash a cheque they wouldn't be able to pay the fare. Charlie was despondent. He reckoned Oiapok was a hole, while Rob thought they had dug it themselves.

Money overtook their conversation. They couldn't decide whether the coffee was going to cost them two cruizeros or twenty. 'Bad Moon Rising' blared in the background and the rain came pouring down. The situation seemed quite pathetic. Rob fell to thinking that the next step was to sell something. He wondered what would be first possession to go. He eyed Charlie's camera.

In desperation and with a lack of alternatives, they thumbed a ride in a dug-out and returned to St George. No one was surprised to see them back, or for that matter had been aware that they had left. Their immediate concern was where to shelter from the rain and to sleep for the night. It took just five minutes for them to find a disused shed just off the village square. It was close by the river and upstairs lived an old Brazilian fisherman and his wife with their adopted nephew, Corruba. They didn't seem to mind having the two strangers sleep downstairs. No one had made use of the shed since the last great flood.

The worry of how to escape St George gnawed at their thoughts. Going back to Cayenne was tempered with the realisation that they didn't have the money to buy a return plane ticket. During a nagging night of sleep in which Charlie dreamed of being back in Newcastle, booking into an hotel room and seeing all the occupants for the last ten years, morning came and they were faced with their present difficulties anew. With two small bananas each for breakfast, hunger was beginning to gnaw at their bellies as well as their minds.

Then by chance they met Ricardo Pestamista, an escapee Brazilian running from drink, women and song to claim his citizenship in France. His father had been a romantic Frenchman seeing the world, his mother an equally amorous Amazonian into handsome men. The union had brought about Ricardo being endowed with dual nationality, and which at last, he was going to France to take up. When he reached France he would renounce his Brazilian name and adopt his new name Ricard Argent. His current name had been fostered on him by his mother's need to marry when his real father left her, and in the end she had sold herself to the highest bidder, the local money lender.

Ricardo had no desire to follow into the business of his step-father that he described as a cross between Fagan and Scrooge. He had no desire to see his step-father continue with his rip-off ways, so he'd stolen his step-father's household savings, received his mother's forgiveness, and set off on the road to France. Armed with a dodgy birth certificate and an even more dubious passport, he'd fled Sao Paulo State and journeyed through Central and Northern Brazil to

Oiapok and crossed the river to St George. Although he resented his step-father, he had paid for his education. He had learned French and English besides the usual applications of calculus and molecule structures that are useless to a country boy. It was the very fact that he had been a country boy thrown into boarding school with a group of spoilt city kids that had made him determined that one day he would leave Brazil and go to France. His classmates had told him of holidays they'd had on the Riviera and climbing the Eiffel Tower. Their experiences had made him want to live like that and now Ricardo was half way to fulfilling his boyhood aims.

Ricardo was now in France, but had only got as far as St George and met Rob and Charlie going the other way. Unknowingly they fell into competition. All three had heard of a small plane landing and had walked the kilometre or so to the airstrip to find out more. The plane was flying back to Cayenne. Disparaging Charlie's schoolboy French, Ricardo harangued the poor French-Canadian pilot all the way into the village about taking him to Cayenne. Charlie tried to butt in, but Rob nudged Charlie to lay off and let the Brazilian do all the talking. There was no point in forcing the pilot into a corner in which he'd come out fighting like a cat, and take off without any of them.

Unfortunately, what transpired between the pilot and Ricardo over a couple of beers in Modestines, the local bar, was that the pilot agreed to take Ricardo to Cayenne, but waved his finger in all his Frenchness and said "Non, non, non!" to our two British bums. Ricardo made his apologies, and as he headed out the door with the pilot, in a farewell gesture, he slipped Charlie one hundred and twenty francs.

That night, with restored faith in life, the clouds shifted and let Gemini and Orion shine through. The two bums sat at Modestines bar waiting for their first full meal since New Nickerie. They would have eaten their own cooked food in economic sanction, but it was Sunday and the local stores were closed in Catholic reverence. When the lentil soup was placed on the chequered table cloth, the two set-to in a clatter of spoons and slurping, their other hands free to grab the bread and pour the wine. When finished, they dropped their spoons in all urgency and sat at the table with their knives and forks in their hands. The three

Legionnaires propping up the bar turned with amused smiles. Modestine's girl, Lulu, came rushing out with the second course, bush-pig and chips. Neither Rob nor Charlie gave a thought to what it was and gulped down their nosh. The final course was a dry piece of home made Madeira cake, which they swilled down with a third carif of red wine.

The three Legionnaires turned back around and continued to prop up the bar. As previously stated, besides scrabble or cards, drinking was the only other social pastime in St George. They were there to protect the frontier from any Brazilian invasion force looking to rid South America of the three Guiana colonies. France's paranoid thinking imagined that Brazil desired a coastline onto the Caribbean and the rest of the hinterland bounding the Amazon. As long as the French government had the Foreign Legion in Guiana, the Brazilians would nurse their longing to add the Guianas to their Federal system. Whether the three Legionnaires were aware of the fine political knife-edge they sat upon was not obvious. One went behind the bar, put on an old French record and all three wavered on their stools, and sang boisterously.

In the morning Rob and Charlie awoke with a hangover as the radio upstairs gently eased out soft refrains of 'Summertime'. It was a peaceful day and a large boat sailed up the river which they suspected was the Brazilian government boat that sailed to Macapa. But they dismissed that as their alternative escape as they didn't have enough cash to pay for two tickets.

Rob sat on the oil drum outside the shed. The street outside No.2 Rue Maurice Sparce was muddy. There were hens in a coop across the way, a concrete telegraph pole erected on 20.4.1958 with a disused light on the side, bush, overgrown trees and coconut-less palms all around. Plainly visible was the galvanised fence round Modestine's yard and the hotel balcony. The local sewer ran down the middle of the path that led to the river on the left. At the end of the seventy yard Rue, ran the main track from the Square to the Gendarmerie. Next door to Modestines, in a small house, lived a little woman who had let them cook their Quaker Oats for breakfast on her gas bottle cooker. Next door to her sat a big fisherman watching the cockerels fighting and the young children playing.

The village radio mast rose into the air, its red evening lights still bright in the grey morning sky. The French flag in the square half poked over a building.

The house at No 1 Rue Maurice Sparce suddenly broke into loud Latin American samba music. The only other thing to do from the oil drum was to watch the dug-outs on the river, the shifting clouds, and a little orange monkey tied to a tree. In the lulls the dogs could still be heard fighting for the bitch.

Charlie around the side of the shed was taking a piss. There was a leaf crawling along the ground, wriggling like a serpent. He stared at the leaf in wonder. Curious, he got down on his hands and knees and discovered an ant carrying the leaf along. He watched, his attention focused on the ant, not the leaf. It had fooled him, but never again. There was no substitute for experience.

In the event of no other option, they decided to wait for the monthly supply boat back to Cayenne. They could cash some travellers cheques there. It was due in little over a week. If they spent ten francs a day, they'd last out with food. It would mean a repetitive diet of sardines and rice, or macaroni and sardines, or rice pudding with bananas, or porridge, or bread and cheese spread. Upstairs above the shed, young Corruba living with his foster aunt and uncle, had taken a liking to the two strangers staying down below. He had seen them asking Mrs Cocina if they could use her stove. As a result, he had let them borrow his uncle's spare primus stove and for a franc had bought a bottle of kerosene for them from the local store.

Corruba knew himself to be a strange boy. None of the other children spoke to him, except to ridicule his appearance or imitate the way he spoke. To them he was a jungle boy. Brought up in the bush of Brazil, half Indian, half Negro, he had been deserted at an early age and had been reared by successive nomad jungle families. Left to his own devices, he had become a loner, happiest in the wilds, climbing trees and stalking armadillos and anteaters. He never had much use for speech and besides the few essential words of tribal language and Portuguese, he had never learned to express himself with words. With the exploitation of the Amazon jungle gaining momentum, Corruba's tribe increasingly came to settle on the

Oiapoque. They came under the influence of Brazilian governmental control. At their small settlement, the authorities built a school, and along with the other children, Corruba was expected to attend. The incentive for sitting at a desk was two school meals a day. As this eased the tribe's food shortages, the children were coerced by their guardians to go along.

Corruba attended school as the fancy took him. For days he'd be content to eat manioc dug up by his own hands, green bananas, or a pineapple if he could steal one from a farmer. But always he'd been lured back to school to sit at a desk labouring painfully for his two meal reward. He learned little and his understanding of Portuguese was little better than that of a three year old child. He was now about ten years old and the school authorities thought there was little they could do with him. A fisherman relative and his wife who were elderly and had no children of their own offered to look after Corruba. In time they tried to teach him how to live in a more civilised environment. At first he reacted strongly to having his shoulder length hair cut and being forced to wear shorts in place of his loin cloth. Eventually, they got him to wear a tee-shirt and occasionally to wash his face, but all their patience, failed to get him to wash in the river. His jungle smell remained and he occasionally ran way in despair back to the jungle when he couldn't understand what he was being taught. Other times he just caught the call of the wild in the wind.

After five or six years, the bandy legged, wild eyed, busy haired boy moved to St George with the old couple where higher prices were paid for the fish caught. Corruba was no use in a dug-out, his fear of drowning made him nervous and frightened the fish. His aunt instead got him a deliver boy job for the local store and bakery, as well as being the odd job messenger to the surrounding jungle villages. He quickly came to know everyone, but conversely they came to know him and his odd manners. Paradoxically, his bad Portuguese in a French speaking colony set him back. The upside was he couldn't understand the taunts of the local children and so found them easy to ignore. But not always. Once in defiance, he had dropped his shorts and began masturbating. The kids were speechless until Modestine came flying out of her restaurant with a bread knife and quickly dispersed the gathering.

But back to our tale. Charlie was cleaning the primus stove. Rob consented to let him take the stove apart to clean it properly. Rob reminded him of the time he let Charlie take his Francis Barnet motorbike to pieces. It had taken him weeks to get it going again. Rob believed that if something wasn't broke there was no point in fixing it. Charlie carried on regardless, unscrewed the components of the stove, cleaned them. It was light relief from the previous hours of unfulfilled boredom. He put the parts together again. With no great surprise to Rob the stove no longer worked. Charlie became irate and frustrated. Rob peeved that he had foreseen the outcome, suggested Charlie should go and buy some more kerosene to help rebuild the jet pressure.

Charlie, heavy shouldered and sullen faced, returned with a half litre of kerosene from the store. The primus still wouldn't ignite. Corruba showed up and offered to help. Charlie, in his usual off-hand treatment of the smelly jungle boy went off in a tizz, and left the task of fixing the stove to Rob and Corruba. He sat glumly on the oil drum shouting at them that they weren't going to get it going. He was sick of rice and sardines anyway! St George was a shit hole place to be stuck without money! He'd always thought travelling was adventure and excitement, not fiddling with a fucked-up primus stove.

So much for diamonds and emeralds, all he'd seen were tropical rain storms and mile upon mile of jungle. Call that adventure? There and then, he'd rather swap it for the comfort of an armchair watching David Attenborough, than be stuck in the jungle himself. It was all a waste of time! Here he was, sitting on a rusty old oil drum, on his left a river chock-a-block with rotting old dug-outs, and on his right a ramshackle hotel and a few broken down wooden huts. Useless. Absolutely primitive and these two in the shed fiddling on a knackered old primus stove. What a screwed up place to be imprisoned in.

Corruba and Rob coaxed the stove to work. Corruba with the pricker, Rob with the matches. Rob struck the last match with no success. Charlie threw his arms up in despair while Rob trudged off to the store for another box of matches. Corruba with the measure of Charlie's character and delighting in taking the rise, made faces at Charlie, pulled out his penis and much to Charlie's disgust, furiously began masturbating. Rob returned with the matches to witness Corruba's antics He immediately threatened Corruba with his knife. He'd cut it off if he didn't put it away. Corruba instantly responded and they started on the stove again. This time it gushed into flame, giving them a better burn than they'd had before. Rob praised Corruba, while Charlie turned his back and huffed and puffed. Corruba began screeching like a monkey. Rob put their behaviour with each other down to them both being young and stupid.

During this time, the three Legionnaires had been out the back of the shed repairing a long boat they had swindled a fisherman on. Their boredom was driving them off the land and onto the river. Even propping up the bar had become tedious. Each sat on an upturned bucket, sand papering the hull, singing. Corruba hating their awful singing. He dashed upstairs and switched on his uncle's radio. A loud click, followed by a louder hum, a wail of bagpipes and Paul McCartney's *The Mull of Kintyre* drowned out the Legionaries. Corruba caught in this double musical dilemma, shrieked, bounced up and down like an irate baboon, then hysterically flew screaming out of the house and leaped head first into the river. Rob and Charlie dashed after him and pulled him out.

It began to rain, the Legionnaires stopped signing, and the bagpipes faded on the radio to be followed by Tom Jones's *Delilah*. A wet Corruba shook himself like a dog and they all returned to the shack.

The rain lasted four days. Charlie had begun to believe his funeral would some day be in St George. It had taken the distraction of their encyclopedia and cards to stop their brains from frying. *Jumping Jack Flash* played on the radio upstairs as Rob put their pan outdoors to collect some water for an afternoon cup of tea. The previous night's meal had been a farce. The stove had packed up and Charlie had lost his temper. Corruba mercilessly ridiculed him, and Rob disconcerted by their bickering, had knocked over the pot of rice left to soak. Eventually, they proceeded to cook two fish they had bought for a franc, but the bones stuck in their throats and after some sustained willpower to keep eating, they threw the fish and banana leaf plate out of the back window. The rice pudding to follow tasted exceptional, but the mess Charlie made in opening the coconut he had earlier climbed a tree in the rain to cut down, made it necessary to evacuate their eating area as he let swing with a rusty machete, sending pieces of husk flying in all directions.

They had been in St George eleven days and there was still no sign of the local supply boat. The rain had kept them indoors for most of their days, the mud attaching to their bare feet and dampening any desire to move around the village. Charlie lay dejected on the floor, wallowing in self pity and composing poetry. Rob handed him a cup of tea and tried to empathise as Charlie was on his first trip and experiencing his first long wait. In many ways, Rob had been through the waiting in Asia and Africa and understood the level of insanity waiting brings on. Yet he too was feeling the days dragging out, any belief in escape a fantasy as he tried to keep his mind active and away from thoughts of despair.

At night when the clouds cleared, Rob looked to locate the *Southern Cross*, *Centaurus* and *Argo Novis*. The sky was fitting into place. He had worked out the exact relationship between *Orion*, *Taurus*, *Auriga* and *Gemini* though the *Pleiades* were lost behind hazy cloud. During the day, the encyclopedia kept his mind occupied. He thought on politics and public affairs and British democracy, his past travels and freedom of speech. He mulled over ideas and beliefs and saw the limitations on drugs and obscenity restrictions. Yet of all the countries he'd visited, his own seemed the most libertine. Perhaps one day he would dig deeper into the injustices in his own country. It all passed time. Useless or wasted, thought passed time. The fourth dimension they occupied by waiting. For without these mental distraction, Rob knew his time in St George would be as anguished as Charlie's.

Charlie dragged himself from the floor and staggered to the oil drum, bubbling with inner frustration before dashing off into the rain. He could hear the throbbing of a boat engine coming up the river. Rob heard it too. He hastened to the river's edge to join Charlie now filled with hope. They listened. They heard singing, loud singing which shook the rain from the trees. "*Viva la France!*" rang through the green jungle woods as up the river with the flag of

France over the bow, the landing craft of the 2<sup>nd</sup> Battalion of the French Foreign Legion came into view. Charlie blinked a couple of times, while Rob rested his arm on Charlie's shoulder and sighed "Bloody hell."

The landing craft pulled into the bank by the village square. Was there ever such a motley a bunch of military men assembled wearing army uniforms, lined up for roll-call in front of Modestines? To describe the assortment of men that made up a battalion of the Foreign Legion could fail to convey the brutality of their faces or the sorry state of their minds. From the smallest four-foot-eleven Legionnaire, with one boot, to the tallest six foot seven killer covered in scars and tropical sores, the rest of the squad covered every type of ailment or disease, mental and physical that a medical dictionary could list. Their appearance as a whole was one of a gang of desperadoes armed with knives, revolvers, rifles, clubs and metal spikes sticking out from their boots; sharpened elbows, knees and chins, battle-scarred from practising on one another in the barracks. Each man looked capable of flooring ten Scotsmen, twenty Gurkhas or fifty US Marines. And the officers? One look from them turned a man's knees to jelly and his heart to stone.

The three Legionnaires stationed in St George ran by struggling into full jungle kit, having been caught unprepared by their compatriots arrival. Word had passed around that the Legionnaires were being shipped out to fight the Commies in the African Congo. The troops would be staying the night and in the morning sailing to Kourou. Charlie's eyes lit up. "That's near Cayenne, right?"

Just after dawn, to add to the excitement, a fifty foot boat anchored on the Brazilian side of the river. Two crew members in a dugout came ashore to buy beer for their captain. They had seen the Legionnaires' landing craft and decided to be as quick about their business as possible. A desperate Charlie asked them where they were going. Neither of the two men spoke English, but they told Charlie to get in the dug-out with them. Rob watched as they took Charlie across to the other side of the river to speak with their captain.

The captain was drunk and in a high spirited mood and on seeing Charlie, broke into smatterings of English. "Where are you going?" Charlie asked with the biggest smile he could muster. "My boy! We go to

Belem." "Belem" Charlie whispered to himself, not believing it. "You couldn't take me and my friend, could you?" he asked the waltzing captain. "Certainly. Bring your friend and luggage. But be quick, we sail in five minutes. We don't want a run in with those Legionaries."

Still in disbelieve at their good fortune, Charlie was canoed back to the French side of the river. He and Rob gathered their belongings. There was no time to say goodbye to Corruba.

They got into the dug out and departed French Guiana for Brazil.

## THE AMAZON

When the *Ely* set sail, she had come at long last as their ship in the day. The grins on the faces of the Legionnaire officers standing on the shore was one of relief at not having to refuse Rob and Charlie passage to Cayenne. It hardly seemed believable after thirteen days by the banks of the Oiapoque they were on their way to Belem.

On board, with the captain and a crew of seven, there were numerous woman passengers from the Cassipore River with their men, all from the same village. One man, the apparent leader, sat drinking with the captain, exchanging stories, calling out to the women in teasing tones. He was a tall fellow, beginning to lose his hair as he neared his fifties, his right arm missing from the elbow down. He had a mean smile which revealed a touch of ferocity developed over years of dangerous living. He was a crocodile hunter and was fixing a price with the captain for his skins. He called out to the 'Princess', the party's woman of fancy, to look after the young English boy and pointed to Charlie. She needed no coaxing. She had taken a liking to his blue eyes and had hooked him by the waist, squeezing his body close to hers. Charlie, momentarily embarrassed, smiled and disentangled the Princess's arm, while the captain and the crocodile hunter laughed loudly. Princess drifted away and took up with one of the crew.

Charlie went to join Rob sitting by the fo'c'sle, rocking with the waves. "There's eighty thousand different types of tree in the Amazon" Rob stated. But Charlie was drifting, his thoughts momentarily resting on the shoreline and a wooden hut on stilts. He could hear the bilge pump, the voice of the captain telling stories of his visits to Paris and London and the ports of South America. He saw the faces of the various women and the swinging hammocks slung from the beams, the odd plastic mattress underneath. The comings and goings from the engine room were a blur, the smell of beef and bean stew cooking increasingly nauseating. Then without much more ado, he lowered his head over the side and threw up.

The *Ely* was out on open sea and though calm by Atlantic standards, still took the waves with a roll as she had no keel to keep her steady. She was an old wooden pre-war Second World War fifty foot ketch, with an open hold, and little room between the hammocks to swing a cat. Her sixty horsepower engine on full diesel had her splashing along at a steady six or seven knots. With the wind behind her and the sail on full sheet, she could cruise at ten knots which added some respectability to the old girl. But her timbers creaked, and leaked water through her planks. She had seen many a trip. The latest from Belem to French Guyana and back had already gone one month and seventeen days. She was feeling worn out and the crew had become sloppy and careless in maintaining her. Supplies had run low and there was little diesel to keep the engine running. She couldn't be blamed if things started to go wrong.

Captain Brazil dropped his passengers off at the small village of Sao Joao, some hours up the Cassipore River. It had been a crowded night for him and his crew. The passengers had drunk him out of tea and eaten him out of everything but the beans. But he had his croc skins. The small village always guaranteed good crocodile, the interior lakes and swamps awash with them. They even lurked by the wooden planks that formed the village walkway along the river bank. They were easy prey when they were only three feet long.

The captain had gone hunting in his younger days, and the Cassipore had always offered the best return for the dangerous business in hand. He was glad he'd given up the actual hunting himself. He'd come close to losing a limb a few of times, and once nearly his life. He was happy most of his money was now in cows, though he said that if a man knew what he was doing, he could become a millionaire by exploiting the wild life in the Amazon. That included the Indians. They were a sad lot of savages. He was lucky. He came from an aristocratic family, spoke French, Spanish and English as well as his native Portuguese. He ate beef for breakfast and drank rum at night. He liked to spend money on shore and be generous to his crew onboard, and although smuggling cows to Guiana one way and dealing in sharks and crocodile skins the other wasn't strictly legal, at least he was a self-made man.

His pair of blue shorts, light blue shirt and sandals weren't much for a man whose hair was beginning to grey, but for a fifty-six year old, with tanned skin, smoking Dunhill and with his own private yacht anchored in Guanabara Bay, he could call himself a playboy. Presently though, with most of his ready cash spent, and down to his last two barrels of diesel, getting back to Belem was his major focus.

The rain raged down and a canvas was erected to cover the deck. Rob flipped through the encyclopedia, and reckoned by the violent swaying of the trees on the bank, that it had reached force seven or eight on the Beaufort Scale. Manuel, the helmsman, a small quiet negro with a moustache, switched on the ship's transistor radio and tuned into one of the Caribbean stations. The interference soon forced him into defeat and he switched it off. He rested in his hammock listening instead to the rain drive against the side of the canvas.

The captain nodded to sleep and awoke some hours later and decided the wind had dropped sufficiently to risk them sailing back down the river and out onto the open sea. The crew were being kept in the dark, they didn't know if the captain would be taking on diesel, nothing seemed certain. They didn't like the idea of relying heavily on the sail at that time of year. Not with the strong winds. Nor did it help matters that the moon was close to full and was producing equatorial tides that could maroon them on a sandbar or drive them far out into the wild Atlantic.

Belzario, the first mate and Roberto, the engineer, had been with the captain for years and accepted the risks. The grumblings started by Bronco, taken on as a hand at Cayenne, were echoed and amplified by Mula, the acting cook. They were tired of the slow progress being made down the coast and the captain's continuous side-dealing. Mula had little more to cook than beans, the occasional piece of beef, and unenviable salted fish. He was a six foot tall negro, equally as wide, and the ship's diet was bringing him down as he stood over the stove cooking the same thing for every meal. Either there had to be an improvement in the food supplied, or the crew was going to crack.

The two youngest crew members, Cristobel and Abul, were missing good food worst of all and were moping around with little to look forward to after a hard day's work. As for Rob, he enjoyed the change from ten days of sardines and rice, while Charlie couldn't look a bean in the face without throwing up. He was slowly dying as he languished at the stern as the rolling black clouds from the interior of the Amazon broke in thunder and lightening and tossed the *Ely* out onto the high seas. "On the sea to eternity, off the course of serenity and into rough water," quoted Rob as darkness fell and threw up such high waves that Charlie thought they were going down. Onboard they were floundering in a foot of water. The captain, concerned they had hit such bad cross currents in the dark, ordered Manuel to turn her round and make for shore. It was a timely retreat, for he knew well that the *Ely* would have leaked badly from the buffeting if they'd maintained their course. The thunder ceased, and the distant lightening illuminated the boat now anchored in the drizzle, off the Isle de Maraca. It was a wet night's sleep for all.

The sunrise brought a pleasant day grounded on the island's mud flats. A small fishing boat was anchored nearby, and one of its three man crew was crawling over the mud in search of bait. Rob was up aloft sorting out the sodden papers of the encyclopedia, drying out the pages that had survived the deluge. Charlie said that he was going for a walk and lowered himself from the deck onto the mud. Rob dropped the encyclopedia in panic as Charlie sank up to his knees and was going down forever before he and Mula caught an arm each and pulled him out. The captain, lounging in his hammock strumming his guitar, waved a warning finger as Charlie covered in mud slithered about the deck.

A meal of crab and fish heads were devoured by all except Charlie who rotted at the stern frightened to face the task of eating. Since they'd set foot on the *Ely*, he'd eaten only a plateful of porridge, lacking the courage to stretch his stomach to other sea foods. Rob reckoned he'd missed a lovely fish soup the day before. But Charlie had green bilge pouring up from his stomach and continued to be doggedly sea sick. He was exhausted after a damp night, the mosquitoes buzzing and snapping at his bare feet and neck, the smell of dampness filling his nostrils, the dream of a hot day to dry out, finally a reality. He was hating the boat journey and couldn't wait to put his feet back on land. The mud flats had been an attempt at that, but that turned out to be just another disaster.

Lucky for Charlie, it was plain sailing from Maraca round the Cabo de Norte to a little fishing village on the mouth of the River Seguriju. He slept that night like a dead man. Having travelled little more than half way to Belem in seventy-two hours and the cross current of the Amazon River before them, Rob couldn't see the *Ely* being in Belem for at least another three days. Not that Rob was particularly worried. The boat journey was an experience he'd probably never get to have again, so he was making the best of it. Afloat on the Atlantic in a fifty foot boat with no lights, no compass and about to go down in the first serious storm was sheer lunacy. But then again, he and Charlie were lunatics for setting off to South America broke in the first place. They had little choice over their forms of transport.

As the light fell, nothing in Rob's experience rivalled the beautiful cloud formations out at sea, the cumulus building upward to strato cumulus with an orange band wedged between them and the sea. Black streaky lines descended as precipitation on two sil-houetted fishing boats anchored on the horizon. They were hauling in their nets, the fish taken from this tranquil setting to be processed, canned and stacked on supermarket shelves in North America. Being so close to the equator, the heavens looked as though they could be touched. Could the cosmos be any more spectacular. *Triangulum Australe*, *Ara*, *Musca*, *Scorpio*, *Sagittarius*, all but hidden to the gazer in the northern hemisphere. *Taurus*, *Leo*, *Cancer*, *Gemini* glittering in one long chain. Yet Rob regretted the fact that the skies and galaxies had once been a beautiful mystery to him. Now he wished he could sit or lie and be content to know nothing of the night sky and its notations. All it really achieved was to extend his vocabulary but not his knowledge of the cosmos. What worth did all these names have in these times other than being valid only as words? Ancient mariners steered by the stars, but now there was radar and soon there would be satellite navigation.

They awoke to German music from a Caribbean station north of their part of the world. Rob and Charlie joined the crew swimming in the river and chased frantically after their soap as it was washed out to sea. They were waiting for the tide to turn so they could cross the sandbar at the river mouth. They listened, then saw the approaching *porra rocca* sweep over the sandbar and rush towards them. Abul loosened off the anchor chain and they waited as the two foot tidal wave of the incoming tide raised the *Ely* off the mud in one great rush.

The captain had been unsuccessful in finding diesel at the village so they set sail with the engine running on half-ahead. With his regular cook too drunk to come on this trip, the diesel shortage and the general lack of anything edible left on board, it hadn't been the usual type of voyage for the captain. He tried to remain cheerful and to keep his crew's sagging morale from falling into an ungovernable lamentation over their inadequate supplies. He looked for the dolphins to lead the way, the dolphins always brought good luck. He was also hoping his two passengers had found their sea-legs by now, for apart from the fish being a little over salted, it had been fair sailing.

As it was, Charlie was pulling himself together and beginning to enjoy himself. The sun had reddened his body, but to a land lubber, he probably had a salty look. He wanted to be more than a fair weather sailor but the sea-sickness had weakened his resolve. He had thought of it as a bodily function over which he had no control. Now he understood that although the initial sickness attack may have been uncontrollable, after that it was all a state of mind. Rob had been running around the deck for days, and Rob felt it was about time Charlie did the same. He slapped Charlie on the shoulder and quoted from the encyclopedia.

> Give me rough sea, the gathering cloud
> The wind, the wail of the scavenger gull
> The sail on full sheet, the waves breaking aft
> The cracking of timber, the sway of the mast.

Charlie smiled and turned to watch as the sails were taken in. They had been out all day and land had long since disappeared from the western horizon. Cristobel dropped a bucket over the side and hauled in the line. He was filling up the water tank. They had reached sweet water and were beginning to sail across the two hundred mile mouth of the Amazon.

When the sun went down, they cut the engine. The stars came out and Rob in compliance with the captain's wishes, pointed out *Orion*, *Gemini*, *Ursa*

*Major*, *Alpha Beta Centaurus*, *Sirius* and *Scorpio*. He was fascinated at knowing the names after so many years. He fetched his guitar from below, and sang *I Left My Heart in San Francisco*, *The Sound of Music*, then *Edelweiss*. And as the *Ely* bobbed on the ocean, the captain's singing drifted upward, ever skywards, the night revealing another million hidden stars.

Some hours later, they awoke to a raging storm and seas that were determined to sink them. The captain and Roberto struggled to start the engine. They were fighting sea water and pitch darkness below with a torch and all their wits. Everything had turned nightmarish, the frantic crew in the hold with buckets baling fifteen hundred gallons of water an hour. The bilge pump, along with the Perkins engine, had choked on sea water. The *Ely* was pitching in all directions. They were sixty miles from land and being swept further out to sea every hour by the storm. Fearful of the worst, the captain was planning to abandon ship. Charlie looked like death, while Rob thought he felt death touch him on the shoulder. They were shipping water at such a rate that it was only a matter of time before they went down and ten more souls would join the millions before. Then with a yell of triumph the engine roared into life. It drowned out the howling wind and the hammering on the boat's timbers by the sea.

The captain sent Cristobel up front to the wheelhouse to tell Manuel to change course and head for land. Barefooted Cristobel fought his way forward through the lashing waves, momentarily stopping to clutch at the mast. He tapped on the wheelhouse window, expecting to see Manuel's face. But there was no one there. The wheel speedily spun round in one direction, then the other. Cristobel rushed back to the captain. Manuel had been swept overboard! The captain acted instinctively. He ordered Bronco to stop bailing and to take the helm. There was nothing they could do for Manuel. In these seas, the rest of the crew's safety came first. He must have been washed over hours before.

Bronco took the wheel and with the waves pounding on the bow, steered until the first signs of dawn. He was used to death, he'd seen it in the prisons of French Guiana. People thought the days of Devil's Island and the St Laurent Penitentiary were over. Perhaps they were, but not France's methods of obtaining confessions. The kind of discipline metered out inside Guiana's prisons had not changed much since the time of Dreyfus. He had been caught smuggling drugs into Cayenne and had rotted in prison for months, awaiting trial. They eventually made him sign a confession, extracted by making him kneel on two spikes driven through a piece of wood. At first, he refused, but a jailer put a little pressure on his shoulders until the spikes began to draw blood from his knees. He signed as he had decided a long term in jail was better than a life as a cripple. While waiting for his trial, he had months in jail to work out his clemency plea. The French thought all Brazilians were poverty stricken Latinos with large families fighting for each piece of bread. At his trial, he broke down and declared that he was a poor Brazilian with a wife, a mother and eleven children to support, and that the proceeds from his smuggling was for their benefit. Luckily, the judge did not see through his cock-an-bull story. On compassionate grounds, he was given six months in jail and a deportation order on release. As it happened, the *Ely* was in port on his release and the French coerced the captain to take on Bronco as an extra hand.

The sea calmed. Utterly exhausted, they regained their strength by downing some of Mula's beans. They made sight of land mid-afternoon. The *Ely* anchored offshore a small island. The captain had no idea which island it was. The volume of silt washed down the Amazon was constantly forming new islands. It was now better that they sailed to Macapa and re-fuelled instead of going straight to Belem. The captain had some friends in Macapa who could lend him the cash to buy enough diesel for the remaining journey. The crew were not happy. It meant going up the Amazon. The first problem would be finding a channel into the mouth, for the mouth was two hundred miles wide, and as already stated, the interior formed new islands continuously. What had been river five years before, could now be tropical undergrowth teeming with insects and birds. Rob and Charlie, with little to do but get in the way, went aloft to stay out of the possible mutiny. The crew backed down and accepted the captain's authority. They settled down for siesta.

The captain fell asleep over his guitar and was still

asleep towards dusk. As he slept the crew ridiculed him. High tide came shortly before dark and no-one let the captain know. When he awoke he was in a foul mood. Almost immediately he ordered Belzario to heave anchor, revved the engine high and sailed off in search of a channel into the Amazon. By this time it was pitch black, and in the starry light, they ran aground on a hidden bank. Lost and will little knowledge of exactly where the channel was, they turned back and dropped anchor. The atmosphere aboard was heavy with disappointment at wasting another day. The captain gathered his crew round him and dressed them down for not waking up in time.

With fish on Mula's menu again, the crew were far from happy. Nor was Charlie, who lay on his back and almost cried like a baby as he dreamed of sardines and rice. He vented his frustration by mimicking the captain as Long John Silver. Rob told Charlie to dry up. If he was going to criticise the captain to whom he was just an extra burden, they might throw him overboard. If he was too weak to put a lump of seafood down his throat, he deserved to die. To Rob there was nothing worse in a traveller than being a fussy eater. Rob could see Charlie's tastes were a problem. Travelling on an empty stomach was one complaint he wasn't going to put up with from Charlie even though he was still only a kid. Charlie taking onboard Rob's lecture, pulled himself together and forced a little salted fish down into his rumbling stomach.

That evening the captain admitted to Rob that his knowledge of the mouth of the Amazon was of little use to him now, he'd spent too many years cruising on his yacht in the Southern Atlantic. He hadn't been on the river itself for almost twenty years. He had once known it intimately. He had been twenty-years old when the Americans got into the Second World War. They had used Belem as their jump off spot for Africa and the Far East. He had made handsome business supplying the GIs with whatever they needed. By 1944, he had worked through the captains, majors, colonels and focused his services on the generals. He drank with them, joked with them and kept them amused, but underneath it all, he didn't like them. They were foreigners who tried to lecture him about Brazil rather than listen to what they had to learn from him about his country. They thought Brazilians were dumb while they knew everything. That is a crazy thing for anyone to think. It was still the same after all these years. The Americans he met in Rio had the same arrogance. One American woman, who visited his yacht, told him she didn't want to change her personality, she wanted to remain American in dress and in her outlook and make sure that everyone knew she was American. He had told her if that was what she wished to do it was up to her. He really wanted to throw her overboard. He was a gentleman. Travelling abroad was meant to widen a person's horizons, not confirm the beliefs already held. Anyone unwise enough to tell him that change wasn't one of the motivations for travelling wouldn't have been shocked if he had told her she was wasting her time being in Brazil. Perhaps he should have thrown over overboard. But he didn't.

The captain was in an expansive mood. "There are so many foolish people in the world who confess to know everything and never once prove a thing. Especially Americans. They should all be given an IQ test and shown just how ignorant they really are. Americans are indoctrinated by their own narrow culture. The average Brazilian can't be understood by an American as their thought process is geared towards money or reverse geared towards propelling their country to self destruction." The captain wasn't done on Yankees. "Americans have lost faith in life. Humanity to them is on a downward plunge. Escape to the stars is the only way of avoiding the total destruction of mankind. The way I see it, the Americans should zoom off to the stars, fight it out with the Russians in space, and leave the rest of us on Earth to develop at a non-destructive rate." He picked up his guitar and sang with a clearness of voice, a song called *Gringos:I Hate Them*. He stopped. No, he hadn't been up the mouth of the Amazon for years. "But what the hell, a little adventure is what keeps us all alive."

The mosquitoes that night were unbearable. At sunrise, they chugged up a small channel and ran aground. The crew went into the water, their feet sinking into the mud, crabs nibbling at their toes, the water up to their necks. They put their shoulders to the hull, their heads disappearing under the brown water to reappear in an explosion of bubbles and gasps. Twenty minutes of desperate attempts to push the *Ely* off the sandbank couldn't dislodge the stern. With the tide ebbing, they abandoned their efforts and fell to idling away the daylight hours to the next full tide.

The captain went off to buy a pig. Rob and Charlie followed. It was a wise move to take a stroll on the mud flats with the captain. They sat drinking coffee in the wooden hut of a man of Portuguese, Italian and Spanish descent, who told them they were on Ilha de Nueva, New Island. As he and the captain exchanged stories, more coffee was produced, bananas were brought and an avocado doused in fresh lemon became breakfast for each of them. More coffee followed. After all, they were in Brazil. On New Island, Rob could see Charlie was much happier on land. He loved his avocado breakfast and ground down palm tree drink *acai* laced with sugar and farina. It was invigorating stuff. Put muscles on the arms and hairs on the chest, so the old man said.

From the hut next door came the chatter of children. It was the only the school room on the island. Small faces peered at them through the gaps in the sparse panelling of the hut. The crew took to playing football with the barefooted schoolhouse kids and Rob joked about the *porra rocca* with the little girls. Charlie headed off into a horizon of turkeys, ducks and cows, horses, goats and pigs, all moving to the rhythm of a kite. A tree trunk bridge crossed the mud on the far side of a boat house, but it was devoid of any interest to Charlie who was in search of coconuts and avocados. Tired of soccer, the crew went hunting for shrimp and returned head to foot in mud, but with enough shrimp to feed everyone for days. That evening's meal consisted of beans and shrimp amidst clouds of mosquitoes and a downpour of rain. The rain cleared and high tide came up fast. The *Ely* afloat once more, chugged down river to the sea.

The captain had bought a duck and pig from the old man, who had drawn a map of where the channel into the Amazon could be found. As the others slept in their hammocks, Rob gazed at the stars, trying to fit *Bootes* and *Virgo* into his celestial map. He found *Arcturus* alright, but the herdsman seemed vague to him. *Scorpio* came up bright and strong, followed by *Sagittarius* in all his glory. *Gemini* went down very early, though *Ursa Major* was prominent for many hours. The beauty and diversity of the stars had him lost in the heavens. He was pleased that he was making good use of the vast field of vision that the equator afforded.

Rob had no sooner gone to sleep than he was awoken and called to the wheelhouse by the captain. Ahead, gliding through the sweet water, swept a dolphin. They were on the Amazon at last. The captain handed Rob the helm and told him to follow the guide, she knew the way. The experience made the matted sleep in his eyes nothing. His gaze was fixed on the dolphin, reliably staying fifty yards ahead and to the left. The captain stood smiling, remembering other times. Charlie came stumbling from the stern, saw the dolphin, saw the tropical vegetation, saw Rob at the helm and thought the school day dreams of high adventure had not been lies. With a nod from the captain, he took the helm from Rob.

Shrimps for breakfast no longer mattered, the days of spray flying across the bow, of hammocks rocking violently in movement with the deck, of pans dropping off their hanging nails, of the canvas covering the stern flapping nauseatingly in the strong sea gales, were over. The Amazon stretched like a lake without a ripple, a lake with a thousand islands, green and lush and dense and impenetrable, a surrealist dream of perfect light blue sky and silence and not a bird in flight or crocodile stirring on the island banks, nor a fish to break the surface. Only the dolphin, arcing seawards having led the way into a veritable paradise from the restless ocean. No, Charlie thought, at last, it was all worth it. With duck for lunch and slaughtered pig for evening meal, no one was complaining about the change of diet. Mula the cook was happy and Bronco was too busy up in the wheelhouse to grumble any more. The captain was relieved they'd soon reach Macapa. They had been gone one month and twenty-six days, and every day was costing him fifty cruzerios per man in pay. They were onto the last barrel of diesel with just enough to limp into the small Amazon port. But with the dolphin gone, the channel was narrowing and the tide dropping, and they spent the night grounded on a silt bank.

Rob awoke to find Charlie had gone ashore with the captain to buy a parrot from a man who lived in a wooden hut nearby. The man had gone off fishing and his wife wouldn't settle on a price. The parrots squawked. They drained their coffee and walked through a guava orchard back to the *Ely*. The captain picked, peeled and handed one to him. Charlie agreed it tasted good. All around there were strange fruits he'd never seen before, but he couldn't bring himself to ask the captain about them.

As they waited for the tide, the vampire gnats made a meal of all aboard. With great relief they slid off the silt bank, and took soundings all the way up the shallow three-metre channel. They chugged on slowly all morning and by afternoon had crossed the equator and harboured along the jetty of Macapa. On touching shore, Rob and Charlie cleared with immigration, cashed £80 of Rob's lost traveller's cheques in the local bank and spent the next four days in a brothel cum discotheque with the rest of the crew. The World Cup had just begun, but none of the men of the 'Ely' spent a single moment without a bottle or a woman while in front of a television. Scotland lost. Brazil won and Charlie yearned to know the England Test Match scores.

Re-kindled with life, the *Ely* left Macapa stacked with food and primed with diesel, and took an uneventful one and a half day voyage round Maraca Island and Caoajo Point until they came upon the lights of Belem and the end of a two month nautical voyage. Rob and Charlie had only been with the captain and his crew for fifteen days. They had fallen in love with the *Ely*. The interior of Brazil and the rest of South America waited. They said their goodbyes to the crew, gave their thank-yous to the captain who was busy supervising the unloading of the crocodile and shark skins in the most discreet manner.

## BRAZIL

It was a casual day of hitch-hiking that saw them arrive at the Maranhoa Goias State bridge, a mile north of the grand Transamazonas highway. The Tocantins River wound lazily below on yet another hot afternoon, the traffic heading south as sparse as the shade offered. With the sun directly overhead, it was a nice bridge, and for a Sunday, Estreito was a busy little town.

They were considering a lunch break, when a Volkswagen pulled up. Its two male occupants coaxed them to get into the back. Rob and Charlie needed little persuading as the passenger waved a gun at them. The door closed behind them, they drove across the bridge and half way up the hill on the other side they parked in the yard of the Goias State Police. Rob and Charlie gazed at one another but they were ordered out of the car before they could utter a sentence.

In the police office, the two cops scanned the wanted poster of the Baader-Meinhof group. Disappointed, they made a body search of them both then began to look through their belongings hoping to find some mystery item. One of them noticed the rings in their ears. "Hippy!" he accused Rob. "Oh, no" Rob replied. "It's the fashion in England. You know. A la moda Inglis." He avoided mentioning the word Punk. "Marijuana?" the other policeman suggested in a slow puffing gesture. "Who me!" Rob laughed. Charlie laughed too, catching on.

The other officer was flicking through their picture postcards. "Ah, turistas" he uttered. "Si, turistas!" Rob replied. "Vamos mucho cuiadadas en America Sud, me amigo y yo." He was babbling in Spanish but the Portuguese speaking cops seemed to understand him. "Ah, so he no is your brother" the other cop enquired. "No, we're friends" Charlie confirmed. "He is a bambino" the same policemen laughed, pointing to Charlie's age on his passport. Rob and Charlie laughed as well. "Nineteen years is no mucho for your friend here to be in Brazil. You protect him mucho." He patted Charlie on the back. "He is nice boy. Un momento please, we have something for you."

The policeman disappeared into a back room and returned laden with bananas and oranges. "You want?"

he asked "Si, gracias, signors." Rob replied expelling a sigh of relief that the cops were shaking their hands and wishing them b*uenos suerte* and not rattling jailer's keys as they are reputed to do in South America.

Free, and climbing the rest of the hill beyond the state line, they began hitching again. A truck pulled up and two pretty chicas got out. The truck drove off. The chicas ran towards them and introduced themselves. No sooner were all four acquainted, than Rob and Charlie were led off into the bushes by the roadside. The two girls knew what they wanted, took no for an answer, and got on with it. It was all so Brazilian.

Brazilian women loved their men. With nineteen percent of the guys in the country gay, there was a shortage of men to go around. In a promiscuous society like Brazil's, love making was as essential to life as eating and drinking. Rob and Charlie with their gold earrings and good looks, seemed to be driving Brazilian girls to distraction. Every time they smiled in a woman's direction it appeared to arouse something in them. Even a frown wasn't good enough to deter the most insistent girls. Brazilian women, many of which would have been celebrated beauties in any other country, were just waiting for the first stranger to come along. And it seemed that no strangers had been to that part of Brazil for countless years. Some people would call that luck.

One of the girls went off and returned with sweet bread and pop and plied them with cigarettes and oranges. Charlie and Rob were flattered by their new company and Rob suggested they should split up and hitch in pairs. One chica was into it but the other was slightly up in arms and a heated Latin discussion between them followed. Hair flew everywhere and Charlie went off the idea too, so after a truck refused to take all four of them, the idea fizzled out. In the lull, the girls went off to buy more cigarettes, leaving their bags scattered on the ground. Rob wandered aimlessly down the road. Charlie half-heartedly stuck his thumb out at a passing truck and it stopped in a hiss of brakes. The driver agreed to take the two boys a hundred kilometres south. As they were getting in, the two chicas returned, stuffed some biscuits into Charlie's hand and waved their goodbyes. The truck took off on a cloud of dust.

Narcotico Mercedes was a small, roundish, balding thirty-three year old drug-taking trucky who'd driven in all twenty-two of Brazil's states by the age of twenty-nine. He was no mean fucker, took his time and had a wicked laugh that would have suited him better if his moustache had been upturned instead of drooped. His philosophy on life was step on the gas on hills and free wheel down the other side, and if there was a barrier across the road, stop, get out and find out what the hell was going on. No, Narcotico was no fool, he knew what life was all about. Yet when he tried to explain his philosophy to anyone else it came out as sex, booze, drugs and trucks, which he admitted made him typically Brazilian. That of course was his own slant on national characteristics. Who could blame him? While making the three thousand mile run on the Transamazonas, why wouldn't he cram his tool box full of marijuana to get through each day. Long hauls required patience, perseverance and something to take the mind off thousands of miles of boring jungle lined road.

It had taken him twenty-two days and a kilo of marijuana to get to where he picked up Rob and Charlie. He didn't care how long it took, his bed was the road, his truck his only friend, and the bordellos along the way his only means to stop from going insane. He didn't mind hitch-hikers, they were few and states apart, but this was the first time he'd picked up foreigners. He just didn't know what to say or whether he should be polite and offer them some marijuana. So when Charlie offered Narcotico a biscuit, he refused. He was chewing on his thoughts. The heat was getting to him, he'd have to stop soon for a siesta. The next bordello would do.

The first stop over was light-hearted fun for Rob and Charlie. A little local whisky and a flirtation with the local girls on top of an excellent *prato del dia* while Narcotico slept with a girl in a back room. It was a hot afternoon, and Charlie fell to carving a ring out of a tagwa stone, while Rob had a few more beers and kept the girls amused.

Narcotico emerged from the back with a big smile. He indicated that it was time to hit the road. So back in the cab he climbed, his two trusting hitch-hikers getting in behind him, and off they drove. After little more than twenty miles, they stopped again. Another drink, another flirtation and off they drove once more. Another twenty miles. Stop, drink, marijuana, woman. Hit the road. Stop, drink, marijuana, a further hit of marijuana and that was them for the night. Charlie slept on top of the thirty ton load. Rob slung the hammock he'd bought in Belem between the front and back wheels. It was to be a peaceful night in the Brazilian Highlands, the endless dream of tropical sounds only fully recognised by Brazilian ears. The burning glow of a dying cigarette dropped out the cab as a near-slumbering Narcotico thought about another day gone.

In the morning, a steak and rice meal ana-esthetised the aches of Rob's night slouched in a hammock and Charlie's lying on top of thirty tons of canned corned beef. Mouthfuls of coffee that took a bordello girl all her time in vain attempt to keep full, a quick shot of local rum to kick-start the day was for Narcotico the only way a truck-driver and his two hobos would get through another long drive. He'd agreed to take them to Anapolis without any fuss and was quite happy to pay for their meals and buy them whisky. As a matter of fact, another Brazilian truck driver who'd worked in the States for a year and whose English was comprehensive, told Rob that Narcotico was nice guy! They didn't need to be told. Narcotico was a guy who saw Rob and Charlie as a pair of harmless foreigners passing through. It was his duty to show them Brazilian hospitality.

Charlie wondered if Narcotico was like all other Brazilians because of his preoccupation with women, drink and music? Why did he smoke weed? Was that normal for a Brazilian? In fact, Narcotico really had Charlie confused by his own English way of looking at things. He was swimming in newness. The experience of a bordello was not a dream from a Kerouac novel or a Dylan song which went back way before his time anyway. It was a living room of women pouring coffee, making meals, in general keeping the customers satisfied. It was just too much to cope with, which left little time to ponder why a Brazilian should not be blowing dope. Charlie was confused indeed, for all he could think about was women, especially in a bordello.

Rob on the other hand was in more accepting frame of mind. Narcotico had a wicked laugh. To Rob he was archetypal Brazilian. His teeth were falling out.

He was not the only one. Brazil was a country with many beautiful women with missing teeth, broken or black through. Yet Rob could look past the teeth to their tits, hips and butts. Every stop they made, the girls were there in droves, hanging by the corner of their table studying the curious, but seemingly desirable Brits. All it did was make Rob as horny as hell. "Mental control is all that is needed" he convinced himself again and again. "Bullshit, man, grab me and don't be so damned conceited" hissed one fiery whore at him. He was sore tested.

Their journey through Brazil was a journey where everyone knew basically what they were living for. It was not some intellectual straight-jacket view that life should be spiritual to the point of being extra-terrestrial. If there was ever to be another tomorrow in Brazil, it wouldn't be until after a night with a woman, a breakfast of rum, and lunch in a bordello.

The days rolled by. They pulled into a truck stop at KM post 381 with a flat and awaited the repair. Narcotico boringly sat on a pile of disused tyres staring vacantly at the ground. Rob and Charlie were in the bar talking to a guy who spoke a little English who bought them beers. "Oh, I never work" Charlie said to the guy with a flourish. "Not in England. I'm a photographer, you know. I'm touring South America taking shots." The Brazilian guy was obviously puzzled that Charlie never worked. Rob pulled Charlie aside. "You can't go around telling people you never work." "Why not?" Charlie answered impertinently. "Because you're lying, that's why. You've hardly used that camera of yours since we got here. I can't stand the sight of you when you start bragging. It's bad enough when you waffle and bullshit. But when you throw in things like never working, you've gone too far."

Rob returned to the Brazilian. "My friend's last job was pushing a trolley in a supermarket, stacking the shelves. He does work in England." This clarified things with the Brazilian who shook their hands and left. Rob was angry with Charlie. "You'd still have been working in that climbing shop if I hadn't shown you this kind of life style which lets you live without working. There is no respectable way of telling people you don't work. It makes people think that your parents support you or you're a crook." Charlie shuffled in his chair as Rob scolded him. "Living without working means living at someone's expense. That is exactly what we are doing at the moment. That guy bought the beers. So don't go around telling people you're a lay-about. You're only harming yourself, which means us. Both of us."

Charlie crestfallen, hid his tears and left the bar in a hurry, angry and hurt by Rob's lecture. After all, what harm had been done by exaggerating his photography taking. What did it matter anyway? The Brazilian wouldn't have been any wiser. A photo-grapher was definitely more interesting than a shelf stocker. He hated Rob at times, he always believed himself to be so perfect.

Lost in vexation, Charlie wandered up and down the truck-stop forecourt. Narcotico gazed up from the ground and watched Charlie pacing up and down. The temperature was dropping. It was definitely becoming cooler as they moved south. Maybe he's cold, Narcotico thought. It was winter and there was talk on the radio of zero degree temperatures in Sao Paulo. Narcotico knew what that meant. Life became more restrictive, more time indoors, more clothes, extra expense on hot food and warm accommodation. No, Narcotico mused, moving south meant cooler times for himself and his hitch-hikers.

It was his fourth day with these boys. He hoped to reach Anapolis by evening, but it seemed question-able. Personally it troubled Narcotico none to spend another night on the Great North Road with his two guests. He enjoyed their company. They didn't talk much, they just looked at each other when the road ahead got boring, smiled, then pulled faces to see if they were still in one piece after all the marijuana they had been smoking. He'd never known hitch-hikers who smoked as much weed as he did. It restored his faith that he was perhaps, after all, a fairly normal guy who'd picked up two dope, drink and women-mad friends. These gringos were crazy! He raised his sore backside from a pile of Kelly's, Goodyear's, and Fires-tone's. The new tyre was fitted, they were ready to go.

The following morning when Narcotico let them out at the bus station in Anapolis, they were all tired. It was the end of the road after another night of a hammock slung between his wheels. Rob and Charlie couldn't understand much of Narcotico's Portuguese which they reckoned must have frustrated Narcotico at times, seeing he was driving so much and they were saying so little. But what could they do but smile and pretend to understand when they didn't. He had always remained cheerful and they had only seen Narcotico pissed-off once. It had been when he awoke from a sweat beaded siesta, found the bottle in his hand empty, the drug filled cigarette in his mouth burnt to the butt, and the woman who was supposed to be looking after him gone. Recovering from the initial shock, he bellowed with the raging of a bull, swallowed spit in his wail, rampaged around for ten minutes until he broke into his wicked laugh. And with that memory of him, a cloud of marijuana smoke, a vision of women and a thirty-ton roar, Narcotico Mercedes disappeared into the endless horizon, and the annals of culture and folklore.

Charlie went into the Anapolis bus station and bought two tickets to Brasillia. Two hours later, the Brazilian capital lay before them. A city so new that they were blinded by the shininess of the buildings. "Heh, Rob, according to this tourist brochure, there's a bloke who speaks English at the Imperial Hotel. We aren't getting very far with Portuguese, maybe we should give him a try and see if he can suggest any cheap place to stay." "OK, sounds good, Charlie. This city doesn't seem all that cheap. Have you seen these marble buildings? The whole place looks like a fairy tale castle which has lowered the drawbridge to let two serfs have a peek." "I'd say we look more like two bums than serfs. Anyway, let's find this hotel, Rob. Those statues in front of that weird building with the spikes give me the creeps." "There not spikes, dumbo, they're spires. That's the Cathedral. According to the brochure it is the most modern in the world. Seeing we're here we might as well have a look inside."

Rob started towards the cathedral, Charlie was reluctant. "I don't know. After the crap you subjected me to in Georgetown Cathedral I'm wary. Those windows remind me of a spider's web. They are so out of this world. With architecture like that, how come all the buildings in England are boxes?" "Don't ask me" Rob shrugged. "Probably Picasso's doing. When he went Cubist, the whole world went overboard. Just like our parents' generation, everyone in Europe went square."

They entered the cathedral. Charlie looked up. "Thank God for dole queues and New Wave music. No one's going to put me into a little cube. They tried that at school and I wasn't having it." "That's why you got expelled" Rob replied coldly. Charlie smoothed down his moustache. "Yeah, they were trying so hard to squeeze me into a little box full of other kids and ship me off to college, they never even bothered to ask me if I wanted to go. If it was twenty years go, it would have been the army, now it's college. I'm quite happy being a nonentity instead of a celebrity!" "Keep your voice down, Charlie, this is a cathedral, and I'm not some old battle axe teacher. This building might be assaulting your visual senses, but its still a place of worship." "Stuff it, Rob, shove all this conventional shit on to someone else. Numbed senses or not, this building serves the same purpose as all the little religious cubes back home. It makes me sick." Rob gave Charlie a long side-look. "OK, you're tired, let's go and find this Imperial Hotel."

Ten minutes later they are outside the Imperial. "Well, well, well" Rob hummed. "I might have guessed that the flashiest hotel in Brasilia would be the one with the bloke that speaks English." Charlie is not put off. "To hell with that. These shits with their airs of wealth are all creeping morons underneath. You watch the bags, I'll sniff this English speaking guy out." Charlie spun through the revolving door of Brasilia's only five star hotel. He re-emerged five minutes later. "Well" Rob asked. "Aww, the guy wasn't a bad bloke. He said there's a place a block away that's cheaper. Let's go." Picking up their gear, they trekked across a wide expanse of concrete in a city built for cars.

Rob and Charlie reached the door of the hotel. They glanced in. A condescending desk clerk frowned back at them. Numerous neat suited business men shuffled sideways as the bedraggled pair, still heavy with two thousand kilometres of Amazon dust, advanced towards the desk. A quick glance at the price list confirm their suspicions. "Ten US dollars a night" Charlie declared. Rob looked quickly for an excuse. "Its not clean enough to me" he said loudly enough for the clerk to hear. "Let's get out of this hole, Charlie, before we're contaminated by the lack of class. Any place that hasn't got a doorman" Rob quipped to Charlie "is beneath us." "Right, let's get back to the Imperial" Charlie ordered. "I'm going to give the guy there my evaluation of what's cheap and what's a rip-off."

They returned to the Imperial. Rob again waited outside. Ten, fifteen, twenty minutes, half an hour passed. "What's keeping him?" Rob moaned feeling the cool winter air. Charlie emerged with a big grin on his face. "The desk clerk's name is Tito. I told him about the other place and he apologised. He then suggested we could rent his flat for ten dollars a night. I gave him the low down on our money situation and eventually he gave in and said we could stay at his place for free. He knocks off work in about an hour, told me to hang on 'til then." Rob stamped his feet. "Is it any warmer in there? I'm cold out here." "Why aye, we can wait inside. They've some nice comfortable armchairs."

Tito Chiflado was gay, but it took Rob and Charlie a day or two to work it out. Tito kept referring to Charlie as 'baby' and Rob continuously laughed as he considered his younger friend a baby too. But with the growing realisation that Tito was a Brazilian nineteen percenter, the 'baby' joke took on a new meaning. Rob and Charlie began to watch Tito's every action for signs of his femininity.

For most of the next three days, the two chumps had Tito's flat to themselves, and used it as a spring-board for sojourns round the tourist sites of Brasilia. By chance, they witnessed the changing of the guard at the Palacio de Planalto, the sparkly nineteenth century blue and cream uniforms of the guards colourfully contrasting with the silk-white palace. The lowering of the flag to the trumpeter – the band taking heart and playing their piece – the guards marching around – the two exchanging officers goose stepping – the band letting toot again. Rob and Charlie thought it hilarious.

As the sun went down, the sky tinted a glorious red and the two hundred and eighty-six square metre national flag swayed in the breeze. The ceremony continued, the guards lined up along the ramp into the palace, blue to the left, cream to the right, their gold leaf hats reflecting the red glow from the west. The Commander screamed an order of 'fix bayonets' as the band put their hearts into the National Anthem. Descending the ramp flanked by his ministers stepped President Ernesto Geisel, erect, smiling, and nodding, before getting into a waiting limousine. The limousine u-turned and drove at a casual pace to allow around eighty spectators time to clap their approval and for the President to wave and smile in return. Excitement hung in the air, it was a privilege to be within two metres of the President. No one needed to push or elbow another aside. Everything was dignified, yet informal, the crowd felt they could reach out and touch their leading politician. There he was in his car, smiling on his way home to his private residence for his evening meal. The people cheered.

In England seeing the Queen was such a hassle. But the President of Brazil, like all other Brazilians, could spare a few moments. In Brazil, there was no rat race, no population trying to cut each other's throats in getting on a bus or making a few more pennies at someone's expense. As a pioneer land, a final frontier, the frustration evident in Europe didn't exist. Competition was scarce. The man with an idea developed it for himself, he didn't lose it to a multi-million super-conglomerate who could pay the fee to patent it.

In Brazil every day got better, the dream that tomorrow would be better, was national fact. The contentedness of the population and its desire to go nowhere and see nowhere else was based on an inner knowledge that Brazil had everything, and had everything to offer within its own frontiers. "Why go somewhere else?" the captain had told the boys. "Brazil's changing so fast, all the excitement you'd ever want is here. Can you name another country in the world that's moving so fast? If there are any cracks to wedge open, it's the presence of a military government, and you can go to the Presidential Palace in Brasilia yourself, and see what the people think of our President. This might be South America, but the world has a lot to learn from us."

"Yes, Brasilia is an impressive city, don't you think, Charlie?" "Why aye, I enjoyed the Twin Towers today, just to have a shit and have a cup of coffee at the government's expense. What other country in the world gives away free coffee? What about you, Rob?" "Och yes, I've never seen such an impressive city as Brasilia. I thought Johannesburg was spacey but Brasilia's light years ahead. I like Brazil, its a beautiful country, has a beautiful capital, a beautiful population, and a beautiful future. Though I can't understand with all these beautiful women around why nineteen percent of the population is gay. Something inexplicable has happened to the men folk here."

It was six in the evening. Charlie and Rob were lounging on Tito's cushions listening to his stereo, drinking his whisky while Tito was out at work. The telephone rang. Charlie picked it up. "Hello." "Hello" the reply came through. "Hello" Charlie repeated. "Hello, es Tito la?" "What?" Charlie asked, not understanding Portuguese. "ES TITO LA?" the voice shouted. "What! I don't understand" Charlie stated. "Speak English, man." "Que? Que pasa?" the voice returned. "Fala Portuguese." "God, can't you speak English?" Charlie shouted down the phone. Click... the voice hung up.

Five minutes later, the phone rang again. This time Rob answered. "Hello." "Hello, es Tito la?" The voice again. "No" Rob managed to answer. "Esta Tito's casa?" the voice asked. "Si" Rob answered, pleased with himself. "Es Tito la?" the voice asked again. "No" Rob repeated. "ESTA TITO'S CASA?" the voice shouted down the phone. "Si" Rob beginning to sense the language limitations of talking on the phone, his well developed gestures of little use. "Donde esta Tito? Soy Frederick!" the voice said, trying a new line. "Que?" Rob was stumped by that one. "Fala Portuguese,?" the voice inquired at a high pitch level. "No, I speak English. Do you?" Click... the voice rang off again.

Half an hour later there was a knock on the door. Rob answered. On the doorstep stood a small Brazilian, young, clean shaven and cutely dressed with a bag slung from his shoulder. With a nod he swept past Rob, went straight to the wardrobe in Tito's bedroom and commenced to fill his shoulder bag with shirts, socks and multi-coloured underpants. Rob and Charlie exchanged glances while the young Brazilian searched through Tito's drawers. Satisfied, he finally straightened and gave Rob and Charlie a guarded smile.

Rob offered him a whisky. He declined and headed for the door, opened it, then was gone. Charlie shuffled on his cushion a little while Rob poured himself a stiff one. "I guess that was the guy on the phone, Frederick" he said, lifting the glass to his lips. "Yeah, I suppose it was" Charlie conceded. "Funny bloke" he said with a yawn.

An hour later, Tito came home, glancing only momentarily at the near empty whisky bottle. "Any calls?" "Yeah" Charlie mumbled. "Yes baby. Who?" "I don't know, we couldn't speak Portuguese. I think he said his name was Frederick" Rob recalled. "Oh, I see. He was my old lover." "Oh, well!" Charlie informed Tito. "I think it was him that came and collected some clothes." "Never mind" Tito mused. "I have a new lover now. He'll be arriving shortly. He's only seventeen, but unfortunately he's married and has great difficulties getting away from HER to come and stay with me. You'll like him for sure, baby." Tito looked in Charlie's direction. "Tonight we are going to the Club Aquarius down town. Do you want to come?" "Are there any women there?" Charlie asked. "No, it is all nice young men. You'll have a good time. It's the best gay club in all Brazil, baby." Charlie looked to Rob. "You only live once" Rob said resignedly. "OK" Charlie said. "What time are we going?"

The Club Aquarius was one big disco at five dollars a night with two drinks thrown in. Rob quickly ordered two rum and cokes and thrust one into an uneasy Charlie's hand. Heavily fortified, Tito led the way down the stairs into the Pansy Jungle. Bolts of fluorescent light shot through the air in blues and greens and violent reds, playing hide and seek with the stiff-limbed shuffling dancers. With not a woman in sight, the jiving jockeys wriggled to the heart felt beat of *Saturday Night Fever* and the Dee Gees.

Charlie was dragged onto the dance floor, and in order to stay alive, began to jive. Rob likewise was coaxed into playing along, coming alive, began to jive too. Then it all got out of hand. They started to elbow the Brazilians aside, take command, show these guys that they could streak their legs out across the sky, clear the floor with their dancing. They went all out to show these gays how punks could jive, give it more, be more than just wallflowers pumping their thighs, be overnight stars. The gays loved them! Clapped their hands in glee, flocked to them, until Rob burst free and shouted he needed a drink.

Charlie fled with Rob to the bar. A drink, a drink, they needed a drink as men flocked after them. "God! Rob, what have we stirred up by dancing? These guys can't keep their hands off us." "I know! It looks as though we're the hottest foreign talent to hit the club for years. Nothing's going to cool these guys down. They're man crazy."

*Pheeeeeeee...! Pheeeeeeee...!* It was the sound of a whistle. "What the hell is that?" Rob swung round to face the stairway as the first cop appeared carrying a sawed-off shotgun, a whistle dangling from his lips. The music gulped to a stop. It was a shake-down! More armed plain clothes policemen appeared and commenced to check everyone's ID, amidst gay frowns and disgusted 'tuts'.

The boys had left their passports at Tito's flat. The police hauled them out into the street, hotly followed by Tito who explained they were his guests. The cops were ambivalent. They allowed Tito and Rob to hire a taxi and return to the flat to collect the passports. Meanwhile, Charlie was taken in police custody to another club the cops were raiding. Charlie could not believe his luck. The club was full of sex-crazed women just looking for a man. A sweat-drenched blonde grabbed Charlie by his shirt, pulled him aside and wrapped her lithe and searing body around his stunned torso. A policeman broke into a grin and registered his approval. He seemed delighted that Charlie was not a ponce. Charlie meanwhile was some-what dazed at this sudden sexual transition from bloke to chick.

When Rob and Tito arrived with the passports, the police departed. Charlie was in no mood to be separated from his new acquaintance. But the doorman wasn't going to let him stay without producing the five dollar entrance fee and Tito was hurt that his little baby had found the arms of the mortal enemy. So stuck between the materialistic and the moral, Charlie acquiesced and was shuffled away from his blonde. All three returned to the happenings of the Club Aquarius.

Let's get that other drink" Charlie suggested. "They still owe us one. Barman! Dos rum y coke" he ordered. The barman refused. They'd had their drinks he argued. Rob tried to correct the matter with words, but Charlie butted in. His rising anger at paying five dollars for a drink someone else had half drunk when he had been dancing, plus the memory of the blonde in the other club who had smothered him with her breasts, gave vent to a frustration he was finding difficult to keep under control. There were no women in the Club Aquarius to throw his heterosexual emotions at. Rob was in a similar frame of mind, but was just about managing to control his rising feelings.

Charlie asked the barman again for two rum and cokes. Tito came running up the stairs. "Hurry, hurry, both of you, the cabaret act is beginning in the Pansy Jungle." He disappeared down the stairs again. Charlie turned back to the barman who had ignored his order and who was now pouring another rum and coke for someone else. As he finished pouring the coke, Charlie picked up the drink and put it to his lips. The barman grabbed him by the wrist and attempted to recover the glass. A tussle ensued.

Meanwhile, downstairs in the Pansy Jungle, the transvestites were in full swing doing their act. Upstairs, the tussle broke into a swinging fist fight. All of a sudden the whole place was in an uproar. Bodies went flying in all directions as Charlie and Rob were dragged to the club door by the bouncers and unceremoniously thrown out into the street. As they lay in the gutter, the street filled with beautiful women staring down at them, until they realised they were the transvestites who had left their act to watch them drag themselves to their feet.

Tito came running up and *shoo...ed* the trannies away. "Baby, baby" he cried. "Why did you do it? Now my name's nothing here. Nothing! I'm in disgrace for bringing you here. I despise you! You must leave my place at once! I hate you for what you've done. Here is the key. Go! Pack your things and leave. I never want to see you again!!"

Charlie took hold of the key. They returned to the flat, collected their gear and left Brasilia at three in the morning on a bus to Rio.  Rob held his head in his hands and wondered what would have happened if the tourist brochure hadn't mentioned the fact that the desk clerk at the Imperial Hotel spoke English.

From Corovado, Rio lay below shrouded in a mist. The peak of Sugarloaf poked up from Guanabara Bay. The sands of Ipanema and Leblon girthed the azul sea that washed the high-rise steps of the Copacabana skyline which reached back into the Beryl hillside, while alabaster, Christ the Redeemer watched over all. Rob and Charlie gazed down on Rio from the foot of the statue. Charlie took some snapshots. "Well, we can go home, now that we've seen Rio" Charlie joked and laughed loudly.

Two American girls gave him dirty looks. For their benefit, Charlie continued. "All these tourists are the same. They fly out here, taxi from the airport to their hotel. Taxi from their hotel up here to Christ the Redeemer. Taxi back to their hotel. Taxi back to the airport. Then next stop, home. Even Johnny Rotten's doing it these days. And I bet those chicks over there are doing it as well," he said pointing to them. "Aye" Rob answered. "A right pair of scrags, aren't they?" "I don't know, worse than that, I think. They look American. Big backsides and even bigger mouths." The two girls, highly offended, moved out of earshot. "Let's get off this bird perch and down to the beach for a swim" Charlie suggested. "People aren't too friendly up here." "Well, what do you expect?" Rob answered. "We're back in tourist country."

They hitched a lift down to Leblon. "The girl from Ipanema came walking" Rob sang to himself, remembering the famous song. "Never lose your heart to a girl from Ipanema" he recalled. That wasn't proving to be very difficult. The beach was deserted, not a soul was to be seen. No half naked girls, flouting their beauty, no famous film stars tanning their bodies. Just virgin sand that sparkled in its loneliness.

The waves were pounding in and Rob and Charlie were like fish to water in their eagerness to strip off and roll the crests and flounder in the troughs, unaware of the bright red flag fluttering in the invigorating breeze. They were on the Copacabana and nothing was going to stop them showing off their boat trip tan or braving the waters on one of the world's most famous beaches. They frolicked and splashed, tumbled and dived in childish glee, ran up and down the sands to test their fitness, then stopped and rolled a number, which didn't make much different to their already euphoric state.

As they sat in the sand, Rio life went on. The skyscrapers grew taller, the cars sped past faster, the fashions came and went. The waves, the Redeemer, the champagne corks, carnations, chocolates and candles remained to garnish South America's golden strip in fame. "Ee! I'm glad I'm not spending my time wheeling trolleys around Littlewoods any more" Charlie said stretched out on the sand. "Aye" Rob agreed. "Here I am sitting on the Copacabana beach" Charlie

convinced himself with a pinch. "It's hard to believe."
"Aye" Rob agreed again. "I've never felt this type of
excitement before. The newness of everything. At
times I can't wait to find out what's going to happen
next. One minute we could be sitting like this and the
nex, well, who knows." "Aye" Rob agreed. "Something
always happens, Charlie. Travelling is a world of extr-
emes. Whether surprise springs from the recesses of a
dark alley when you're trying to score some dope, or
comes from the wound down window of an expensive
car when you're trying to hitch a ride, its all part of
travelling. Good and bad, rich and poor, travelling
bridges most of the gaps created by wealth and
culture. It's all part of the experience."

"I know what you mean" Charlie laughed. "I'm
getting sick of drinking coffee. It's all very well bridging the culture gap, but I wouldn't mind a cup of tea
for a change." "Side tracked again" Rob said, brought
down from his higher plane of thought. "Tea" he
mused. "Aye, I wouldn't mind a cup of tea for a
change. Brazil might be coffee country, but I suppose
we were brought up on tea." "Rob, look, isn't that
Maxim's over there?" Charlie pointed. Rob turned to
look. "Aye, but it'll be as expensive as hell." Charlie
was not for being put off. "So what! I thought you said
travelling bridged the wealth gap as well as the culture
one" Charlie said triumphantly. "One up for you, mate"
Rob admitted. "OK, let's get dressed. It's funny, I still
can't understand why there are so few people around."

In Maxims, Charlie drained the last of his tea and
slowly placed the cup on to the saucer. "See, it wasn't
too bad. Only a quid for a pot" Charlie said. "Which
means it's bread and cheese for lunch" Rob replied.
"Aww, not again." "Aye, it's the price you have to pay
for bridging the wealth gap. Come on, let's find a
bread shop."

In the panificadora they found out the reason for
the streets being deserted. Football. Twenty Brazilians
were crammed round the bread rolls and a colour
television watching their national team take on Poland
in the World Cup play-offs. All over the country, the
streets were deserted as Brazil struggled to maintain
its position as football's royalty. The game meant so
much to the people. To lose meant murders and
suicides and a gloom that would throw the entire
nation into the deepest depths of depression. To lose

meant... no, it was unquestionable.

Charlie bought the bread and cheese and had to drag Rob away from the television and out into the street. Suddenly, Brazil scored. Bread rolls came flying out of the panificadora amidst roof raising screams of hysteria. Out on the *Avenida Copacabana*, the sky filled with carnival as the sun was blotted out by a vicissitude of impenetrable ticker-tape, ponderously cascading down to nestle in Rob and Charlie's hair. Their feet were buried beneath an autumn of paper. Gunshots were heard ringing from the skyscrapers. "C'mon" Charlie said grabbing Rob with a jerk. "Let's go back to our hotel and eat."

Everything was at a standstill. The buses had ground to a halt and the crews had headed for the nearest bar with a television. Then from somewhere a lone bus came whizzing through the paper snow flakes. Rob and Charlie pulled themselves on board and jumped off again in Central Rio. On arrival at their hotel, Poland had equalised. They tried to obtain the key to their room, but the receptionist had disappeared to watch the game. The lift attendant was pissed-off that he was still on duty. He told them the receptionist was on the ninth floor, but before they had the chance to step into the lift, the attendant had closed the doors and shot off without them. They were forced to take the stairs.

On the ninth floor, the lift doors were jammed open by the attendant's stool. From the end of the corridor came cries of despair punctuated by shouts of exasperation, which pinpointed the action. Rob and Charlie peered round the door. In true Brazilian fashion, everyone in the room was out of their wits. There were five men and a woman including the receptionist and the lift man, sitting on the edge of their stools, the table in front of them strewn with empty and half-full whisky and beer bottles, the picture on the television hardly visible through the clouds of cigarette smoke being exhaled by their gasping lungs.

The receptionist quickly took time out to beckon Rob and Charlie to the table and poured them each a stiff whisky. Then another. Someone inquired tentatively if they were Polish. Charlie denied it strongly, while Rob said he was Scottish. The receptionist raised his hands to his mouth to signify the puffing action of smoking marijuana and mentioned Willie Johnstone, a Scottish forward sent home from Argentina by the authorities for taking drugs.

Rob smiled and turned in time to see the Brazilian super-star Humberto smash the ball into the back of the Polish net. Everything exploded, the table was upturned and the chairs went flying across the room to smash against the walls. Bottles went rolling across the floor and the Brazilians went dancing uncontroll-ably into each other's arms. The woman in her own form of patriotism ripped into pieces uncountable newspapers and threw them out the window. Disentangling herself from the sea of arms and legs she walked out calling the men crazy, returning a minute later with another bottle of whisky. Two-one to Brazil.

One more goal and they would be sure of qualifying for the final. Fifteen minutes to go and all of Brazil sat by their televisions and radios waiting, hoping, praying for the eleven bionic men out on the field to produce that goal. Fifteen minutes in which Rob and Charlie sat toasting one another, wishing every day in life could be as good as theirs that day in Rio.

Rio was a good place and three days of good living did no one any harm. They cashed more traveller's cheques, toured the museums, visited the war memorial and gazed vacantly at the gleaming yachts in Guanabara Bay. Life went by pleasantly, it was no hardship strolling the streets of Rio. The sun always shone, the ice cream was always good, and the coffee was the best in the world. The women were beautiful, the people cheerful and music overflowed into the streets. Rio had class. Rio was a city that everyone should get the chance to see, at least once in their lifetime. That's how they felt when they left on the bus to Sao Paulo.

At Sao Paulo bus station they were met with a sea of people. A city of eleven million inhabitants, they decided to bus on. With a lack of sleep and overeating taking its toll, they spent the night in Dos Barnabes, a poky little village eighty-one kilometres south of Sao Paulo. As it was St Pedro and St Antonio day, the villagers were out celebrating, drinking ginger beer, letting off rockets and playing bingo. The bonfires roared, the accordion music blared while Charlie and

Rob longed for a quiet spot to rest their heads.

Forced to stay awake by the noise, they had a peanut liquor in the Little Dog Bar, a sad empty place devoid of atmosphere where the locals played their own form of pool with blue and yellow balls. Although it was fiesta time, everyone seemed miserable. At KM 81 smiles were rare, the chilling misty weather the greatest dampener. As strangers in town Rob and Charlie were treated as such, the friendliness of Northern and Central Brazil just sweet memory. Finally, the mundane faces drove them to use the school house as their doss spot. Rob strung his hammock on two door handles which were, not surprisingly, well bent by the morning. Charlie settled for the floor. Over coffee and bread for breakfast, Charlie vaguely recalled an almighty bang going off while they slept. Little wishing to spend fruitless guessing at who had thrown a banger to disturb their sleep, he had slumbered on.

Charlie threw out a thumb and a Brazilian in a Ford stopped to pick them up. Trundling along on the road again, the lorry in front ran over a dog, leaving it lying, mushed and dead on the road. Ten kilometres further, lashing lights indicated SLOW DOWN. A Volkswagen had ploughed into the back of a bus, the driver's blood-smeared head resting on the shattered windscreen, his arm dangling out the window of the blood streaked door, policemen hovering around the dead man's body, wondering who was going to be the one to cut him out. McCartney's *With a Little Love* played on the radio. It kind of softened the impact. It was the first corpse Charlie had witnessed. Not for Rob. His first stiff had been a beggar woman in Mysore, India, lying stretched across the pavement, her body covered by a horde of flies. He had been obliged to step round her and walk on.

Dropped off at Registro, they spent a good half hour in petty argument about when they had arrived in Brazil. Rob reckoned it was the moment they stepped on the *Ely*, but Charlie insisted it was the day they reached Macapa. Pointless stuff. "Listen, shithead" Rob stressed. "It was a Brazilian boat, Brazilian crew, Brazilian water and landing on Brazilian islands constituted Brazil as much as the mainland did."

The argument was forgotten as they tried to wave

down a car. Without success. Charlie, bored, suggested they walk a little way along the road. Rob was reluctant. "You're getting old, mate" Charlie said in his usual matter-of-fact way. "Aye, I'm over the hill" Rob joked. "A few more years and my body won't be able to take the change of pace or my stomach cope with the food. I'm surprised I've done so well so far with no illness. I've only had the dribbles once." "I know" Charlie said. "At twenty-four you're past it" Rob agreed. "Aye, travelling takes it out of you. Look at this ulcer I'm supposed to have. The cramps. Anyway, apart from my feet, I've never felt healthier." "That's what it is, your feet" Charlie smirked. "You don't want to walk because of the sores." "Good God! After all this time it's got through to you that my feet are hurting." "You shouldn't have bought those new sandals in Rio. It takes a while to wear them in." Rob looks down at Charlie's grey gutties. "Better than having stinking feet, mate. Even with these sores, I can out walk you any day."

Three miles later, both had stopped and were sitting by the roadside, the midday sun beating down on them. "Why don't we take the bus?" Charlie suggested. "Good idea" Rob replied. "Here's one now." He rose to his feet, waved his arms. The bus went straight by. "Things are not as simple as they appear" Charlie stated philosophically, stretching out on the grass. "I'm glad it's such a beautiful day." "Aye, but it's the World Cup Final this evening and I don't want to be stuck somewhere without a telly." Charlie let out a sigh. "I prefer cricket."

Rob scoffed. "You English are all the same. You think you're good at football, but you're not, so you pretend you're interested in cricket. You're all wankers. No wonder all us Scotsmen came down to your country, you need back bone. You're just like fell sheep, they need a good shot of Scottish blackfaces to keep your strain from degenerating and catching foot and mouth." Charlie is offended. "You'll get a boot in the mouth if you don't shut up, you ignorant bastard. You've no breeding, that's your problem. The sooner they make Scotland independent, the sooner we can send all you haggis eating, kilt swinging, loud mouthed, uncouth rabble back there." "And we'd gladly go, once you return everything you've stolen from us" Rob returned. "We'll get the Stone of Destiny back, you thieving hypocrites."

"The Stone of Destiny!" Charlie squealed. "What a load of crap." Rob shook his head. "See, denying everything now." "No I'm not." Charlie replied. "Hypocrite. Your lot stole the Stone of Destiny and you'll never right that wrong with the Scottish until you give it back." Charlie dismissed Rob's argument. "I don't see what all the fuss is about. It's only a piece of rock." "A piece of rock! Robert the Bruce was crowned on that stone, and every Scottish king back to Malcolm Canmore. It was brought across the seas by Saint Columba and, according to the history, it was Jacob's pillow when he had his dream about the ladder." "Crap!" Charlie muttered. "Crap is it? Edward the First stole it and took it to England, and every English monarch since then has been crowned on it." Charlie laughed. "Go and play your bagpipes." "Aye, right, you cricket twat."

Curitiba bus station tannoy was playing 'Moon River' as Charlie and Rob drank beer and watched Argentina beat Holland 3-1 in the World Cup Final. All around, goggle-eyed Brazilians were sullen faced and disgusted that Argentina had become the new world champions. They were convinced that the Argentinos had paid the Peruvians to throw their game 6-0 so they could qualify for the final at Brazil's expense. The Brazilians were no longer the number one footballing nation in South America. It dented their national pride and made them want to go to war with Argentina.

The station tannoy played Greensleeves as they waited for the overnight bus to Foz de Iguazu. A mouthful of bread and processed cheese made its way round their famished mouths in time to the music. Both were tired from journeying. They hadn't had their clothes off since leaving Rio three days earlier. Their jeans hadn't seen a wash since St George. They looked as though they'd travelled two thousand five hundred miles in two weeks. Charlie's feet smelt as though they had walked the whole way.

Another sleepless night on the bus delivered them at Foz in time to catch the local bus out of town to the Iguazu Falls, the largest cataract in South America. Charlie was partially excited, but Rob was all ready to compare this natural downpour with the Victoria Falls on the Zambezi. His critical eye, he told Charlie, would put everything into perspective.

It was still dark as they walked along the avenue pathways, the thunder of cascading water anaesthetising their consciousness. Undetected beneath the roar, they stole ice-creams from an open kiosk as the attendant slept on the ground under his poncho. As the grey dawn approached, Rob and Charlie stood on the catwalk beneath the falls, sodden, and wringing wet, engulfed by mist. The waters of the Iguazu, surging in a cataclysm of white caps over the brink, pelted the two foolish sods below. In the face of such a deluge, they soon had enough of their own madness. However, not until Charlie had unpacked his precious camera and taken one photo. "Well, how does it compare to the Victoria falls?" Charlie asked. "It doesn't. Its impressive, but the Parana is not the Zambesi."

So much for the Falls. They were back in Foz, a strange little frontier town with a ferry service across the Iguazu to Argentina and a bridge across the Parana to Pte de Stroessner in Paraguay. Rob and Charlie had a cafezinho and sat and discussed which way they should go, Paraguay or Argentina? The prospect of moving on to a new country refreshing. They liked Brazil, but the time had come to leave, for everything was becoming too familiar. It was time for something new. Another country and culture, and with it another slice of mankind.

With four countries behind them, they were moving into Spanish America for the first time. The transition from speaking really bad Portuguese to fucked-up Spanish would take a little while to sort out.

## PARAGUAY

To Rob, the Paraguayans seemed less happy in their disposition than their Brazilian counterparts, perhaps attributed to the slower moving nature of their country's economy and the future prospects of advancement in social and monetary status being duller. But the women were pretty, the people in general friendly, though slightly more reserved and humble than the Brazilians. After all, Brazilians are a rum lot.

The standard of living was slightly lower, but the prices only fractionally cheaper. Then again, it was difficult to assess the overall picture of a country from its capital city. There was more than a touch of poverty out in the Chaco and amongst the Guarani Indians holding on to the old way of life. In Ascuncion the presence of countless street sellers flogging pocket calculators to tiger balm, pastellitos to cake-buns, pineapple juice to peeled oranges, was an indication of a market aimed at both supplying a poorer public and supporting a struggling poorer class. Yet the overall atmosphere of Asuncion was one of relaxation with enough to go round for everyone. The rich did not stand out from the poor, each dressed similarly as in Brazil. Admittedly, the sales assistants were quick to try and accost Rob and Charlie in the street to come indoors to view their merchandise. The sense that the shop owners were heavy on their assistants in a brow-beating Victorian fashion gave an edge to the assist-ants' relationships with their customers. It evoked a firm politeness, more out of fear of losing their jobs than attempting to get someone to buy.

The history of war haunted the whole nation. From a population of five hundred and twenty-five thousand at the beginning of the Triple Alliance War to the two hundred and twenty-one thousand left alive after the war, it was hardly surprising why the TAW meant so much to the Paraguayans. To lose sixty percent of the population and be left with only twenty-eight thousand seven hundred and sixty-four men was nothing short of genocide. The memory of the two loser President Lopezs was only erased finally by the winning of the Chaco War (1932-1935) against Bolivia. The victory had brought great relief and had generated a resurgence in national pride. It was the greatest moment that filled the only other pages of Paraguayan history. The old tank on Independence Square, built at Elswick Works, Newcastle, and the adoption of General Estigarribia as a national hero were the reminders. However, the people still believed that Marshall Lopez, despite all his shortcomings, was the father of the Republic and tried to forget the Napoleonic and Josephine aspirations of his son, Carlos Antonio and his Irish wife. They had little understood that Paraguay was not France. The resulting war with the Brazilians, Uruguayans and Argentinos reduced Paraguay to the status of a second rate country within a third world continent. It had become a forgotten country.

But to our story. Charlie was scrubbing his jeans in the Brazilian House Hotel while two Mormons in the off-chance of spreading the word, paid a visit to a resident guest. On the way out, they stopped to talk to Charlie, wearing only a pair of red underpants.

"Gee, are you English?" "Why aye, with skin like this I couldn't be anything else. You sound American." "Sure are. My brother and I are on God's mission to spread light and understanding." "Really" Charlie said doubtfully. "So you're brothers, then?" "No, not real brothers. Brothers of the spirit in God's Kingdom."

Charlie rinsed out his jeans. "Oh! I haven't been there yet. I've been to the Guianas and Brazil, but not to God's Kingdom." "Then we will pray for you. You are searching in the wrong places." "I know, I might try Argentina next." "You will not find the Kingdom there either." "Oh, I don't know. I could try Chile after that." "Your search will be fruitless." "What about Bolivia?" "Pointless." "Peru?" "Useless." "Where do you suggest then?" Charlie asked in naked honesty, standing in his red underpants. "Up there." The Mormons point upwards. "What's up there then?" "God. The spirit, the light, the divine being." "How do I meet him?" "He is within us all." "Which part of me?" "You search your soul." "How do I know when I've found him?" "You learn to sing his praises." They broke into song.

Charlie thought it incredible how many people sang songs in South America. They finished their song with pleading eyes. "That's alright lads, I understand," Charlie said, patting them on the shoulders with his soapy hands. "I'll think of you if I ever meet HIM during my travels." "Gee, will you? We'd love to come travelling with you but we have to convert someone at

three o'clock. We have to spread light and understanding." "That's OK. I'll just get on with scrubbing
my jeans. There's three thousand miles of understanding to be washed out since the last wash."

Meanwhile, Rob was round the corner having
breakfast in the railway station restaurant. The
bespectacled proprietor was all smiles and flattered to
have a foreigner brighten up the dusty walls, draped in
photographs and by-gone engines on the Rio de la
Plata line. His customers were usually poor old men
ordering the cheapest plate of soup with a bone and
no meat. Or an even poorer Guarani Indian couple
huddling over a cup of black coffee before taking their
handicrafts no one wanted to buy back on the street.
Or a drab grey suited man from another town, waiting
to catch a bus to his home.

No one ever went by train. Sometimes a train ran
to Encarnacion on the Argentine frontier, but they
were few and infrequent. The station had become a
museum piece that collected cobwebs and never opened its doors on to the platform, and never removed
the notice above the ticket office that said CLOSED.
Only the restaurant opening out on to *Calle Eligio
Ayola* and a peaceful little off centre square bred life to
Carlos Antonio Lopez's magnificent railway terminal.

The proprietor nudged his burly simple waiter to
serve the gentleman sitting at the red chequered table
by the window. Sweet Latin American music eased out
of an old gramophone behind the serving counter as
the waiter clambered his way between the tables,
trying to appear gracious and succeeding in catching
his braces on a chair. He shrugged it off and nearing
Rob, bowed and asked if he could take his order. Rob
scratched his head. "Oh yes. Café y pan, por favor."

The waiter retreated and the proprietor beckoned
him aside and asked what the gentleman had ordered.
"Coffee and bread" the waiter boomed. "Ssh! You silly
oaf, not so loud" the proprietor whispered. "The
gentleman is a foreigner and maybe his Spanish is not
so good. Maybe he wants coffee with milk and bread
with butter and two eggs inside and a steak as well,
and a sticky bun to finish. He looks much hungry.
Hurry! Do not keep the gentleman waiting."

The burly waiter, all fingers and thumbs,
drummed on the serving hatch as a skinny red faced
man in the kitchen dropped beads of sweat into the

coffee, grey hairs onto the buttered bread and drips of blood onto the steaks as he sawed through a carcass hanging from a hook.

The waiter nervously glanced at the proprietor changing the gramophone record and shouted at the cook to hurry up, thankful the proprietor hadn't done the same to him. Jobs were so scarce in Paraguay, he didn't want to end up living on plates of soup without a bone. It was bad enough getting a decent bone to eat at the restaurant as a waiter, never mind as a customer. The proprietor was a mean old skinflint making good money out of bones.

The waiter grabbed the coffee as the cook plonked the order on the counter and shouted, "Buttered bread, two eggs, one steak sandwich breakfast." The waiter picked it up and reminded the cook about the sticky bun. The cook sighed, ran out the back door and reappeared puffing and panting with a sticky bun bought just round the corner from an Indian street seller. The waiter smiled. The proprietor smiled too as he saw the waiter carry the tray across the room, avoiding as he usually didn't, hooking his braces on something. He wasn't too bad a waiter, just a little clumsy and slow at times. "Your breakfast, signor" the waiter beamed as he lay the order out before Rob and retreated with an unusual nimbleness of foot.

Rob looked at the milk coffee, the buttered bread, two egg, one steak sandwich breakfast and sticky bun, and scratched his head again. He knew his Spanish was bad, but had always through café y pan meant coffee and bread. The sooner he learned the lingo properly the better.

That afternoon Rob and Charlie each blatantly cashed a hundred pounds of traveller's cheques, having signed each other's. With beaming smiles, they strolled the streets waiting to be accosted by sales assistants, trying to make them part with their loot. But the cowboy boots were too concertinaed, the leather shoulder bags too heavily patterned, the hide skin hats too small. They were having no luck on the souvenir scene, until two eager women grabbed them by their elbows and dragged them into the depths of their shop.

"Signors, you must buy something or we will have no job tomorrow" they pleaded as in the gloomy light they focused on racks and racks of US Forces surplus attire of jungle green, field grey, khaki, full dress, battle dress, fatigues and strictly regimental. "We don't want any of these" Charlie said aghast. "It's hard enough as it is convincing people we're not American without dressing like ones."

"But Signors, you will be helping us by turning American foreign aid into money if you buy one." "I don't want to disappoint you, ladies" Rob said, "but we can't be seen to look military if we're going to Argentina." "Signors" they pleaded. "We must sell something. It is after midday. Maybe you will be our last customers. The manager is such an angry man, he can have someone take our jobs within an hour. There are so many people looking for work. Please buy something." "Away man!" Charlie said to Rob. "We can't hang round here all day. They'd tell us anything to make us buy something."

"Signor" one assistant cried as Charlie headed for the door, the tears streaming down her cheeks. "Please" she pleaded "come back." "We have an upstairs too" the other added in desperation. "Maybe you will find something there." Charlie, caught midst this barrage of emotions, looked to Rob who gave him an expression "What does it matter, money's money, let's spend it".

They followed the gleeful assistants upstairs past the greatcoats, past the mackintoshes and beyond the trench coats to stop amidst a paradise of jerkins, parkas, wind-breakers and lumber jackets. Why such a cold climate shop was doing business on the main street of Asuncion so close to the tropic of Capricorn was bewildering? It may have been the Paraguayan winter, but Rob and Charlie couldn't get to sleep at night for chasing off the mosquitoes in their stifling hotel room. Yet, they felt obliged to buy something.

As they lay on their beds that night they wondered why they had ever been talked into buying two check wool-lined jackets. They tried to convince themselves if they were heading further south and then across the Andes they would certainly need them. One thing for sure, Paraguay had a strange way of creating a demand for the things it had to sell.

And what souvenirs did you buy in Paraguay, someone would later ask them. All they could do was show them their lumberjack jackets and smile and point to the labels "American Foreign Aid."

## ARGENTINA

The dust was sweeping in from across the Chaco, as a half witted, half asleep Argentinian soldier stamped them into the country. There were no problems, not even a remark that they were kind of late if they'd come to see the World Cup.

The contrast with Paraguay was marked. Clorinda was a shit-hole cowboy town of gaucho hats and concertinaed boots with not a hitching rail or horse in sight. It was the sort of place they couldn't wait to leave behind as quickly as possible. The local street sellers huddled under ponchos and pulled down the brims of their hats to escape the swirling dust.

Rob asked a few times for the whereabouts of the bus station. Most shook their heads, or pointed where the fancy took them and quickly disappeared beneath their hats and ponchos again. Eventually someone squatting behind an array of heavy vegetables put them on the right track. Not that the bus station was hard to find in a place like Clorinda, with one main street. It was just a bad time of day to arrive – siesta time. No one felt in any mood to communicate with the world or participate in the struggle for survival. But Rob and Charlie were in a hurry to be on the move, Clorinda didn't appeal to them at all.

Once on the bus heading south, miles and miles of open range flanked them in, only the numerous colourful birds relieved the boredom of black and brown and speckled cows that dumbly grazed on while they glided by. Charlie fell to reading Evelyn Waugh's *Decline and Fall*, a book far removed from their present reality. Yet Charlie was always seeking escape from his present environment, his span of concentration too short to spend a whole day living in the world of total outward awareness. By comparison, Rob was content to sit and gaze out the window and wonder how many of the cows would end up in a corned-beef can. Meanwhile Charlie laughed his head off over Paul Pennyfeather and Captain Grimes, which distracted Rob from the cows and woke half the passengers on the bus. Reading Waugh was much more fun than counting cows, Charlie corrected Rob.

Rob looked at the two hundred page novel cradled in Charlie's hands, then turned again to gaze out the window to wonder how any one man could ever condense the world into something so small as a book and attempt to make it interesting. There was one thing to be said about books, they cut out all the boredom of normal life. Yet Rob inwardly never felt bored by what his eyes saw, his ears heard, his hands touched, nose smelt or mouth tasted. That was five things Charlie couldn't get from his book. He got an overall picture of what the characters were experiencing, but only to the extent of reliving that experience by thought alone.

Rob felt if he could plug Charlie into a dream machine and feed him with so many fantasies that it obliterated his common sense, maybe he wouldn't be as contented when the machine was suddenly switched off and he found himself floating around in a world of reality, where his dream machine experiences were of no value to him. Perhaps it would make him wonder what had been going on around him while he had been plugged in.

Rob gave Charlie a nudge and pointed out the cows to him. Charlie looked, saw black, brown and speckled cows and returned to his book. Why Rob wasted his time counting cows when he could be reading and gaining a bit of intellectual stimulus and understanding about alternative things in life, he just didn't know. There was more to life than experiencing it for oneself by seeing, touching, hearing, smelling and tasting it. For after all, there was no way in which Rob could ever experience the life of Paul Penny-feather without reading about him. Nor was idle thought about how many cows ended up as corned-beef going to be of any use to him in later life.

But by now, Rob was thinking that it took all the grass on the open range to feed the cows. It took countless irrigation canals to water the grass. It took rivers from the Andes to fill the canals. It took Pacific Ocean rainstorms to produce the rivers. His thoughts were expanding all the time. He was creating his own dream state out of the concept of grazing cows and corned-beef while Charlie was still trapped by the mortal experiences of Paul Pennyfeather's decline and fall. Rob knew he was in the hands of his own thought. Charlie was placing himself in the hands of an author who was in the hands of is own thought in creating Paul Pennyfeather. Rob was mentally creating his own book while Charlie slavishly waded through two hundred pages of someone else's book. But if both were being amused, what did it matter.

On arrival at Resistencia, thoughts turned to food, something quick and simple. They settled for pizza and smoked sausage that left their stomachs in an indigestible state. As they sat on a park bench, stuffing pizza the size of a dartboard and the foul looking Italian sausage into their mouths simultaneously, Charlie, disgusted by the taste of his sausage, asked Rob how his sausage tasted. Rob replied in a stutter of pizza, "Cheap." And well it was, thought Charlie, the buying of it midst a thousand grabbing Argentino hands on their Friday night shopping spree, with wads of notes clenched in each hand, which was only enough to buy about two loaves and five tins of sardines.

But there were no miracles in this supermarket, just big long queues of exasperated housewives wanting nothing better than to be off on home. They bought two strawberry yogurts to wash the dry pizza and greasy sausage down. Neither would have been edible without the other, and the yogurt made it easier to forget them both. It had been another one of their food fiascos. Still, it was better than paying three thousand pesos for a small plate of ravioli and a shared beer at the first restaurant they came to. You know the type of place. Nice stone floor, nice white table cloth with matching waiter in traditional camarero rig-out and synthetic smile. No doubt it would have been enjoyable. But they would have let their masks slip with a frown on seeing the bill.

Finding somewhere to sleep that night proved difficult. The walk out of town was long, but shortened by chewing through a kilo of bananas. Passing by a cake shop, they stopped momentarily to make eyes at three girls behind the counter, who teased them with rows of buns and tarts and sticky treats. With a carefree shrug of shoulders, they succumbed to temptation. They entered the shop to a '*ding*' from the bell above the door.

The cakes looked beautiful, but proved expensive. Finding the cheapest, the end of the day sticky buns at a hundred pesos each, they used their bad Spanish, and asked for two. The sight of Charlie holding the St George pot in a plastic bag and Rob saying there was no need to wrap them, they'd eat them on the spot, was too much for the soft-hearted assistant girls. At seeing two young men, apparently in the straights of hunger, standing eyes a-glaze and tongues hanging out before them, evoked their feminine pity to bag up two more buns, and let them have all four for free.

Once outside the shop, Rob and Charlie smiled at one another at their luck, and giggled all the way down the street as they stuffed the buns into their mouths. On the edge of town, they found a lean-to in the fresh fruit market and Rob strung his hammock from the iron bars of two high placed windows, while Charlie wriggled into his sleeping bag on the concrete floor. Both spent a stiff positioned night, the wall preventing Rob from moving around much, the floor straightening out Charlie's dreams.

In the morning, an icy wind blew over the plains from the east. Rob stood by the roadside, stamping his feet and blowing into his hands, while Charlie sat on his pack, huddled into his Paraguayan jacket. Two hours had passed and no one had even waved, never mind given them a lift. With the usual impatience, both looked at one another, gave a nod, picked up their belongings and back-tracked into town. Well, after all, there was no point in freezing to death when they could catch a bus.

Buying two tickets to Santa Fe, they sat in the warmth of the bus station café, drinking coffee, Charlie still reading Waugh, Rob gazing around. The café could have been almost anywhere in England. A young man, cheap jeans, desert boots and duffle coat chatted drearily to his bored looking girlfriend. A heavy set man with the enormous hands of a lorry driver wrestled with the small handle of his coffee cup, whose contents threatened to splash his fur lined suede jacket and acrylic sweater. A neat little bespectacled man in grey trousers, black dress jacket, highly polished brown shoes and white neck muffler, stroked his water-flattened hair, and groped for the handle of his suitcase under the table to satisfy himself it was still there. A worn-weary traveller, blue blanket wrapped over his shoulders, was falling asleep right into his coffee. Another grey trousered man in threadbare tweed jacket and matching waistcoat, flat cap and baldy head, wore a greyish moustache to diminish his rotundity. A grey suited, white shirted, red tie type with leather suitcase and cigarettes endlessly transferred from hand to mouth, mouth to hand, tried to hide the nervousness of being a pressurised travelling salesman. A young man in blue pin striped suit with a gay black and red striped scarf, clean shaven and hair neatly styled, leather briefcase and morning paper gazed at the well worn shoes letting down his appearance. A pretty woman in knee length boots, long green overcoat, white canvas shoulder bag and brown plastic holdall, huddled expectantly over her table, dipping her croissants into her *café con leche*.

It was a quiet morning scene in which the blue pin-striped suited man got a shoe shine, the suitcase man sat patiently tapping his foot, the travelling salesman dashed off into a waiting Austin Cambridge taxi and the young duffel-coat man stopped talking to his bored girlfriend, having run out of conversation. The tweedy bald headed man commenced chatting to the blue pin-striped man as the boy continued to shine the latter's shoes. The lorry driver's hands had gone, nervous of the hovering waiter. The man under the blanket still had his nose dipped in his coffee fast asleep, and the young woman rose up in delight at seeing her boyfriend, dashed out to greet him, with the harassed waiter in hot pursuit.

Charlie read the last page of 'Decline and Fall' and Rob wondered how other people's lives seemed so simple on first impressions, and how Charlie missed it all. It was nothing unusual. Rob sometimes had difficulty in keeping his thoughts from sinking to how other people's lives seemed so empty on superficial investigation. With effort he had to stop himself from looking too deeply into their souls and remind himself that although he had a fortunate life himself, it didn't naturally mean it was any more fulfilling than the life of any one else. In India, he had seen to the bottom of life too often, and since those experiences he had always averted his thoughts from the pointlessness so apparent in others' lifestyles. He was just invoking pity which was essentially groundless. From the outside he could only look at another person's life briefly, observe them at most for a few hours, perhaps a day, and assume they would live the rest of their life in much the same way, with no new events or variances from day to day. But he knew this was a negative attitude. He only had to think of the time he worked as a bus conductor. A passenger boarding his bus watched him for perhaps five or ten minutes, then felt sorry for him as he would probably spend the rest of his life punching out tickets to a thankless but pitying public. He had eventually only punched tickets for six months. No, brief glimpses or first impressions could be so misleading, and judging the emptiness in another's life after just a few hours was ridiculous.

He would be interested to know what people thought of his apparent pointless drifting round the world. To the outsider there seemed no aim to that either. No, seeing the best in mankind was the only way. Eliminate pity, superiority and condemnation inside himself and acceptance of life would be so much easier. He was not insensitive to feelings, but he felt it was essential to override sentiments which veered on the dejected. A shrug of the shoulders, a laugh soon cleared away all misery and moved the mind on to something else.

Charlie laughed and closed his book. "You should read this book. It's really escapist. I haven't read such a funny book for ages." "Aye, I think I will. I need an escape. I'm thinking too much this morning." "You always think too much. C'mon, let's catch the bus to Santa Fe before it leaves without us."

Four hours later they were sitting in the bus station café in Santa Fe, Rob reading '*Decline and Fall*', Charlie prattling on about the merits of the *café con leche.* Suddenly his tone changed. "Fucking hell" he cried. Rob looked up from his book. "What's up with you?" "I've lost my passport." "Eh!" "I've left my passport holder on the bus." "Aw, shit! How did you manage that?" "I took it off my belt, so I could get some sleep." "I've told you before to put it round your neck." "It's a bit late now." "Okay. Go to the bus office and find out if anyone's handed it in."

Charlie went to the company bus office and explained everything in atrocious Spanish. He found out that his passport, traveller's cheques, dollars and all their Argentine money were on their way to Rosario. The company official was helpful. He phoned their office in Rosario to explain the situation. "They say" the official said, "that they will send your passport and money back, if it is still on the other bus when it arrives. So don't worry, come back later."

Charlie returned to Rob who was now wrapped up

in the world of Paul Pennyfeather. "Well?" he asked. "They said they won't know for four or five hours." "See what happens when you return to reality. There's nothing we can do but wait. Let's go and change some of dollars and buy some drink to ease the blow. If we don't get your stuff back, life's going to get tougher."

Charlie heaved a sigh of relief that Rob had taken it so lightly. "Well, I'll tell you one thing, Charlie" Rob said as he passed the bottle of Cointreau to him. "As long as we keep making mistakes, life sure won't be boring. But if we lose any of your money, we'll be off the Cointreau and back on to water. It's all very well living off these dummy traveller's cheques, but we're getting through them."

When Rob and Charlie got off the train at Retiro station in Buenos Aires, everyone else had long since gone the week before. There were no longer banner waving multi-nationals singing patriotic songs in defiance of the watchful armed police. Retiro was now a quiet South American terminal point, where passengers came and went about their normal business with little bustle and little fuss. The large station clock ticked peacefully round and the information desk had room to place an elbow on the counter, enabling questions to be asked in a civilised manner and to be answered in a graceful mood. Most of the trains were empty and the little bars and *pastellito* stalls in every corner of the station did little business. The boom was over, all the pieces had been swept aside and life had returned to normal.

'Welcome to Buenos Aires' a sign read as they handed their tickets to the collector at the gate. It was Sunday morning and the station clock chimed eight. Charlie had been reunited with his passport, but two hundred dollars worth of cash had not been returned. His remaining traveller's cheques were still intact plus everything else a man-about-the-world carries in respect of documents. With the dent in their finances they decided to spend the day in BA then travel on across the Pampas. The Mendoza train left at ten o'clock that night.

BA was very cosmopolitan and very European. It had the feel, the look, the mood of a large city. Yet it was difficult to believe it was the fifth most populated city in the world. The enormity of the streets, 9th Julio and 25th de Mayo, tastefully dwarfed anything London had to offer. The Congress building styled after the American capital; the obelisk commemorating the 400th anniversary of the city's founding; the Casa Rosa Government House in Plaza de Mayo, befitting a nation with an empire it had never had. For the fifth largest city in the world, it seemed too nice to be so large.

Having munched through a number of *pastellitos* for breakfast, they began their day in BA by trying out the Subte, the underground system. There was no comparison with London or Paris or for that matter Munich or Madrid. It was more like Athens. With four lines each a different colour, it was an easy system to fathom, though Rob and Charlie didn't know where they were going until they got out at Constitution.

Climbing the stairs, their world opened out onto a beautiful clear morning that could have been mistaken for an autumn day in England. A tree lined avenue stretched into the distance, flanked by block after block of offices and warehouses, the grey building stone, solid and impressive, the multi-coloured single-decker buses racing past or parked in termini by the station. Here and there church spires punctured the skyline, and Rob spotting some gulls, reckoned they were close to the sea.

"Either that or it was a rough day on the coast and the birds have ventured into the city for easy pickings" Charlie added. He felt he knew. Being brought up in Newcastle, the wintry gales that struck the north-east coast from time to time drove the sea birds inland over Newcastle some eight miles from the coast. The gulls had a liking for the trees and cemeteries and the highest points of view, church spires and local public monuments. The other British winter birds, the sparrows, tits and blackbirds kept a respectable distance in the cemeteries and the starlings and rooks kept a watchful eye from their city perches. With not enough feed go round during a harsh winter, the appearance of the gulls usually meant a hard time for all the other birds.

But as it was, the docks were close and the River Plate eased out peacefully to the southern Atlantic. Beyond the docks they found the Embankment refreshing. They recalled the last time they'd seen the sea at Rio. Here was different. Anglers were out having their Sunday break from the rigours of a week's work. A little Scottie dog with a tartan overcoat barked comically as his angler owner landed a wriggling fish on to the embankment. Others propped up their rods and sat idly talking or munching on sandwiches, clutching flasks of soup or drawing on a *bombilla* of *mate* tea. Again the scene could have been somewhere in Europe. Yet the similarities with European culture and its way of life was best explained by the similarity of weather. Brazil could never be Europe, the climate put it in a world of its own. But Buenos Aires and its people of Italian, Greek and mainly Spanish influences made it an extension of European culture, combined with a southern European type climate. Shirt sleeves were worn in summer, overcoats in winter. It was simple. There was no need to develop a different kind of way of going about things. When in Buenos Aires, do what the folks in Madrid or Athens or Rome are doing. A simple rule of thumb.

Rob and Charlie had on their Paraguayan jackets, their hands stuffed in their pockets and as lunch approached, their minds were on food. They headed for La Boca, one of South America's greatest hang-outs for artists and their hangers on. It was the Left Bank of South America, a bohemian paradise, every garret a wishful painter's dream. It had to be visited. Not that Rob and Charlie had ever heard of it beyond someone mentioning it to them on the train from Santa Fe.

"La Boca, that means the mouth, doesn't it?" Rob had asked at the time. Their informant elaborated that La Boca had been the cultural centre for many artists now famous and living in other parts of the world. Painters and sculptors too many to mention who turned the alleyways behind their houses into open-air art galleries of murals, wall sketches and plaster of Paris. The world had come to acclaim their work, so Rob and Charlie thought they'd better go and see what was going on. Finding the place was another matter.

Rob asked a hombre the way to 'La Boca' and with great pleasure the hombre told him to catch a No.4 white coloured bus. They flagged down a No.4 and asked for the Boca. The driver put them off at a street corner in a distant suburb and told them to catch a No.28 green coloured bus. The No.28 was crowded and they paid their fare. Being a Sunday, Charlie thought the people must be on their way to see the work of the local artists. He had heard the people in BA were very cultural and supported their local geniuses.

The No.28 bus trundled on and on, block after block of offices gave way to shops and bars and cinemas and people of a poorer disposition. Washing hung out of side windows and the smell of boiled cabbage was everywhere. By now the bus was jam packed with over-coated men treading on toes and pushing shoulders into gasping mouths trying to regain their breath midst the jostling. The bus stopped to squeeze in a few more souls until it finally reached to its final stop. All the passengers descended.

Rob and Charlie were the last off the bus. They looked around confused. Where were the art galleries? They followed the crowd. From all directions other people, mainly men, were channelling down side streets and joining the growing throng. Before them loomed a large stadium. Rob and Charlie were carried along in the tide. Rob asked someone if it was the right direction for 'La Boca'.

"Si, Boca Juniors." "Boca Juniors?" "You know. Boca Juniors" he gesticulated with a kick of a foot. "The best football team in Argentina." Rob thanked the man, let him walk on. "Jesus Christ" Charlie yelped. "The World Cup has gone to these people's heads. La Boca is not some useless football team. I ask you. So much for a quiet little street full of bohemian artists. We're headed for a football match! God!" Charlie twittered. "How could anyone mistake the famous Boca area as a desire on our part to go to a football game?"

"Maybe we look the type" Rob said. "Maybe La Boca isn't so famous after all. It's years since I've been to a match. Fancy going to the game?" "You must be joking. Just because the World Cup was won by these blokes last week doesn't mean we have to go to the first club game of the season. That bloke who told us to catch the No 4 bus was a fool. God, I'm a cricket man." "So you keep reminding me, Charlie." Charlie sniffed the air. "Let's get away from here before we're mistaken for a pair of foreign football fanatics. They must have seen enough of them during the World Cup."

With great endeavour and a rumbling of stomachs, they re-traversed the suburbs and finally located

La Boca with its street art. It was a pretty area in an older part of the city with colourful fishing boats tied up by its waterfront of quaint little coffee houses, restaurants and antique shops occupying the leisure time of Buenos Aires's aristocracy out for a quiet Sunday stroll, happy to nod to the workers conforming to being their contented subordinates. These wealthy family rulers of Argentina, taking in the real world for themselves, taking time off from a life of theatre, dinners, social functions to patronise their favourite artists although most of the artists were normal run of the mill landscape or master imitators, it didn't matter. There were a few original artists amongst the ordinary. But not enough to stop these rich customers having a fixation for the more carnal pleasures of life. A quick purchase of something to stick in the furthest corner of a drawing room, and off it was to the nearest restaurant, hosting a singing waiter.

One could never be forgiven if the serving staff didn't sing well. There was nothing like a good waiter's song over a bottle of Mendoza merlot and a roast saddle of lamb. Antonio, the melodic waiter instructed Henrico, his guitarist, to play. His voice lifted the sea gulls from the highest steeple and chased them out to sea. All the Boca stopped to listen.

> Oh, my sweet Argentina
> Oh, my sweet Argentina
> Oh, my sweet Argentine
> Oh, my sweet Ar – yen – tine

Rob and Charlie, passing by, could have confused Antonio's singing with a dusty grooved record that hadn't had a new needle for years. But their mouths dropped as a much enthused Antonio, dressed in his immaculate waiter's whites, waltzed to the restaurant door, spotted the two filthy tee-shirted children of Punk, and turned back in disgust to the diners who paid his wages. He wasn't a snob, he just would like proper international recognition from real international people who would pay a meal to hear him, instead of louts hanging around the restaurant door like vagabonds trying to catch a mere glimpse of his whites for free. He lamented more.

> Oh, my sweet Argentina

Oh, my sweet Argentina
Oh, my sweet Argentina
Oh, my sweet Ar – gen –tine

Rob and Charlie failed to suppress their sneers of contempt. "A singing waiter, I ask you" Charlie smirked. "We've met enough singers by now to tell the good from the bad. Oh, my sweet Argentina. What a load of crap! He'll be on his knees next begging pesos from the customers. It's pathetic. Maybe we should have gone to see the match instead." "Oh, I don't know" Rob replied. "Shows you another side of life this does." "Life? Is that what football matches and singing waiters are?" Charlie said sarcastically. "Of course. They are part of it." "Well!" Charlie announced, turning away from the restaurant, leaving Rob flat-footed. "If that's the case, I might as well commit suicide now. The terraces may continue to roar, the waiters may continue to lament, but I don't really want to have anything to do with either." "That seems to put you in a kind of dilemma" Rob answered, catching Charlie up. "You're caught in the culture gap. Neither here nor there." "Well it's better than being caught up in it. Football for the plebs, singing waiters for the rich bastards." "Which end of the scale are you on then?" Rob quizzed. "I'm indifferent" Charlie replied "I'm hungry."

It was growing dark as they emerged from a cafeteria, a *pizza neapolitano* lying in their over-stuffed stomachs. With a few hours until their train left, they contentedly huddled in a corner of the station, clutching a very large bottle of Cointreau and watched the girls go by. The Argentino girls were very pretty, thought Charlie. It was just such a shame that most of them were good Catholics. Their fortress of flame lay locked behind a barrage of guilt and centuries of conditioning. A brush against the breast was enough to send them to confession. At the most, the most experienced romantic could steal would be a kiss from a cheek, Charlie sighed. He felt destined to remain an onlooker and distant admirer of Argentinian women. In Argentina they were travelling on too fast for any woman to catch hold of them. Yes, Rob said, the women were pretty, but they were definitely looking for husbands. This choked any ideas Rob had on the women they were gazing at. "Gold rings and ringing bells detract from romance and replace the pleasures of sex for a noose hanging over your head. The lure of two breasts and a vagina equate to a female voice telling you to get out to work and pay for a house and a car and in return she'll give him a baby." "That's a bit harsh, Rob." Charlie slugged more Cointreau.

They were happy with their bottle of Cointreau, huddled in a corner watching the girls go by. The following day they would be crossing the Pampas. The day after, the Andes. A few days later they'd reach the Pacific. To them that was better than reaching out for a woman, touching and getting trapped for ever. They were young. Before them was the unknown. They were drunk. "Go out into the dark and choose your own path for it is better than a path already worn." Rob spouted. "And like Jesus, there were plenty more fish in the sea." Charlie agreed.

They got on the train to Mendoza and went across the Pampas in ten hours. They got there in the morning and took a boarding room. They slogged across town to the 'Cerro de la Gloria', drank wine, and slept the night away. Next day was a bright, clear wintry morning, the frost lifting as the sun rose over the Pampas to light up the foot of the Andes. Mendoza's famous avenues lay peppered in leaves, and the early-to-work artisans and non-professionals were well wrapped up in woollies to deaden the chill.

Rob and Charlie, rising with a shiver, washed under a cold tap and breakfasted on coffee and hot pastries. In a few hours they would be traversing the Andes like General Jose San Martin who in the 1820's, crossed the Andes with an army to liberate Chile, an incredible undertaking as great as Hannibal crossing the Alps. Rob and Charlie were preparing themselves for the same feat.

"Have you got the bus tickets?" Rob inquired anxiously on the way to the bus terminal. "Why aye, stop moaning. I hope Chile immigration doesn't turn us back" Charlie replied. "They'll have to shoot us on the spot then. There's never any going back" Rob stressed. Charlie raised his eyebrows sceptically, but said nothing.

At the bus station they found their bus, and much to their dismay, it was not Neckermann. It was a twenty seater pre-Second World War vehicle with wooden doors, wooden panelling and kapok stuffed seats. The bodywork was decorated with paintings of the open highway, mountains, rivers, trees and Christ. The wheel nuts looked so rusty that they had fused with the wheel which had prevented the bald tyres from being changed for the last ten years.

The luggage was stored and everyone ushered on board. Having taken their seats, a woman stuffed a leather coat onto Charlie's lap and muttered something in Spanish. Charlie reacted immediately, thrust the coat back at the woman, and thanked her. Although it was a beautiful coat, he didn't need it. The woman shook her head, threw the leather coat back at him and appealed to one of the passengers to explain what was happening. By now, Rob was catching on. All twenty people on the bus appeared to have two jackets, two coats or a combination of outdoor wear from suede knee-length trench coats to imitation mink stoles.

"Charlie. She wants you to pretend it's yours." "So I've gathered," Charlie replied in an irritated rasp. Rob smiled at the insistent woman and nodded his head. She retreated down the aisle and returned with a leather jacket for him. "You're not being left out of this one" Charlie said, struggling with his jacket, little knowing whether to put it on or not. The bus started up. It was three hundred and fifty kilometres from Mendoza to Santiago, and the Chile border crossing stood at over thirteen thousand feet.

They passed through Las Heras and began to climb the snowy mountains towering above. Rob and Charlie sat chewing on the Argentinian equivalent of *Murray Mints*, straining to see back across the dusty Pampas and the vineyards around Mendoza. The strain became too much and they contented themselves with scanning the thousand foot cliffs which Charlie wanted to get out and climb. It made his climbs in the English Lakes seem puerile by comparison. "Who in their right mind would be a rock climber anyway" Rob said. "You might as well go down the pits and see a different type of rock face as a coal miner." Charlie shook his head. After all, he had worked in the climbing shop and had met famous climbers, and listened to their tales.

They drove through Villavicencia, winding up a river valley, the drop over the side gaining in vertical fall-away with each kilometre until at Uspallata they stopped for a coffee break. Over coffee, the passengers fell into light chatter with one another, the majority middle-aged Chileno women on their way home after a shopping spree in Argentina and visiting their relatives who had stayed on in the country after Pinochet took over in Chile. With two hundred thousand Chileno refugees living in and around Mendoza, they had swelled the population to make it the second largest city in Argentina.

The other five passengers were male, two expatriate Chilenos on their way to Santiago to perform their international cabaret act as singer and musician. The singer Jose Gruesom had been numero uno before the coup, his records too numerous to count. After the army had machine-gunned the Santiago students in '73, he'd moved to Mendoza with his son who was of university age. His hot-shot classical guitar friend (who was asking Charlie what punk rock sounded like) had also left around the same time.

The third Chileno guy, long haired, well into the Chileno freak scene, was a student who'd swapped politics for the leather coat business, just like the women on the bus. He said he was doing it to pay his way through university, but he didn't exactly look anyone in the eye when he said it. The last two male passengers were Brazilian journalist Noche Papel from Belo Horizonte on an assignment to interview the leading Brazilian World Cup player Humberto, and an Ecuadorian student. Humberto was resting with relatives on the Chile coast after Brazil's World Cup defeat, and although on assignment, Noche appeared to be in no hurry to return to Brazil as he had met the Ecuadorian student on a travelling holiday and had gone wandering with him. Now a week late in pushing on to Chile, the Ecuadorian was still with him as he had been persuaded by Noche that Chile was a good place to visit and had tagged along.

As everyone reboarded the bus, the classical guitar player insistently inquired who Sid Vicious was, what type of songs he sang and could Jose Gruesom with his musical accomplishment achieve the same harmonic sound. Jose laughed at his musician's questioning of Charlie, and told him they were getting too old to jump on all the bandwagons. He reminded his guitarist that he was looking for a quiet, peaceful existence. The musician smiled, his love of music and his enthusiasm for it had got the better of him. He was interested, that's all. English music had so much to offer. It was so diverse, he didn't know where to start to understand, or how to begin to play.

The bus climbed beyond the snow line to Pte del Inca and into a landscape of unblemished brilliant white of frosty sunshine and cold sky. Charlie's feet were going numb and the constant patter of stamping fee from the seat in front and behind was irritating him. It may have been the tropic of Capricorn, but an endless blowing of hands, wiping of noses, *brrrrrring* of mouths, the wrapping of chilled bodies in fur-lined jackets with chins tucked into lip-turned collars, and hands stuffed in pockets and pulled in at the crutch, hinted at sub-Antarctic conditions as the bus continued to climb. Charlie started his own stamping and blowing.

Inside the bus the temperature was just bearable, but at the Argentinean check post, everyone was told to get out and wade through the snow to the immigration office. They had put aside their fur lined jackets and coats and donned the leather substitutes they had been issued by the women. It was a ridiculous sight, twenty full grown humans lined-up in front of the customs bench, wearing identical outer garments and denying that they were new or belonged to anyone else. The icicles dangled from the gutters, breaths froze in mid-air and dropped with a clang on the ground as lumps of ice the size of a fist. Rob's nose had gone bright red and Charlie's arms blue as they protruded from his tight leather jacket that was a little bigger than a waistcoat on him.

Noche Papel had never even seen snow before. He stood with pink ears, chattering away, the sound of his teeth filling the whole office with a pitiful lament. Everyone else stood like stiffs while Jose Gruesom tried to sing his way out of trouble. Two of the customs guards recognised him, encouraged him to finish his song. Jose belted out his love song so loudly he caused a small avalanche in an adjacent ravine. It was spectacular. Everyone clapped their numb hands which produced some muffled applause that the customs men heeded. They ordered everyone back on to the bus.

Rob stopped for a leak and tried to melt as much snow as he could in a cloud of steam while Noche picked up a handful, sniffed it, threw it, kicked it and probably would have sat in it, if his Ecuadorian friend hadn't shouted that the bus was leaving.

## CHILE

A two mile tunnel separated Argentina from Chile, a tunnel which cut through Aconcagua, the highest mountain in the Andes chain. It towered twenty-three thousand feet, but they couldn't see the top, the tunnel blocked out their view of everything. It was pitch black as the bus rattled along on top of the railway track. Only the bus headlights gave any light. Giant stalactites hung from the bedrock-roof. Ice coated the walls edging in with no more than a foot clearance on either side. There was no room for error.

Then brilliant bright light, the tunnel's end. They were in Chile. The vista opened out on a world enclosed by shimmering mountains, glaciers, and constant avalanches. A frozen world. No streams, no vegetation, no animals nor birds. All pure albesence, argent streaks of snowy hoar, blank glistening of foreboding, perfect beauty. An ivory snow domain.

The officials weren't quite as alabaster. Immigration was formal and polite. All personal luggage, nicknacks and gear had to be collected from the bus and presented before the customs officials. So once again, on went the fur lined jackets and coats on top of the leather contraband that had walked around the customs office on the Argentinean side. For like all smugglers, the thing to do was to pretend they were doing nothing illegal.

"Is this jacket yours?" "Yes" answered Charlie. "How much did it cost you?" There are guarded looks and frowns from some of the women. Rob nudged Charlie. "Thirty dollars …." Charlie spluttered. He remembered some of the prices from the shop in Ascuncion. "Are you sure? It is your jacket? You have two on. For most people one is enough?" "I'm cold." Charlie started to shiver. "I bought this leather one in Mendoza... and this one in Paraguay." "Why?" "I liked them both."

The customs official gave Charlie a look of disbelief and moved on to Rob. "You have a leather coat. You bought it in Mendoza." "That's right. Thirty one dollars." The official scowled. He moved along the line to Jose Gruesom who had a leather jacket under his hand-tailored overcoat. He gazed at Noche Papel, the Ecuadorian, and then the student – all of them wearing leather jackets under their own overcoats.

Still moving along the line, he huffed and puffed at the thirteen women.

He stopped at the end of the line and called his subordinates over. "I know what's going on here. They are all in this together." "In what?" one of the women shouted. "Quiet! Don't try to fool us" the official shouted back. "There are twenty brand new leather coats, jackets and fur coats on your backs! Unless the real owner steps forward, I will send you all back to Argentina!"

A deathly silence greeted his threat. Everyone tried to avoid eye contact with the officials and eye contact with each other. Charlie fixed his eyes on the ceiling while Rob scratched his ear and pretended to whistle. The Chief Customs Officer turned to one of his men. "Who is that?" he whispered "He looks familiar?" "Jose Gruesom. The old crooner." "Really? It's years since I've heard his records. Great singer, you know. The best. Haven't heard nada from him since the takeover." "He's singing for El Presidente tomorrow night in the palace" one of the customs officials whispered. "Oy oy oy. Just what we need in this wasteland. A call from the Presidente's office."

He turned to the band of smugglers and barked. "I know your game. If I catch any of you trying to cross this frontier again with a lame excuse that a coat belongs to you when it doesn't, I'll nail you. Which ever one of you women is the real owner of these coats, you nearly got everyone here sent back to Argentina. Go on, get on the bus, think yourselves lucky."

What jubilation! Once clear of the border post, they were off down the white mountainside in party mode, whole bottles of rum supplied by the woman smuggler being consumed in gulps while Strauss' *Blue Danube* waltzed on the bus cassette. The driver, bottle in hand, took each snaking bend at a glide as they rolled downwards in drunken stupor towards the expecting bright lights of Santiago, eleven thousand feet below, waiting to greet them.

William Smith was always clapping his hands and saying "now then". As an eccentric Chileno of English parentage, residing in Vina del Mar and working for the National Cash Register Company, he was a bit of a tippler who liked more than the occasional sip of the local wine. He preferred nothing better than to take some hours off work in the comfortable surroundings of his own home, sampling vino and listening from the depths of an armchair (or wildly waltzing with his wife Rebecca on the living room floor) to the sounds produced by his second love, music. His stereo system he believed was second to none in Vina del Mar and his choice of music went beyond the limitations of samba and flamenco. It encompassed Elton John's 'Rocket Machine', Simon and Garfunkel's 'Bridge Over Troubled Water', Bowie's 'Strawdogs' and the latest Rolling Stones single. But as William Smith was well into his fifties, his favourite album was Frank Sinatra's 'Madison Square Gardens Live' and the ultimate track 'The Lady is a Tramp'.

Rebecca never took the words of the song issuing from Frank's and William's lips simultaneously as a slight on herself. She knew her husband was crazy. Why she'd remained with a man who was bald on top and had a chipped scalp in places who for the last thirty years had always cut his chin when shaving, was a mystery.  Although he always wore a white polo neck, blazer, flannels and a handkerchief in his breast pocket, he didn't look smart enough to pass as dapper. And with his spectacles on, he certainly didn't look so handsome. But what other man at his age would have her waltzing round the room to the Rolling Stones? She reasoned he was just a crazy misplaced Englishman who revelled in living the bachelor life and who treated her like his housemaid, mistress, nurse rolled into one. She wasn't his wife, she was his play thing.

Rob and Charlie were having a glass of hot milk in a bar off Quillota Street in the seaside resort of Vina del Mar. Santiago had been a quiet un-cheery sort of place. The only thing of any consequence was their meeting with a paranoid American who unloaded a lump of hashish on them. Rob and Charlie weren't ones to shirk responsibility while being in one of the most fascist countries in the world, and as such, smoked the hashish as fast as their minds could cope with it. It was a pleasant change from the sickly taste of marijuana and a healthy reminder of things at home.

Nothing was happening in Santiago, no tanks rolling down the street, no tear gas quelling rioting mobs, no policemen beating the shit out of rebellious students. It was all peaceful afternoon shoppers getting on with life and too busy worrying about the cold to concern themselves with politics. To Rob and Charlie, Santiago was a boring uninspiring place, and after a stoned out night mixed with dining on fish and chips and excellent Chileno wine, they decided that a few quiet days by the seaside would rest the aches of five thousand miles of non-stop travelling. Second only to Rio, Vina del Mar was South America's most talked about holiday resort for the *nuevo riche*. It had the same forlorn flavour as Whitley Bay in winter and was a postcard of desolation and deserted sea front. But that was to be expected in the off season.

It wasn't long before a bald headed William Smith had spotted Rob and Charlie in a bar and ordered a round of local vino to set them off on the right foot. With a display of panache, he invited them to his home for breakfast. The two boys at a loose end on such a loose day, readily accepted. Rebecca was still in bed when they arrived and could restrain herself no longer to stay in bed with '*Rocket Machine*' blasting out, a clattering of pots in the kitchen, and the appearance of black smoke from under the bedroom door. "That man" she mumbled to herself, pulling herself from under the covers and donning a dressing gown.

"Now then" William Smith was telling the lads "the eggs are a bit burnt. But there you are. I'll just pour another glass of wine first" as he left the toast under the grill, made for the wine bottle but decided to change the record instead. Rebecca rescued the toast in time and told all three to sit at the dining table while she cooked a proper breakfast.

The conversation alternated between English and Spanish, Charlie still half asleep and gone with the music. William Smith talked of Chileno hospitality and what pleasure it gave him to demonstrate it fully. Rob sat nodding affirmatively. "Now then" William Smith stated, with a clap of hands which had Charlie sitting upright. "Rebecca, what this boy needs" referring to Charlie "is for a woman to waken him up and bring him to reality." "Oh, I can do that for him alright. Look, here's his breakfast, that should do the trick."

Rob and Charlie's eyes focused bemusedly on the one burnt egg and piece of toast they were each served. Rebecca retreated to get dressed while William poured more wine. "Now then, I must go to work soon. I have some business at Reneca, a short drive along the coast. You must come for the drive."

William switched off his stereo. "Rebecca, we're off. Come and say goodbye to the boys." Now fully clothed, Rebecca shook their hands and reassured them by gesturing that her husband was crazy. "Play along with him to keep him happy" she winked.

Meanwhile, William Smith was out front trying to start his battered old Cortina. Charlie got in the back while Rob slammed shut the passenger door by using a shifting spanner as a door handle. They were no sooner in than they were out again with collars upturned on to keep out the cold, and pushing the wreck. Their breath misted up the bodywork as they attempted to bump start William Smith's motor. "Now then" he clapped his hands. "All together, push!" and the rusty heap began rolling forward, shuddered, then blessedly started by pouring out clouds of carbon monoxide from the exhaust. Rob and Charlie jumped back in. They were off.

Like all South Americans, William Smith burst into song, oblivious to the earlier setback. Charlie and Rob cast eyes at one another and refrained from commenting. Their gaze was diverted to the pounding Pacific waves breaking on the deserted sands. Rob, brought up by the Atlantic, who'd sunned himself on the Med and dropped acid by the Indian, now found the world's largest ocean a surprise. Until then the Pacific had conjured up surf boards and nude bathing, but the coastline of Chile changed his view of what the Pacific was really like. It was a chilly reality. Charlie, on the other hand, couldn't believe it was really the Pacific and wanted to get out and paddle in the water to satisfy himself it was all true. William Smith by contrast was thinking about cash registers and an impending sale.

They reached Reneca, parked at a seaside restaurant and while he went indoors to contract himself in business, William Smith left Charlie and Rob to stroll on the stretching beach. Charlie searched for sea shells while Rob sat on the sand reminiscing of idle months spent on Grecian beaches doing nothing. Both were returned to normal by a shout from William. "Ola, ola" he called. "Come on boys, time to have refreshments."

Rob and Charlie dragged their feet through the sand to join William Smith sitting at a table furnished with three bottles of beer and three paper cups. "Salud" William smiled. "Now then, business was successful. We'll drink these, have another and then we can drive back to town. It's almost time for my afternoon nap." Rob and Charlie duly drank their beers, then off they drove in a cloud of smoke to the vacant gaze of the restaurant manager wondering why such an unusual representative was working for such a reputable company.

"Now then, boys" William Smith clapped his hands. "I'll drop you off where I picked you up. I hope I've shown you something of Chileno hospitality to mention in the fields of home. England must be jolly at this time of year." And with a shake of hands and a wave from his wound down window, he slid out of sight, his Cortina leaving a trail of smoke.

Rob and Charlie looked at one another, laughed and went back into the bar they'd started from and had a bottle of wine to keep the day rolling along. "Now then" Rob said with a clap of hands. "Whatever shall we do next?"

Noche Papel had traced his assignment to Vina del Mar and was inquiring in the post office to the whereabouts of Quillota Street while his Ecuadorian companion dropped a postcard to his parents saying he'd be coming home soon. Noche was eager to get a story from Humberto (Brazil's number one player now that the great Pele had gone to teach the Americans). How did he feel at their failure to regain the World Cup trophy? Up 'til then, it had been unthinkable that the Brazilian national side wouldn't regain the title in Argentina. Even Noche Pale, a man of unbiased views, believed Brazil were unbeatable. When Humberto had scored the decisive goals against Poland in their last game, Noche had believed he was on his way to Buenos Aires to see Brazil in the final. In fact he had packed his bags, left his home and was on a bus from Belo Horizonte to Rio before he heard that Argentina had paid the Peruvians to throw their game. He felt frustrated and cheated, but given the time off by his paper to cover the final, there was no turning back. He had met the Ecuadorian who convinced him that he took his work too seriously and that he should make a holiday of it. So after the post-final celebrations and witnessing the wildest night in Buenos Aires since the War of Independence, Noche and the Ecuadorian had wandered aimlessly until Noche picked up the scent of a story over the Andes in Chile. He informed his paper and they agreed to pay his expenses. The readers were still wrapped up in Cup fever and an interview with Humberto was still hot news. Noche on the other hand was looking for any excuse to stop from returning to Belo. He'd not left Brazil before, and having gained his new found freedom, he wasn't going to give it up without a fight.

The Ecuadorian by comparison, was on a self-education course during his break from Quito University. A student of politics, he enjoyed Noche's informed picture of life as a well-read journalist, and many a heated discussion followed between them. Yet both had narrow views as to the practical application of the politics they discussed, and they were finding what they knew of their own countries could only be used as a reference and not as a guideline to the politics of the countries they were travelling through together. Everything seemed so different from the pages of the books they'd read. After a while they dispensed with politics and fell into conversation on women, drink or food and confessed that neither of them had enjoyed life so much, free of commitments and schedules, responsibilities and ties. It made them both wonder what they had been doing with their lives. They clarified the best parts and made resolutions to dispense and never return to the bad. They talked of fulfilling dreams and aiming higher in life. They discussed their understanding of life and their coming to terms with death. They exposed their needs and defined their wants. They confessed their wrongs and upheld their rights. Until finally walking past a bar, they heard peels of laughter louder than any they had expressed so far.

"Ah, Noche! Noche!" someone shouted with a slur. "So you've made it to Vina del Mar." It was Rob and Charlie still in the bar and well oiled on the local drinks. "Yes, at last" Noche replied. "Is this Quillota Street?" "Aye!" Rob shouted. "But never mind about that. Have a drink. Vino, rum, whisky?" "Wine please. Do you always drink so much?" "Aw, don't be like that, man" Charlie butted in. "Just get the wine down you and less of the high almighty." "Och, don't listen to him, Noche pal, he's just a Geordie punk." "Are you really punk rockers?" Noche asked in horror. "Och, no man. We might wear straight leg jeans, filthy tee-shirts, have a gold earring and close cropped hair but we're not punks, are we Charlie?" "Why no! We're just young lads out for some fun. Have you found your footballer yet?" "I think so. He's living on this street." "Well, isn't the world a small place" Rob philosophised. "Here we are maybe no more than a hundred yards away from where the greatest player since Pele takes his holidays. Isn't that amazing?"

Charlie broke down into another fit of laughter. Noche tried to smile, while his Ecuadorian friend tried hard to follow the somewhat erratic conversation. "Well never mind. Have another drink" Rob offered. "You don't seem to know how much Humberto means to the Brazilian people" Noche said, offended. "I can guess, man. If it was anything like what Willie Johnston meant to the Scottish people before he was sent home for drugs, I'm with you." "It's not the same. Willie Johnston was a nothing." "Here! Are you trying to tell me Willie Johnston's a bum!" Rob joked.

Noche, taking him the wrong way, backed off, then dismissed Rob as drunk. "Aw, lay off, you two" Charlie interceded calmly. "Why can't you be civilised and play a civilised game like cricket?" "What's this cricket?" Noche asked. "Oh, Charlie's havering" Rob replied. "Cricket's a game in which eleven poofs dress up in white, substitute a piece of wood for a parasol and try to smack each other in the middle stump with their balls. Charlie likes that sort of thing." "I see" Noche frowned. "Don't listen to him, man" Charlie said, patting Noche on the back. "He's only pulling your leg." Noche frowned. "But I'm not like that. I enjoy women."

Rob and Charlie burst into roars of laughter. "The language barriers, eh Charlie?" Rob winked. "Why aye" Charlie replied. "But drink is one of the best ways of crossing them. Here Noche, it's your round."

And where did it end but outside Humberto's door, sloshed out of their heads, being invited in to cups of black Brazilian coffee. Humberto sat amused at the entourage feeding off his generosity. Humberto didn't recount the lead up to the moves that made his World Cup goals, nor did he talk of the disappointments and failure to become champions. He had already unloaded that on his relatives and countless international journalists who'd sought him out on Quillota Street. What made this interview so different was that the interviewer Noche Papel was doing all the talking, recounting his adventures to the host and his family and introducing individually the Ecuadorian, Rob and Charlie to each person present. Noche was quite drunk.

Time passed, and the coffee was substituted for more local wine. Dinner was prepared and Humberto, family and four new friends exchanged life stories well into dark. Elsewhere it was a typical night in Vina del Mar and William Smith played his *Frank Sinatra Live* album before finally falling asleep to the rolling of the waves and the last refrain of *I Did It My Way*. It can be chilly in Chile. Valparaiso was a cold place, the sea fog hanging in the house coated hills rising steeply upwards, the ships anchored gloomily in the harbour. It's chilly in Chile is like saying I was Hungary, so I ate hot Chile Turkey cooked in Greece, for after five nights in Vina del Mar, they were saying all sorts of things to pass the time. Like, who needs strength when marijuana emaciates the body and leaves the mind a mess.

Rob thought it pleasant to have idle thoughts while waiting to move on. Life at times was so unbelievably easy that he blushed to think of others working hard while he remained horizontal eating grapes and smoking cigarettes to prevent sleep from creeping up on him. It was all too easy to succumb to the addictiveness of sleep. It was a somewhat uneventful way to live out life. Yet why fight it? Why couldn't he be like Charlie and appear to live in a separate reality from the things around him. Why could he not leave the immediate and recede with speed to the restfulness of dream and there perhaps find a world free of thought on the necessities of survival. Was there no escape from reality? Food and money. No. He saw himself as a non-conformist escapist in the sense he lived out his dreams and pushed them into reality. He didn't believe dreams were illusions experienced from the comfort of a bed. On the contrary they were realised on fifty foot boats amidst rough seas in the stormy Atlantic. But then again, as a boy hadn't he dreamed of being aboard the

*Hispaniola* with Jack Hawkins or standing by Christian on the deck of the *Bounty* before letting his book fall as he fell asleep. Did he believe that adventure lived outside of fiction and that he some day would live it?

Once again, Rob reminded himself he had traded fiction for reality. He didn't regret a moment of it, but in what direction could he now look to fulfil a new world of fiction. Soon his travelling days would be over, the challenge gone. He would need new illusions with which to struggle and finally consolidate a content reality as real as the palm fringed beaches were to him now. For the present, now only represented the repetitive packing of bags, as he and Charlie moved on again.

While Martina Navratilova was sending speeding serves across the net at seventy miles an hour, Rob and Charlie were travelling at the same speed on a bus through the Atacama Desert to a cassette recording of Simon and Garfunkel's *Sound of Silence*. At a toilet stop, on tv Borg was winning again at Wimbledon in straight sets against ol' Jimmy Connors who seemed to be heading downhill. Not that Wimbledon seemed that close from seven thousand miles away. In fact it seemed an incomprehensible distance. In fact it seemed totally irrelevant to life. It seemed that tennis was an alabaster sport of backhanded compliment to the Europeans who were whacking down the Americans and Australians, and having a smashing time. There was a mini war going on at the Centre Court and its surrounding battlefields and everyone thought it good clean fun.

The wheels glided on through the Atacama morning mist hovering six feet above the barren landscape. The pitted desert waste was a mirage of nothingness. No life, no nothing. Just waste. And mile and mile of nothing but sand and rock. The Atacama. The driest place in the world. There are parts where no rain has ever fallen. The zero humidity flakes the skin and wrinkles the hands and face, chaffs the lips. The mist, a rare phenomenon, soon lifted to allow the sun to penetrate and destroy any chance of life. A chilling wind sapped the heat and made their bodies cold. It was a strange place, and after twenty-two hours, they reached Antafagasta.

They had a beer and talked with the barman. They were told that the Death Train was leaving for

Bolivia the following day. There was only one train a week and they had no reservations. No reservation, no travel possible. Stumped, they decided to have a beer and think it over. Not that there was much to think over, it was as good an excuse as any. As the train was so slow, he suggested they took a bus to a desert town further up the line where they could buy a ticket and wait for the train to catch them up. It was a fairly common thing that the locals did.

They didn't want to venture out into the cold night to catch a bus. Instead they wanted to drink the seas dry with the local seaman crowding into the bar. They were tired after the bus ride and though Antafagasta was not the most inspiring town in the world, they were happy. The Pacific Ocean pounded in, as it did all along the three thousand mile Chileno coast. The copper ore ships lay sluggishly in the harbour, the cold winter wind blew and the sky went listlessly grey as evening came on. The wisest place to be was indoors in a cosy bar, huddled over a Pilsen's beer having seamen tell stories of the high seas. But they knew that couldn't be. The moving never stopped. The television droned in in the background. In far off England, as the Duchess of Kent presented the winner's trophy to Bjorn Borg for his straight sets win, Rob and Charlie reluctantly picked up their belongings. They said their goodbyes and continued their journey into the night.

What a night it was. When they arrived in Colama, a small town of shadows and freezing cold, they took refuge in a small disused wooden shack by the railway line and attempted to sleep. The icy wind swept through the broken windows and the cracked timbers, and no amount of turning or shifting could prevent their body temperatures from steadily dropping. Rob shivered in his hammock slung from the rafters, while Charlie with his fine feather sleeping bag, lay on the sub-zero floor with this teeth chattering. The door creaked to and fro in the wind, and sometime during the night a stray dog snuggled up to Charlie in search of warmth. Charlie was tempted to kick the dog away, but the dog's own body heat was as welcome as his to the dog. There was room for sharing. Up 'til then he had thought of dogs as being a burden to humans, giving nothing in return. But when an hour before dawn, his dog left with little more than a backward glance, it made him think again.

Up and stamping around, Rob peeped outside. It was a world of white frost and ice. The railway tracks lay crystal bright as blue steel, the trees stood bent and bare in the clear blue light of morning. His breath hung in the air. The icy wind had been replaced by a sharp crisp nip. There wasn't a sound, no bird song, no speeding cars in the distance, no footsteps on their way to work, just the rasp of his own breath and the faint crackling of frost underfoot as he ventured out the hut to urinate. The cold always went to the bladder first.

Fumbling with his zip and beyond with red numbed hands was proving tedious. His penis had shrunk to a miserable size, and stretching the foreskin with a cold thumb and forefinger brought back a little life. He relieved his bladder and tentatively looked over his shoulder satisfied that there was no one about. Shaking off the last drops of urine, he replaced his penis in his underpants, and while reaching for his zip, turned to shout to Charlie that it was time to find a café that served breakfast.

Sometime late morning the train for Bolivia arrived in a cloud of smoke and steam. The small station platform was crowded with babbling Chileno families and Bolivian Amerindians. It was a twenty-four hour journey to Oruro in a jam-packed train. Colama stood at seven thousand feet. The railway tracks climbed into the Andes and would eventually touch fifteen thousand.

Rob and Charlie had welcome hot cups of coffee and egg sandwiches for breakfast before boarding the train and elbowing enough space for both to sit down. The carriages were little wider than six feet across with benches running down either side. It was cold enough at Colama; it was little understood how much colder it could get at fifteen thousand feet on the windswept Altoplano. It was no wonder that the assembly of carriages was known as the 'Death Train'.

The native passengers with their wide brimmed hats and ponchos on the facing bench eyed them suspiciously. It was obvious they were wondering why such Gringos were travelling in the discomfort of third class. You had to be poor to travel third class. Why were they not in the heated compartments of second class, or the private sleeping compartments of first?

Why were they subjecting themselves to the toughest train journey in South America? The crazy gringos.

"For a start, we're not gringos, we're English" Charlie told somebody, emphasising that money was a problem for Rob and himself too. Yes, they were travelling third class because it was the cheapest. Not that he told them all that, his Spanish wasn't good enough, but he suspected they knew why. It was *mucho frio* though, very cold, he confessed to someone wrapped underneath a poncho. Was it always so cold, or was it because it was winter? Charlie was full of as many questions as his inquirers, but the language barrier diminished the conversation and left communication to a series of nods and smiles.

Rob on the other hand was thinking back to India. The worst train journey he had ever experienced had been from Hyderabad to Allahabad. It was just before the monsoons at the end of May when the daily temperature hung around 45°C (115F) in the shade. He had lain on a carriage bunk for two days and nights cursing he was alive as the sweat poured off. All the windows had been closed as the air sweeping in had been hot enough to burn skin. Although he was the only European, the other passengers were no better off than he was in the choking heat. They prayed for the journey to end as hour after hour they were delayed and the train sat in sidings cooking in the sweltering heat. The frustration or agony of the heat had almost driven him insane even though he had been in India nine months.

He later understood why so many other Europeans flew home from India. It was to save their mental health and not their physical well-being as many people might be led to believe. But forty-four hours on a train isn't long as far as train journeys go. A journey from Istanbul to Tehran took four days. Four, five-day train rides in the Sudan weren't uncommon. And the Trans-Siberian took a lengthy eleven days. It made the Glasgow to London five hour journey a joy ride. How could anyone complain while sitting in the comfort of a British Rail train watching the fields and cows and hedges and ditches whizzing by? How could they dare get off and moan about how the coffee was sugared or the cheese sandwiches didn't have any tomato on them? It tended to confirm they were unaware of what happened on trains elsewhere. How many got off and said "Wow, four hundred miles in five hours, amazing." Nearly anywhere else outside Europe, it would take three times as long. The Death Train took nearly five times longer than that. But Rob supposed it didn't really matter, they weren't in any great hurry to get to their destination. He knew it was crazy to be in a hurry at any stage in life.

The train chugged up into the white mountain wastes and all aboard shivered under woollen blankets and ponchos. There was little hope of keeping warm. The windows frosted over and the carriages themselves shuddered as the wheels cracked the ice-coated rails to reveal the blue steel underneath. The sun, a ball of orange and a hundred million miles away, dipped weakly out of sight behind a streaked volcano layered in snow. All was silent in the winter wild of the mountain ranges. A forlorn landscape best forgotten by man instead of being crossed foolhardily by a tiny puffing machine pulling a handful of wooden shacks on wheels.

At fourteen thousand feet, Rob and Charlie began to pant. Their breathing came out as short gasps for breath. Their hearts pounded and they went almost deaf. Their noses blocked and Charlie thought he felt his bleed. Their bodies were already numb and only their tear filled eyes, watery and red, gave any sign of life. Rob gritted his teeth and Charlie let his nose bleed as they climbed the final thousand feet and left the last memories of Chile behind.

## BOLIVIA

Somewhere along the line, the bandits jumped the train in a swirling fog and relieved the passengers of their valuables.

It was on the high Altoplano in the midst of the salt plains of Uyuni, that the train had juddered to a halt and a motley crew of *desperados* boarded and ransacked the carriages. It struck fear into the hearts of the poor travellers. The bandits were no Robin Hoods, they were thieves out for personal plunder, they had darkness wrapped around their every thought. They gave no idle moments of reflection as to their actions, robbery was their profession, their one line of work. Like any factory worker on an eight hour day, they didn't question whether they were fruitlessly wasting their lives, they had no time. Survival came first. Their code was 'line the pockets and worry about the consequences later' if there were to be any.

Not that the attack had been totally successful. One *desperado*, dressed as all bandits were with ammunition belts, had got as far as waving a gun in Rob's face and held out his hat. "Aqui, gringo. Puedo su dinero" he snarled in Spanish. "I don't speak Spanish" Rob answered foolishly. The *desperado* poked his pistol up Rob's nose and repeated in English "Your money, gringo." Rob hastily acknowledged that he now understood and put his passport holder into the hat. The bandit took it out and tucked it into his shirt. He then turned to Charlie and motioned him to do the same as Rob. Just then, the train lurched forward and shots were heard up front. The bandit rushed to the carriage door, fired a shot into the fog, and sparing no time, jumped onto a waiting horse held by another bandit. With a clatter of hooves and a shriek of distress from the train engine's whistle, the passengers rushed to the windows to see what was going on. But the fog obliterated everything; only the sound of distant shots could be interpreted that the bandits were making off. The train continued to move forward and slowly picked up speed. Everyone, at a lost for anything else to do, sat down.

It was a strange affair. No more was said about the incident. After a while it dawned on Rob he no longer had money, passport or any other form of identification. The bandit had made off with the lot.

Yet that didn't seem to worry any of the other passengers on the Death Train. They sat gloomily once more wrapped under their blankets and ponchos. It was a frequent occurrence to them. Such is life. What was a few pesos? What could a few pesos even buy in Bolivia? There was enough gloom without having to worry about a gringo having his money stolen. He could afford it.

Charlie was scraping off the caked blood on his nose, residue from the high altitude. "Now what do we do? You haven't got a passport and I've only got a hundred quid in traveller's cheques left." "Ninety quid. It'll cost us ten to get me a new passport at the Embassy in La Paz." "Then what! God, we're not going to get far on ninety quid, stuck six thousand miles from home" Charlie moaned. "Oh, I don't know. The world is a place of miracles. We're not broke yet." "You're always so optimistic. I should just leave you and keep the money for myself." "Maybe. But you lost the same amount at Santa Fe. Remember?" "Yes" Charlie mumbled. "Well, that's us even." Rob said dismissively. "What day is it?" "Friday." "Shit! That means there's no point in being La Paz 'til Monday. The Embassy will be closed. I've had enough of this train journey. How about getting off at the next big town? What is it on the map?" Charlie wrestled with the map and answered, "Oruro."

They descended from the train in Oruro. "Brrrrrh! This place isn't any warmer" Rob grumbled. "We're still thirteen thousand feet up. Have another look at the map." Charlie wrestled with the map once more. "There's a big town called Cochabamba. It should be warmer, it's six thousand feet lower." "Okay, that sounds great. How far is it?" "A hundred and forty miles." "Jesus! This is ridiculous. How do we get there?" "By bus, I think" Charlie replied. "Here we go again" thought Rob.

The bus ride was a hard one. The dust flew up from the all-weather road. Combined with the altitude, it was rough. Rising to fourteen, maybe fifteen thousand feet, the bareness of the Altiplano wasn't left behind until the green downhill ride on the Cochabamba side of the mountain ridge. The grazing of the alpacas, llamas, sheep and the rare cow, comprised the livestock. Humans were a rarer sight, bowler-hatted shepherdesses and their dogs lying sleepily by the roadside, or woolly-topped pack carrying wayfarers trudging on to some unknown destination.

The relief of reaching Cochabamba was dampened by the sweat from wearing too many clothes and sitting without stirring for so long. Charlie's jeans were soaked and he felt embarrassed that they stank of sweat. He need not have worried. Everyone on the bus was conscious of his or her own hideous odours to take much heed of anyone else.

With an altitude drop of a two thousand metres, Cochabamba was far milder. There was no need to sleep under piles of blankets. The town had its Amerindians but they were more prosperous than their counterparts in Oruro. The market was less attractive than at Oruro, the little nooks and tucked away tea stalls losing out to the regimented tables. The locals were more hostile in their attempt to gain custom. Everything was bigger and more impersonal. It didn't stop Charlie from buying an alpaca wool sweater and Rob purchasing a sombrero.

Some hours later, Charlie had his sweater on and had taken possession of Rob's hat as well. Rob thought it typical. Because they were short of cash, he had given Charlie the choice. A sweater or a hat. Now he wanted both. He paused, thought the matter through, and decided the hat was his. He regained possession of it by snatching it off Charlie's head. It seemed to settle the matter. Charlie never wore Rob's sombero again.

They found a decent hotel on the Calle Aroma for two dollars per person per night. Leaving Rob in bed, Charlie was up bright and early for a stroll and a morning cup of coffee. The market was still coming to life and he wandered around looking at the stalls in idle curiosity. He wasn't like Rob who passed them by as he had seen so many markets in India and Africa that there was little left to interest him. To Charlie, the buzz and the colourful stalls fulfilled his notion of what distant and exotic places should be like. He recalled vividly the markets of Georgetown and Belem. Port of Spain had been one big market. Cochabamba was different. The little old women in bustled skirts, bowler hats and pig tails were as foreign as the bright headscarf negro sellers of Georgetown. Though their merchandise was less tropical, the strange off-colour vegetables and fruit had him guessing as to their culinary uses. Rob knew too much in this respect and Charlie was expected to pick up a mumbled name of a fruit from Rob who took the knowledge for granted. Like the time Charlie had first seen a green coconut and Rob had laughed at his ignorance.

So while Rob lay in his bed, Charlie was out doing his homework spotting guavas from ten yards and manioc from five. But the market wasn't all fruit and food. Stalls of clothes and jewellery kept his eyes curious and envious of others buying. He had so little money to spend.  He was learning to touch without buying and was enjoying the browsing with no aim in mind. It gave him time to think and think of things he soon forgot. He rambled in his subconscious thinking of anything, it didn't seem to matter, there was so much to catch up with in his childhood. It was taking him all his time to discover who he was rather than what he was experiencing while being in South America.

The past was taking up all of Charlie's thought, there was no time to be in the present. Sometimes he wished the trip was over and he could return home to gauge the changes to his character, by comparing them with familiar surroundings. He wanted to know if he had outgrown his friends. He wanted to feel that what he was doing was a quick shortcut to understanding life. He wanted respect from his friends. He needed more respect from his parents. He wanted people to stop asking him what he was doing with his life. For he had no answers, and he still wasn't anywhere nearer a solution. One thing for sure, being in South America was better than being on the dole. He was no longer a drain-stain ex-school kid looking for direction. He had gone the one step beyond and chanced the unknown instead of panicking and settling for a job which offered security but no future. Travelling had no security but it had a future, the prospects of better things in the next town or country. If things went wrong they were soon forgotten when they moved on. Or at least that's how it felt to date. But the thought of having no money was beginning to scare him despite Rob's optimism. They had a long way to go wherever it was they were going.

Charlie stopped by a bowler-hatted lady surrounded by bags of green leaves. He watched and saw locals purchase kilos at a time. He was puzzled then suddenly realised what the leaves were as a local put a leaf into his mouth and began to chew. Charlie dug into his pocket and bought a bag of leaves for five pesos. The bowler-hatted lady laughed as he handed over his money. Uncertain, Charlie asked the lady if it really was the stuff that made the tongue go numb and the head go pop. The lady, laughed again, and waved him off.

Charlie rushed back to the hotel. Rob was stirring, but a chattering Charlie told him to wake up. He threw the bag of leaves on to Rob's bed.

For the rest of the day they were in a state of euphoria, oblivious to external calamities and internal mental disturbances. The powers of the drug *cryth-roxylon coca* could not be undervalued. They were floating. The type of euphoria was different from that of marijuana, cannabis resin or opium and more long lasting in effect than they anticipated. It didn't touch on LSD or mushrooms, but the let down was greater than most drugs, while the apex was superior to any soft drug substitute. The desire to take the leaves again came sporadically as did the apparent feelings of emptiness that accompanied the first pangs for more. Although not a physically addictive drug like opium and its derivatives morphine and heroin, cocaine could be viewed as a mentally addictive habit easily acquired in a country with ready access to the leaf.

Their first experiences of the leaf were ones of great clarity of mind and perception and a numbness of body. Only on coming down had they given any thought to food. Smoking the leaves gave a short term highness of greater intensity, but it was difficult to distinguish the effect of the leaves from the inhaling of tobacco which they weren't familiar with. Cocaine had a uniqueness in that unlike grass of hashish, the mind didn't become fixed on one point, but rather fixed on everything as a whole. Whether this aided their concentration they weren't quite sure. Concentration power seemed greatly increased with the leaves, yet there seemed room within their minds to concentrate on more than one thing at a time. However, it was early days to realise the full effects of the leaf. A few more chews and they'd be in a better position to rationalise fuller. Something was going on. It was not hallucinogenic in any way and whether Rob and

Charlie were even aware of the full effects of the leaves was hard to ascertain in their strange environment.

Sunday night, they took the train to La Paz. The journey soon flew by as they talked to Guido the Swiss. Guido was an uninteresting character to Rob. He had met a thousand Guidos while travelling and meeting another one didn't overwhelmingly impress him. Charlie on the other hand was all mouth and eager to tell stories of their adventures across the Amazon and over the Andes. Rob almost blushed at the exaggerations Charlie made in his recounts. Guido, a twenty-one year old, newly graduated student from the University of Zurich, sat listening attentively, his command of English sufficient to make sense of Charlie's Geordie accent. What he thought of Charlie's stories Rob couldn't work out, his typically Swiss poker-face registered nothing but polite smiles and agreeing nods. Charlie meanwhile didn't care, he was relieved to find someone to talk to about his adventures after such a long time without meeting a fellow European or traveller. Guido, after all, was on the same search for the something as he was.

Rob sat silently and knew that the something was understanding their fellow human beings, but he let them rabbit on. He was relieved to sit back and rest and watch and listen not because he had nothing to say, but because he saw himself as he had been a few years before, when he had been Charlie and Guido, when he had been just a cardboard cut-out with a different face. He saw life repeating itself. Yet he couldn't go around telling people that. He couldn't tell Charlie, it would undermine his confidence. So instead, he sat and listened and nodded when Charlie wanted a point of agreement from him. Guido eventually got a word in and told them stories of his exploits in Peru and Bolivia and why he'd flown into Lima from Zurich in the first place. Charlie sat, ears flapping, and Rob decided Guido wasn't such a bad bloke after all.

Their arrival in La Paz was cold, and was warmed with a cup of coffee in the station café. They were back at twelve thousand feet, the altitude was taking effect again. Now it was in the form of breathlessness on climbing the steep hills. For La Paz was a city of narrow cobbled streets and puffing inhabitants. Finding a cheap dark hotel room wasn't easy and eventually they settled for a double windowless habitation with a chamber pot to share. Their hotel was having major problems with their sanitation, the entrance through the front door was made by leaping over a deep ditch exposing a broken pipe gushing sewage. However, the back drop scenery of snow capped mountains made it picturesque. The Indian market in Calle Buenos Aires and its uncountable stalls tumbled down the hillsides and filled the off-shoot streets with dazzling colour. It was not a dreary city, but the constant watching out for traffic or clumsy pedestrians made it wearing. There were many tea shops, yet none were comfortable for any length of time. The fluctuation of prices always meant asking before foolishly diving headlong into great expense.

The week before the national elections had been held and had left every wall in the city covered in posters and political graffiti. It didn't add character to the city but detracted from it, as the eye became bored with the same repetitive slogans. It reflected political fervour of twelve years of anticipation for the return to democracy, which in the aftermath was totally pointless as the President elect was put into power by a rigged voting system. The people were disillusioned and wondered if an elected government was conceivable in Bolivia. The presence of large numbers of riot police in the city-centre armed with guns and tear gas was evidence of the new President's fear of a revolution. The closure of the University on Avenida Arce, the military police outside, the uncountable slogans of student frustration daubed on the walls, was a sign of the times. Many of the windows on one of the university floors were smashed and presented jagged contrast to the tear gas guards below. Yet life went on, though everyone who passed did not fail to stare at the broken windows typifying opposition to the new military government.

The Bolivian people still believed in God and always looked to their religion more in these moments of unrest. In the Church of San Francisco, the Bishop took mass and communion. The wine and bread were produced and the congregation filed forward in turn to receive their blessing. As the final mouth was filled, a small Indian woman with a bundle on her back, child in one hand and hat held in the other, shyly shuffled towards the altar stairs. Leaving the child in the aisle and telling the child to wait quietly, she moved forward to receive her holy bread. Forgetfully, she remembered her hat, and rushed back to to have the child hold her hat. Meanwhile, the Bishop had turned his back and was walking away towards the rear of the sanctuary to continue with the service. The altar boy closed the gate at the front of the altar, coinciding with the arrival of the small Indian woman at the altar steps. The woman in her innocence asked the altar boy what was wrong, where was the holy bread? The altar boy, highly embarrassed in a church full of kneeling Catholics, retreated to the Bishop's side. The woman stood lost, until the organist waved at her to pass behind the organ pipes and wait there. The Bishop, his face a collection of serious lines, ignored the incident and continued in monotone to conduct the service. The little woman rejoined her child and after awhile left the church.

There was great divide in the country. To quell the unrest, the President had decided to call the day that Rob and Charlie arrived in La Paz, a fiesta day. This meant a national holiday for the people and no one openly grumbled. Yet most knew it was to buy the favour of the people that the holiday had been called. Charlie was not happy. He was restless and ready to move on. The British Embassy was closed for the holiday and he cursed the fiesta day as a typical example of Latin incompetence in running a country.

"The lazy bastards, why couldn't they just be normal, decent, sensible, well-educated people, these Dagos. They have holidays for the least excuse. No wonder they are still in the backwaters of the third world." Rob was more understanding and decided there was nothing they could do but wait. In England if the government wanted to ease unrest, they cut income tax. It seemed to work and so did calling national holidays in Latin America. One way or another, everyone was directly affected. A national holiday maybe didn't do the economy any good, but it didn't do the workers any harm. Rob reckoned the workers in Britain would rather have an extra day off a year than have a half percent knocked off tax.

What was another day's wait? La Paz wasn't such a bad place. The fact that Rob didn't have a passport didn't bother him too much. He had had four in the last six years and the one coming would be his fifth.

He'd lost one between London and Dover in '72. He had smashed up a car in Turkey in '74 and the customs at the border wouldn't let him out of the country without producing the car. So he went to the Embassy in Ankara and said he'd had his passport stolen. In '76 he had to have a new one as the old one was full of stamps. And now in '78 he'd had one genuinely stolen. Guess that added up to five when he got his new one. He wondered what the clerks at Clive House would say if they ever got his file out. He supposed it didn't really matter.

The fiesta celebrations proved little more than the army parading up and down the streets keeping the peace. Rob posed on the square at the bottom of Calle Kennedy. "Queso" said the little old photographer man as he lifted the lens cap off his tripod mounted box camera, uno... dos... tres... quarto... cinco (it was a dull day)... seis. He processed the negative to passport size and placed it on a board in front of the lens. Removing the cap he counted again, uno... dos... tres... and replaced the cap. A series of arm movements in the cloth covered box, a quick juggle and tussle inside and heh! See what magic! The old photographer grinned and handed Rob four photographs in exchange for twenty pesos.

"Well," Charlie said as they walked from the square, jostled by some school kids free for the day. "Do you think they'll do?" "Hm, I don't know, they look a little dull. Maybe he should have counted to seven or eight."

The following day at the Embassy, they sat patiently as the secretary took Rob's passport application form into the Consul. Charlie had verified he'd known Rob two years. There was no other evidence that Rob was who he said he was. They sat flicking through copies of *In Britain* and *Country Life*, transported back to tea and scones and rural mansions. This was what Britain was all about, proclaimed the magazines. Rob fell to reading in depth stories of the Tower and the Jews while Charlie drearily scanned the recipe of *How to make Welsh Rarebit*.

"Mr Tennant?" "Yes" Rob answered, looking up from a picture of a Beefeater. The secretary stood before him. "The Consul thought, if it was possible" she said, as only the diplomatic service know how "if you could supply alternative photographs to these ones." She handed the photos back to Rob. "I thought they were a little dark" Rob said. Sitting back down behind her desk, the secretary replied. "The Consul thought it was the trees and the people in the background rather than the light effect that made them unsuitable." "I see" Rob said in disappointment. "I suppose I'd better go and get them redone."

Once outside the embassy, Rob frowned at Charlie. "Remember those school kids on the square" he said. "Look at the gestures they were making with their fingers while the photograph was being taken." Charlie looked at the photo. "The little shit bags, they're no better than the kids at home" he said. "We need to find a proper photographic studio."

Although it was four in the morning, they managed to pull themselves from their hotel beds and catch the bus to Copacabana on time. It had always been a dream of Charlie's to stand by the shores of Lake Titicaca, a longing sparked by photographs of reed boats and bowler hatted Indians. With a full moon due that evening, the scene was set for Titicaca to be permanently tattooed in his brain.

It was a bumpy bus ride, but after a few hours, they reached the ferry crossing point. Charlie had never seen such a blue-blue lake before. It was bluer than the sky and as crystal clear to its turquoise bottom as the sky was blank and endless to the stars on the brightest night. It was clear beyond words. They ferried across the lake, and Charlie gazed into the depths and saw a gleaming of gold, an illusion sparked by a glint of the light. The Spaniards had been blinded by gold, and with their endless mistakes had made gold and the possession of it the focus of their conquest. Likewise, before Charlie had left England, he had dreamt of emeralds being washed down from the mountains and lying in the gravel beds of all the rivers and lakes in South America. He had believed adventure to be the seeking of one's fortune. But at last he was realising the fortune was to be found in himself and not in the gravel beds of rivers as emeralds. Although the fortune still lay at the bottom of the lake, he now understood that lake to be himself. He saw the glint of gold on the turquoise bottom and no longer saw it as a means of making himself rich. In contrast he saw a life time's views crystallise before him. He saw the revaluation of all he knew and all he had been taught. Perhaps he could still believe that emeralds were washed down from the mountains, and with each emerald lay an answer and a fortune after all.

"Heh, Charlie" Rob nudged him. "Heh, wake up. Look, there's the Bolivian navy." "What navy? Bolivia hasn't got a coastline" Charlie reiterated. "Oh yes they have. Look!" Rob pointed. Anchored to a rickety jetty were two run down gunboats with limp Bolivian flags over the stern. Men in nautical blue uniforms hovered close by. "What a joke" Charlie sneered and returned to looking at the lake bottom. The gold and understanding had evaporated. He began to wonder what he had seen. He had never viewed his life so clearly before. He had never questioned any of the ideals he had on life. He had come to South America because he had nothing else to do. It had been the best offer open to him. To most of his friends, their best offer was a job, a place at college or getting married and having a family. That's exactly where he had been before Rob came along. He had desperately needed the security of a girl or something to give reason to life. Things had been so insecure, he couldn't even leave home successfully. There seemed no real purpose of getting a job but to spend the money on drink and drugs. It seemed that anything he did, did little but entrench him further into a life no different from millions of others. He hadn't deviated from a conventional life style beyond being expelled from school. And that didn't really matter, most of the kids left school at that age anyway. He had a few measly 'O' Levels and not enough with which to go to college even if he wished. His desperate attempts to leave home had been feeble. The trouble had been that he had no reason for leaving. He had tried desperately to find one. A friend in Wales. A friend in the Highlands. A girlfriend in Northumberland. It always came down to people, not a job, or a fixed idea of what he wanted to achieve by moving. Time had been running out. At nineteen coming on twenty, he had wasted three years of his life looking for a cause. He had stagnated, yet had blinded himself to the fact, and had gone around boasting he had achieved a lot for his age. But who would believe him? While other kids his age were in their second year at university living away from home, or becoming rock stars or actors or models or whiz-kid wheeler dealers, Charlie had been sitting in a pub saying he'd done a lot with his life. "So what" he had said. "These people know nothing about life. They're just in it for the money or because they can't think of anything else to do. They haven't worked in Littlewoods or sold mountain gear in a shop. None of them have ever driven a tractor." "Driven a tractor" he reflected. That had been his biggest boast while working for Farmer Potts. Yet he still couldn't reverse a trailer. Brrrrrrh! The past made him shiver.

In reality it was Rob splashing him with lake water. "Wake up man, wake up. This is Lake Titicaca. I just don't know about you. We came all this way and you drop off to sleep. What a bloke." "I was thinking about the Conquistadors" Charlie answered pertly. "Aw, forget about them. They're dead and in the past. Use your eyes and see the present. You'll never get a second chance."

Charlie looked into Rob's eyes and for the first time saw a void he had never seen before. He averted his eyes back to the lake and was confronted by another void. There was no escaping it, something had happened. Something had triggered his mind. His whole body shook as the answers to his old world came flooding in and were replaced by a new world which offered only questions. The past no longer mattered, he had thrown off the shackles and for the first time in his life felt free of worries. He turned to Rob, who was gazing across the lake and said, "Is this really Lake Titicaca?" Rob shrugged his shoulders and said, "Who knows?" The new world indeed only offered questions, Charlie thought.

The journey from La Paz took five hours. Copacabana was a little sleepy Bolivian town and place of pilgrimage for Christians. Rob and Charlie paid forty pesos for a room with a view of the lake. It faced north east and caught the pleasant morning and early afternoon sun. Rob was scratching his head and studying himself in a mirror while Charlie rolled a reefer with some grass they'd scored on the way. Rob wasn't happy with his appearance. "You know, we may manage to keep ourselves clean shaven, but we're not the smartest looking pair of punks south of the

Equator."

"So what" Charlie mumbled. Rob was still looking in the mirror. "Well, look at me. My monkey boots have a hole. My one pair of socks need darning at the heels and toes. My jeans are filthy and have a rip in the backside. This tee-shirt's rotten with sweat and about to drop off." "So what" Charlie repeated. "I'm the same. My tennis shoes should have been thrown away in Argentina." "You shouldn't have such big feet or we would have bought you another pair by now."

"They're all midgets in South America" Charlie smirked. "Maybe. But look at my hair, it's getting so long it's beginning to hide my earring." "Just brush it back" Charlie answered indifferently. "No, it needs a cut" Rob said expectantly. "Well I'm not doing it" Charlie huffed, licking the cigarette papers. "Come on! I cut yours in Trinidad" Rob replied. "You owe me a hair cut. Finish rolling that joint and then you can start."

Charlie got the reefer together and lit up. "OK, sit on that hard backed chair. Have you got the scissors?" Rob handed him a pair of nail scissors. "This is ridiculous, cutting hair with a pair of these. I can't do it." "Here, pass that joint this way" Rob insisted. "Go on, get on with it." "But I've never cut hair before." "That doesn't matter, anybody can cut hair. Anybody."

Charlie set to and mercilessly hacked away, stopping occasionally for a smoke. Hair was everywhere and Rob began to wonder what was going on. "Here, I hope you're not making a mess. One side feels longer than the other." "I told you, I've never cut hair before." "So what, you can still use your eyes to see if one side is longer than the other, can't you?" "No I can't" Charlie whined. "I don't want to do any more." "What do you mean?" Rob exclaimed. "You have to. You started the job, you have to finish it." "Well, I'm finished. If you don't like it do it yourself."

With that, he lay back down on his bed. Rob went to the mirror and began to fume. "You'd have done better if you'd put a bowl on my head. What a mess." "I told you I couldn't cut hair." "It's not that you can't cut hair, it's your indifference. You don't care whether it's a mess or not." "No I don't" he said spitefully. "I don't give a fuck!" he shouted. "Why, you little wanker" Rob fumed. "If I fell in the lake you'd let me drown. You're so self centred you make me sick."

"You're no saint yourself. You're always moaning about me." "That's because you always give me reason to. When is anything I say to you ever going to sink in?" "Fuck off, will you. Go and cry about your hair to someone else." "Maybe I should and leave you to get yourself out of Bolivia on thirty quid. You wouldn't know where to start." "That isn't fair" Charlie bleated. "Well, neither is leaving my hair like this. See what happens when I depend on you. I could easily do everything myself. I could have travelled South America myself. Pity I can't say the same for you." "Shut up will you. Your vanity's driving me up the wall." "OK, OK, but I wonder how much I can trust you after this." "It's only a stinking hair cut." "Is it? You can lie there and think about it while I finish the job you've left undone."

Half an hour later, Rob wearing his sombrero to cover his scalp and Charlie trailing a step behind, climbed to the top of the sacred hill and watched the sun set over the lake. It was a graceful and peaceful setting that bridged the silence between them. Darkness fell and they scrambled down the hill again. Thirty minutes later with a meal in their bellies, they returned to their hotel where they burnt their pride and let some words pass between them before the town's electricity was cut for the night.

From Copacabana, the Peruvian frontier was no more than three or four miles. A truck stood outside the market and the driver's mate shouted, "Yunqayo, Yungayo." Rob and Charlie climbed in the back with a party of locals. Most of them were women, and all were in pigtails and felt hats. Their woollen cardigans and bustled-out petticoated dresses, their black woollen leggings and high square heeled shoes made them the most unattractive women in the world. Their bodies had no shape bar a round red face and ruddy hands fumbling with their large bundles which carried their life's possessions.  They smiled at one another but they were nervous smiles out of shyness and politeness. Most of the time they sat gloomily brooding like mother hens and making noises to relieve the boredom.

At last, the truck set off along Copacabana's narrow streets, following the arrows of its one way traffic system. The truck circled the town three times and didn't encounter one other vehicle. Copacabana was hardly a busy town during the week. Come the weekend, the pilgrims came in droves to climb the sacred hill and watch the sun set. It was as traditional in Bolivia as making the pilgrimage to Mecca.

It was a memorable day. The pale town and azul lake fell beneath them as they rumbled on the bumpy road, up the dusty hillside. The air was crisp and pure, the backdrop mountain beyond the lake, white and dazzling, the yellow sands and wheat straw reeds basking in the morning sun, diluted by the altitude. They were still two and a half miles above the ocean, and in a land of wilderness.

The truck ground to a halt at a striped pole barrier. A yawning immigration officer, hat on the back of his head, signalled Rob and Charlie into his office. The locals, allowed more freedom, remained on the truck while the customs officer poked around.

The immigration officer stamped Charlie's passport and gave it back to him. But Rob's passport wasn't in order. Not at all. He had no entry stamp. Rob tried to explain. His passport stolen by bandits. The new passport from the Embassy. It was natural there would be no entry stamp for Bolivia as it was in some bandit's pocket.

The immigration officer was not having any nonsense. He got it across in broken English that Rob would have to go back to La Paz and obtain an entry stamp from Bolivian immigration. Rob thought a moment, then did the only thing possible. He put fifty pesos on the immigration officer's desk. "Ah" said the immigration officer. "That will cover your fine" and he stamped Rob's passport.

Meanwhile the truck had started up and was moving off in first gear with their bags in the back. Charlie shouted to the driver to stop. He kept going and some good-hearted native threw their bags over the side and into the dust. They would have to walk to the Peruvian checkpoint.

Rob had a shit, hitched up his jeans and they set off along the shores of Titicaca towards Peru. They passed a bowler hatted bare-footed woman struggling with a bundle on her back, her eyes fixed to the ground and glazed with years of toil. A man dressed in rags passed the other way prodded his straw-laden donkey ahead of him. He nodded politely, that was all, the clatter of the donkey's hooves on the stony road, the only sound. Two cyclists went rattling by and stopped a quarter of a mile on and pushed their bicycles up the steep hill. Young children in white smocks, walking home from school, played with their friends and disappeared into the rolling heath. The sun shone more fiercely and the breeze fanned coolly across the blue expanse of lake. Reaching the bottom of the steep hill and climbing wearily to the top, they encountered a crossroads. They took a rest by the wayside in the scrub and lavender.

"What a beautiful day" was all Rob could think. It returned him to his early teens when in escape from Glasgow, he went wandering the Scottish hillsides for days on end, sleeping in highland bothies or camping in sheltered glens. The lochs had never been as blue as Titicaca, nor had the heather smelt as sweet as lavender. Charlie meanwhile was wondering which direction to take. A road branched off to the left and disappeared into a range of hills. The other dipped towards the lake and passed across a mossy heath that acted as an air strip. He asked an elderly man passing by for directions, but the old man just shook his head and hobbled on.

Deciding on downhill, they crossed the bumpy air strip – its orange sock gently stirring from a fifteen foot pole – and climbed another steep ridge. At the top they met two young shirt-sleeved men who pointed the way down another slope to a disused road by the lake's edge. They brushed aside the sheep and jumped patches of marsh where the lake had reclaimed the road. A young boy shouted abuse at them from his boat drifting on the reed coated water. They passed an old man drying out his day's catch on a large reed mat. Out on the lake, they saw a half sunk reed boat near where a woman was staking her pigs out to feed on the marsh reed. Everything by the lake depended on the reeds. Even the numerous water birds nestled on the delicate rush.

The old broken road skirted the lake, passed tin-roofed huts. The midges swarmed and hovered by the leafless hedgerows on the last stretch uphill. Political slogans were daubed on every wall. They knew they were still in Bolivia. They came upon a little shop by the roadside. They quenched their thirst with a fizzy, flavoured drink. One more hill and there, a half mile ahead, they saw the red and white Peruvian flag hanging lifelessly like a worm. Slapping their jeans to rid them of some dust, they set off with increased pace downhill.

They had no more thought for Bolivia; their eyes were on Peru.

## PERU

That night they paid a dollar for a double room and a dollar for two excellent meals. They had arrived in the cheapest country in South America where prices paralleled those of dirt-priced Egypt and two-a-penny India. It was a pity they couldn't make the best of it, as they were almost broke. They taken a *collectivo* mini-van journey from Yunguyo to Puno and shared it with an Alaskan professor of sociology, his son and his friend, a New Zealander, a Uruguayan and two Peruvian soldiers who were lectured part of the way by a drunk who couldn't see why Peru wasted money on arms when there was no one to point to them at.

With occasional stopovers, the clouds of dust, the constant flatulence and cries of "Pooh! No!" stimulated conversation. "Who was that? Was that you?" Rob accused. "Wasn't me" Charlie denied. "Then it must have been him" Rob pointed. "No it wasn't" the New Zealander denied. "Jesus Christ! Pooooo! No." The professor's son choked. "OK, who was it that time?" the professor asked. "Open the window" the professor's son's friend suggested. "Don't be a fool!" the Uruguayan shouted. "We'll choke to death with the dust." "What's the problem?" a soldier asked. "You fart too much" said his friend.

The following day they reached Cuzco and what an amazing little town they thought it was. The police were out with water cannons and tear gas, successfully persuading the protesting teachers on strike not to block the main plaza with placards, nor fill the air with chanting that frightened the pigeons. Rob and Charlie avoided all that and instead met a local called Gustav and got drunk. He was a nice guy and they were amenable to him exercising his English upon them. Not that they could get much sense out of him. They had downed a couple of bottles of Pisco whisky, but they were patient.

Their hotel, the Bolivar, was a maze of rooms. Many of the doors mistakenly could have been the entrances to the broom cupboards, for that is what they most resembled. In the lower courtyard, secluded rooms were paradises for cockroaches and spiders, the gloom, the dampness and the despair, atmosphere enough in which to thrive. It was in these rooms that Hippies spend their last Hippy days, pushed down into the depths and out of the limelight by the advent of New Wave and the travelling Punks. Still the Hippies believed that long hair was the purist form of rebellion, and short-haired types like Rob and Charlie were just straight dudes. They still dealt their dope like gold and measured a man by the number of kilos he moved. Their conversation centred on the same old talk of weed, of stash, of grass and of course, cocaine. Birds and bits and broads and chicks and sounds and rock and pop and blues and vibes and signs and charts and 'MAN, if you ain't no vegetarian, forget it.' The same old claptrap, but basically the same interests as everybody else. Drugs, sex, music and food.

Neither Rob nor Charlie needed any lecturing on these aspects of life, none at all. The Hippies didn't dig them much, their hair was too much in their eyes to see the world clearly. Rob and Charlie just smiled and remained polite by passing themselves off as pleasant British tourists. For what was the point of Rob spouting off stories about Asia and Africa and his own acid tripping Hippy days? He had decided live and let live, he had never been one to go out and change the world, for no one would ever thank him for it. No, Rob understood the Hippy way of life having lived that lifestyle in the early part of the decade. There was no need to regress just for old times sake by swapping Hippy stories. The Hippies in the Hotel Bolivar didn't interest him at all.

Sitting in one of Peru's finest public buildings, Cuzco's Machu Picchu railway station, hemmed in by thousands of white tourists, they were waiting to catch a train to Aguas Calientes, a village a stone's throw from the Lost City of the Incas. "Do you think it's wise to catch the afternoon train?" Charlie asked. "Yeah! Most of the tourists take the morning train to see Machu Picchu so they can get back to the comfort of their luxury hotels at night. The tourists you see here are the ones who either missed getting on the morning train because it was full, or like ourselves, are low on money. They wouldn't dream of spending twenty dollars for the morning tourist train when the afternoon local train is only two dollars."

It was unusual to see so many tourists after being in the jungles, deserts and plain wastes of the continent, but Rob could not imagine what he would think of Cuzco if I'd just flown into Peru like most of the folk looking lost on the platform. They'd got complacent after their experiences. "We're lucky, Charlie, to have the wild adventure we're having. We've had the whole of eastern and southern South America to ourselves. These people aren't even going to get a seat on this train." "Tough shit!" Charlie answered. "Have you seen these tourist brochures? They say 'Come to Cuzco … you will not be alone!' These people ask for it."

"I suppose so" Rob replied "but you can hardly blame them when you've only got two or three weeks holiday. You go for the best and forget about the shit. "We've had our fair share of shit" Charlie nodded. "Anyway, compared with the tourists we've met" Rob continued "we've gotten to know this continent better than most who will only scrape the surface." "And occasionally felt the heartbeat" Charlie interceded with a flourish. "Exactly" Rob smiled. "That's why music helps enormously when trying to understand a people." "So does pot" Charlie said thinking that the effects of the marijuana they had been smoking was wearing off.

"Ah, drugs" Rob gestured with a finger "they only help to alienate us from the society we are trying to penetrate. Admittedly, drugs are intriguing and help to uncover new planes of thought." "If you disregard the disadvantages... like falling asleep" Charlie laughed. "Aye, the energy from drugs should be projected outwards" Rob expounded like the Hippy he once was. "Inner reflection achieves little but personal indulgence. Outward awareness helps with under-standing. South America is a continent that Europeans know little about. Africa and Asia are closer in cultural ties to Europe due to colonialism and the influx of Asians and Africans into Europe." "Especially Britain" Charlie frowned.

Rob shrugged his shoulders. "South America has imported western culture not exported its own. It's a pity" he said. "At least we've had the opportunity to explore the dreams and myths surrounding the Amazon and the Incas. It's up to us while we are here to project ourselves outwards and experience South America, not experience this inner reflection we are doing right now. We are missing the world going on around us. We have a couple of countries left, then we are done. We'll be confident enough to state that we are familiar with South America, South Americans and South American culture.

Charlie looked up. "You know something, Rob. For once you've made sense." "Charlie" Rob replied. "Where have you been all this time?"

It was a five hour train journey to Aguas Calientes, a forgotten little village tucked away in the mountains. The main street was the railway track and the hotels and restaurants were situated on the extended platform. The dogs outnumbered the local inhabitants who survived almost totally on the tourists passing through. And boy, were there a lot of tourists! Rob and Charlie had trouble finding a bed for the night, midst great competition. In one hotel, two Germans had the audacity to try and steal their beds from them. In the end, they hassled them back, then gave them away to an American couple they'd got friendly with on the train. Eventually, they kipped on the floor of the Hotel Calamity after a hassle with the grumpy manager who demanded the full price of a bed. He could give the floor space to someone else if they weren't happy. Rob and Charlie submitted. The thought of sleeping outdoors at eight thousand feet didn't appeal much after their experience at Calama.

The hot springs which gave the village its name afforded them their first bath since leaving England. Arriving there, early in the morning while everyone else goggled at the goods train rattling down the middle of the street, ate their breakfasts or still slumbered in their beds, they found a German shampooing his hair. A short time later an Irishman and his South African family joined in to pollute the sulphuric spring with more soap. Periodically, others arrived while Rob and Charlie fell into conversation with the Irishman about Roman walls, baths and history, the World Cup, South Africa and the Normans in Ireland, each dwelled upon in turn. The most interesting character to appear was a Swiss-American who could only be described as an American because of his New York accent and hippy styled hair. He'd been to the furthest corners of the globe with the exception of China. Rob was pleased with the exception as China was becoming his dream. "I thought you were retiring after this trip" Charlie exclaimed in apparent correction. "Oh, I am" Rob replied. "But I still want to take short one or two month long holidays."

Having semi-cleaned their clothes at the springs without soap, their first laundry wash since Asuncion, they set off back to the village. After lunch, in child-like abandon, they strolled, clambered, waded and hopped along the river bank to Machu Picchu station. Stepping from the wonder and vastness of nature in the shape of towering cliffs and raging torrents, they stumbled upon a thousand tourists waiting to be taken back to Cuzco by train. Their contempt had to be suppressed, their snobbery subdued in order to fit into the milling masses with a smile. A tourist tried to correct Charlie's Spanish as he ordered a cup of tea which the tourist came to regret after being silenced by a cutting remark from Charlie. All the boys wanted to do was to sit and sip their cups of tea. They were not interested in multi-national bargaining for llama wool sweaters or soap stone Inca work that had been knitted or carved out in a little shack the night before. They drank their tea, bought bananas, and stepped out back along the track to Aguas Calientes.

They woke at three in the morning, dressed in the dark and escaped from their hotel via the back way over a wall. Trudging steadily down the railway track to Machu Picchu station, they began the long climb up the mountainside with great shortness of breath until they finally reached the gate to the ruins, a little before five o'clock. There was no-one about. They estimated how far behind the nearest trekkers were by the barking dogs in the valley far beneath. Rob reckoned they had more than an hour's start on anyone.

Struggling over some wooden fencing and barbed wire, they continued with haste into the heart of the ruins, skirted its stone walls and crossed the main plaza of the old city. In the moonlight, all was tranquil as the past lived and their present was occupied by thoughts of how to dodge the ticket collectors when daybreak broke. It would be another hour until the sun rose over the frosty peaks and hued the sky. Above them the snow coated mountains with their violent drooping sides tumbled to the Urabamba raging below, while in the moonlight Machu Picchu towered in a silent green glow, standing timeless, like all man's wonders do.

They traversed up to the highest vantage point within the ruins and contented themselves to wait for the first rays to light the mountain to the east. Charlie was still fearful of discovery. He strained his eyes in the fading gloom. He was certain that they had the mountains and the legacy of the Incas all to themselves, and relaxed. Digging out breakfast from his pack, he handed Rob a boiled egg and a crusty piece of bread.

"Who needs the tourist train?" Rob was thinking. The tourist bus, the tourist guide? The tourist's headache of knowing that a thousand identical tourists would follow the same route in the hours to come. What was an individual's impression after such a conventional sojourn to the top? Would he see it through the lens of his camera to be imprinted on 35mm colour slide film, and not imprinted on his brain? Could he imagine the ruins as deserted, devoid of people, when he arrived simultaneously with a thousand others? Would his visual memory of Machu Picchu be a rare experience like no-one elses? Would he have preferred it by moonlight, or by the sunrise, all on his own or would he go away not aware that it could have been even more visually spectacular than he could have ever dreamt? What if he had put more energy into his coming and not thought of his going away as the spreading of the word that Machu Picchu was one of the world's wonders. Having the 35mm colour slides to verify he'd been there and that he wasn't lying when he said it beat the Taj Mahal hands down.

"This is where it's at" Rob declared as he peeled his boiled egg. From their perch, they sat alone in the moonlight to watch the sunrise. Alone together. It was stupendous as the first rays struck them, warmed them, flooded their vantage point in golden light. Life was good, but like all good things, half past six came, and the first party of French tourists were admitted. Intruded upon, they sat for the next hour watching the ruins' beauty shattered by camera clickers fresh out of Europe, shooting first and looking just briefly after. Watching this invasion of humans, Rob's irritation grew and his desire to leave fermented rapidly.

"Come on, Charlie, time to go" Rob whispered. He'd spotted signs of officialdom in the disguise of ticket collectors. Rising to their feet, they scanned the ruins one last time, then scrambled into the bush. The ticket collectors spotted them, started to run after them, but with a shrug of their shoulders gave up the chase.

Rob and Charlie found themselves on the Inca trail that led the fifty miles or so back to Cuzco. They bade hello then goodbye to a weary French couple coming the other way after four days of self-imposed punishment. The trail climbed upwards out of the Urabamba valley, the overgrown Inca steps fading into thickening undergrowth. Rob and Charlie puffed a little but occasionally broke out into song. "I do like the life in the Andes oh. Do-dada doo."

Suddenly the wind dropped, the birds were mute and hidden, the butterflies disappeared from sight. The sky was cloudless and the ruins lay thousands of feet below. The path seemed to terminate, almost as though it was meant to disappear into the wilderness. The silence was sinister, the atmosphere aroused Rob and Charlie's suspicions. Two sleeping bags lay spread on a ledge of ground to the left of the path. A back-pack, still new and shiny, had its contents strewn all around. A green Paisley patterned headscarf. A green sweater. A torch. A clock. A hairbrush. A pair of panties. Toothbrushes, soap and creams. Dental floss. Toothpicks. Baby powder. Lip balm. Lipstick and other female items (with which Charlie later cleaned his ears). And much, much more including a penny whistle in D. Yet there was no one about.

Rob shouted. "Hello!" "Anybody there?" That was how television had taught him to react. Or was it common sense? There was no reply and the birds remained mute. "Anybody there?" Charlie repeated, looking over the edge to the steep drop beneath them. They stepped back to safety. The sky remained cloudless and the ruins of Machu Picchu lay thousands of feet below.

"This is a bit weird" Rob exclaimed. "I know" Charlie said. "I once saw a movie where something like this happened." "Really? What happened next?" "It was a French film. There were these two beautiful chicks and they decided to go for a weekend ramble on the hills. You know, French girls together must show their independence of men and all that crap. Well, it was a beautiful cloudless day just like today, in real hill country just like this, and it was getting on for dusk when they met two mysterious guys who appeared out of nowhere. But the girls were good, innocent types who were happy to have some company after trudging fifteen miles. They decided it would be alright for the four of them to camp together for the night. Once they had a fire going, and eaten their beans, the two girls became aware that the two mysterious men fancied their chances and weren't to be put off lightly. The men's conversation by the flicker of the fire became assertive and made the girls paranoid of what might happen. I must admit the blokes were rough looking spastics. Those girls were pure stupid. Well, to cut a long story short, the chicks ran off pursued by the guys, and their stuff was found scattered in the morning by a farmer who informed the police, who alerted the murder squad and half the gendarmerie in the entire district, who then eventually discovered the truth."

"And what was that?" Rob asked curiously. "I can't tell you that. It was one weekend my parents were away, and a chick I had round for the night overran me well before the second set of adverts." "Typical" Rob stated. "Anyway, what are we going to do? I suggest we put all this stuff into the backpack and take it down into the valley with us. What do you reckon?" "Not until after our walk, though" Charlie insisted. "Okay, we can check up on the owners when we get back to Aguas Calientes." "Lucky we only brought one pack with us today."

Stuffing everything into the abandoned backpack, they took one last look around before continuing along the trail, the new pack slung from Rob's shoulders. "Pretty good find, that rucksack" Charlie remarked. "Oranges, crackers, cheese, chocolate, mineral water, nuts. Whoever was on the trail stocked up well in advance."

They lounged by the Inca Gate, the highest point of the climb before the descent into the tropical forest ahead. As luck would have it, a discarded bottle of Pisco rum lay nestled in the rocks waiting for some lucky vagabonds to take possession. It was half-full.

They rested in the undergrowth. "Look, there's a humming bird. Isn't it small?" Rob said excitedly, despite a mouthful of Brazil nuts. Charlie took a swig on the rum, passed it to Rob, still transfixed by the feathery object. "Oh yes, humming birds. This rum is foul but it has a mellow quality. Look! Isn't that a pretty butterfly?" Rob's eyes darted from the humming bird to a *Heliconius Ethilla* fluttering by, until it skipped sprightly over a thorn bush and vanished. He turned quickly back to the humming bird, now hovering on its back.

"I need a shit" Charlie grumbled to Rob. He faded into the bushes. "Bloody hell!" screamed Charlie, reappearing from the undergrowth, pale. "Look what you've done" Rob accused him. "The humming bird's gone." "Stuff that. There was a bloody great snake in there" pointing into the bush. "At least ten feet long." "Rubbish, bet you it was a dead creeper." "It was a snake. An anaconda!" Charlie shuddered. Rob was unsympathetic. "If it was one, it was probably vegetarian. The rum's gone to your head. I think it's time we pushed off."

Cocooned by the undergrowth, the overhanging trees protected them from the mid morning sun filtering down through the branches in penetrating shafts. The Inca path became a jungle track, the interlocking stonework no longer visible beneath five hundred years of foliage. It was slippy, but fairly easy going until they came to a landfall. Or at first that was what it seemed. With a mixture of courage and sheer stupidity, the two adventurers set out to cross two hundred yards of scree, disregarding the two thousand foot avalanche they would spearhead if the scree started to move. They hadn't gone ten yards when a thunderclap roll sent the other one hundred and ninety yards of scree tumbling gaily to the bottom. They scrambled to solid ground seconds before their ten yards of scree advanced.

"Shit bags!" Charlie cursed. "They might have warned us they were about to start blasting." A long treacherous climb elevated them to where work was in progress to blast the mountain to pieces. The idea was that if the Peruvians could blow up enough of the mountain and encourage it to tumble down into the Urabamba river below, they would have a ready made foundation for a dam. So two technicians blew the mountain up with explosives and the rest used their hands, shovels, picks and wheelbarrows to throw the reluctant rocks over the side. It was this latter group of men that Rob and Charlie trudged by in stony silence. The foreman nodded, but one worker, muttering under his breath, and sneered "Gringo". Rob slowly turned his head to stare at the man and called him "Diego" in response. Immediately, all work stopped, but the foreman rapped out an order in Spanish and the workers returned to their task of demolishing the mountain. Rob and Charlie continued along the trail.

Five minutes later, coming the other way, was the striding figure of a young man, bedecked in khaki battle shirt, breeches tucked into woollen socks, kitted out in leather walking boots, a cork sun helmet, black silk neckerchief, and handle-bar moustache. Gripped in his bronzen hand a wooden staff, on his back a small knapsack and over his shoulder and dangling by his side, a brass horn. "Good day to you, sirs" be boomed. "Good day" Rob replied "and where have you just come from?" "Ah, good question, my man. You're Scottish aren't you? My father was too. Are you Scottish as well, sir?" he asked Charlie. "Why no, I'm a Geordie, English." "Well, dingle my didgeridoo. My mother was English. As you possible can tell by now, I'm an Aussie, but before we go any further I must tell you. Today is my birthday."

"Congratulations" Rob said earnestly. "Many happy returns" Charlie declared enthusiastically. Charlie and Rob laughed. "I think this calls for a song" Rob said. "Are you ready, Charlie? One! Two! Three! Happy birthday to you, happy birthday to you, happy birthday... what's your name?" "Stanley." "Dear Stanley, happy birthday to yooooooou!" "This calls for a drink" Stanley affirmed, honking his horn. "God, if you'd met us earlier" Charlie apologised, "we could have offered you some rum." "Fear not, my man, I have a bottle of rum tucked away in my knapsack, for this occasion. Moment please ... aqui!"

Stanley produced a bottle of rum and Rob and Charlie clapped their hands together in jubilation. In no time at all the bottle was finished and sent in a beautiful arc over the two thousand foot drop. "Now," Stanley asked "how far have I still to travel before the trail ends? I've walked all the way from Cuzco and I think I've had about enough." "No far" Rob replied. "Three hours at the most to the ruins. Then from there it's about an hour and a half downhill to Aguas Calientes where there's hot springs, reasonable food and beer." "Hot springs? So you're going to be there this evening, eh? Well, the beers are on me seeing it's my birthday. Tonight the kangaroos will be swinging in the trees." "You're buying the beers?" Charlie exclaimed. "Seeing it's your birthday, we should be buying them." "Nonsense. In Oz, the birthday boy buys the grog, so until tonight, cheerio" and off he marched, moustache upturned, staff held firmly in his hand, honking his horn.

Another hour and they were picnicking in the ruins of Winya Huanya. Nothing grand, egg and sardine sandwiches. It was the peace and quiet that made their lunch enjoyable, the ruins so overgrown, that only the ruins' name made it recognisable as something different from the surrounding bush. With the oranges, chocolate, crackers and cheese disposed of, they rummaged through the backpack they'd found, but discovered only more Brazil nuts on which to feast.

Charlie picked up the penny whistle and played his sixteenth century free-form while Rob gazed out of a prismatic Inca window and down to the violent waters of the Urabamba. Lifting his eyes, his vision carried over the distant peaks. He realised how fortunate he was to have had the luck to have seen so many places. The Andes may not be as spectacular as the Himalayas, but they were still bloody big mountains with a beauty of their own. At times they were a tedious barrier to travel, the enjoyment taken out of them by the endless ridges crossed and re-crossed by bus. Yet they were never boring.  Deep in snow in Chile. Dry and grass-less in Bolivia. Green and wet in Peru. Yet always steep, foreboding, uninhabitable places. The Incas had managed for a while, but in the end the Spaniards had driven them deep into the hills and their empire with it. Winya Huanya was one of the last hideaways to have remained undiscovered in modern times. Machu Picchu may have been the Lost City of the Incas, but God only knows how many more there were still hidden beneath the jungle vegetation.

"You know" Charlie interrupted "this backpack, the good sleeping bag and the various odds and ends could be worth fifty dollars second hand." "Yes, I was thinking that" Rob replied. "Judging by how new the things are, I reckon the chick, she must be a chick with knickers and tampons in there, has just flown into Peru. But her friend's sleeping bag looks as though it's been through a few storms. She can't be quite as inexperienced."

"It's strange, isn't it? I don't think they even went hiking on this trail … just camped out for the night and got the fright of their lives." "Looks like it. I think they could probably afford to lose their stuff. After all, if it only comes to fifty dollars that's nothing. So far we've thrown away four hundred. Maybe it's about time we recouped some of our losses." "Aye, I was thinking that. If their passports had been left behind, I'd think twice, but theoretically, all they've done is thrown fifty dollars away." "I agree, so I'll have the penny whistle" Charlie smirked. "I'll have the green sweater" Rob grabbed. "I'll have the neckerchief" Charlie snatched. "I'll have the clock" Rob laughed. "What about these socks?" Charlie asked. "I don't want them, they're horrible" Rob winced. "Nor do it" Charlie concluded and threw them away.

And so it went until they had decided what to keep and what to discard, packed it away in Charlie's rucksack, including the collapsible backpack, then headed down the path that would take them back to the river and along the railway track to Aguas Calientes.

"How was your bath then, Stanley?" Charlie asked. "Sweeping, sir, absolutely sweeping. Never felt cleaner in my life. Just one sec, please Signor!" The Liquor Store owner shuffled out from the dark back of the shop. "Ah, there you are good man. Another round of beers, por favor." The owner disappeared into the dark again.

It was Stanley's birthday party and like he said he was doing the buying. Rob and Charlie were sitting at a table with Stanley and two other tourists, Ted and Dale, who had happened to stroll by at the right time. Suddenly, all the lights in the village faded and the electric generator was heard to stop. "Good grief, what's happening?" Stanley demanded. "It's ten o'clock" the shop owner answered, putting the beers on the table. "Every night this time, the electric no more. I bring you vela."

The shop owner retreated and returned gripping a lighted candle. "Gracias, my good man" Stanley grinned. Illuminated by the flickering flame, the drinking continued. Occasionally someone letting go of his bottle to roll a twister. "When I was in the South Seas" Stanley boomed. "Oh, one moment please,

Signor!" "Si," the shop owner replied, hurrying from the dark. "Another round, por favour." "I sorry, Signor, no is possible. I go bed now. I have one candle only. Is this one you have. I need for to see my way to sleep." "But Signor, the night is young and we need no candle." "I sorry, Signor, I go to bed now. I give you more beer now and you take away. Tomorrow you give me empty bottle back. Si?" "Okay Signor," Stanley sighed. "Well gentlemen, what shall we do now? I feel in rather good spirits, it would be such a waste to retire now." Stanley was not one for early nights. "Come back to our hotel," Rob and Charlie suggested. "The doors will be locked by now, but we know a back way in."

All five groped their way in the dark along the railway track each armed with bottles of beer. Rob pulled up short. "Shhh now" Rob hissed. "There's a wall here. Be careful, most of the bricks are loose and about to fall out. Good God! Shhh! Who's clinking their bottles together?" "Sorry" a meek voice apologised in the dark. "OK, I'm over the wall" Rob hissed. "One at a time now, quietly." Stanley was over in a jiffy. Dale scrambled over with a clink. Ted knocked out a brick, but he was over. Charlie bringing up the rear, demolished the wall.

"Clumsy oaf!" Rob shouted. "Ssssssh" everyone else whispered. "I'm sorry" Charlie apologised. "Oh never mind" Rob murmured. "Have you got the key?" "No" Charlie replied positively. "You have it." "No I haven't. Oh, bloody hell, I've just remembered, I left it on the front desk keyboard." "Tit" Charlie squeaked. "What's going on?" Stanley enquired. "Oh, nothing" Charlie replied. "Rob's just going to get the key." "OK, OK" Rob sighed. "Stay here and keep quiet."

Rob tiptoed down the hotel corridor. He reached the reception and tripped over someone sleeping on the floor. The manager! He took a deep breath, and waited. From down the corridor clink! clink! Echoed. The manager turned over in his sleep. "Bloody fools" Rob cursed as he reached across the manager and the desk to the keyboard and lightly lifted the key to their room. He tiptoed back down the corridor and let the drunks in. They spread themselves on the two single beds. "So much for the Lost City of the Incas" Stanley declared. "Cheers" he toasted, and honked his horn. Everyone said "Ssssssssh!" then laughed.

The following day was another day of planning. "Right, today's today and tomorrow's fiesta" Rob said. "We'll catch the afternoon train to Anta, hitch over to Nazca and head up the coast to Lima." "You must be joking" Charlie said. "It's eight hundred miles to Lima. In this country that will take us a week." "I didn't say anything about doing it in a day, did I? What I mean is let's get on the move. We've been in Aguas three days now and apart from that American guy with the acid, who won't part with any of it, there's nothing to keep us here."

"I've never taken LSD" Charlie said disappointingly. "I don't know how I'd react to it." "Like a madman. I know you. Maybe some day, eh? It's gone out of fashion and hard to get now. The first time I tripped I was eighteen on a Greek beach in Mykonos. I'm still not sure what happened. All I remember is an electric thunderstorm that flashed for six hours before it rained, and I stood there in the downpour mesmerised by it all. Acid's like that, any old hippy can tell you a story or two about its wayward effects."

"Sounds a bit dangerous to me." Charlie quipped. "Yes and no" Rob replied. "I lived in this flat once, where I burnt wood to save on bills and chopped the wood with an axe in the back yard. Once I was tripping and the guy with me freaked out as he thought I was going to chop my hand off. Another time when I had a motorbike, I was tripping and decided to top up the battery. I was kneeling and pouring water in and it started running down the side of the battery onto the floor. At that moment I couldn't decide whether it was acid or water as it ran towards my knees. My tripping buddy pulled me out in time, but it was only water after all."

Charlie winched. Rob continued.

"Making love on acid was one of the finest experiences I've ever had. Another time on acid when I had my dog, we were in the cemetery behind where we lived. It was the usual night's walk for the dog and myself, but the guy tripping with me went all gibbery on seeing the dog and me leaping and jumping over the tombstones. We even got as far as going down the crypts. I admit that was even too much for my imagination with an owl hooting and the moon staring down at us from between the bare branched trees. The dog loved it, I didn't mind too much, but the guy with us … well. I had to explain to him that the cemetery was a big park with trees and grass. He was struggling with that concept, so I asked him if he knew of any other park with so many monuments raised through public subscription. It seemed such a waste that no one ever used the park or looked at the monuments. He was horrified. He asked me did that mean I had no respect for the dead. I told him that cemeteries were the only places where I didn't steal flowers to give to women. I had that much respect for the dead and the same amount of consideration for the living. No flowers in a cemetery meant more than just garden adornment and what woman in her right would accept such flowers if she knew where they came from. That seemed to satisfy him."

"God, you do bullshit, don't you?" Charlie sneered. "Rubbish! It's all true, every word" Rob protested. "I'm a romantic at heart."

The packed train journey from Aguas to Anta was spent in the passageway watching three pickpockets at work. Rob and Charlie didn't want to get involved. They stuck their hands in their pockets and kept a beady eye on the culprits, as one stole a wallet, passed it to the second, who gave it to the third who returned the wallet to the first who replaced the wallet in the victim's pocket minus its contents. All went well until someone tumbled and confusion broke out. Rob and Charlie raised their eyebrows at one another. After the Death Train it all seemed so tame. In Bolivia no one had bothered much about their plight. In Peru they weren't going to worry much about anyone else's. It was a case of dropping their British fair play attitude and adopting one of South American apathy and disinterest.

Aboard the train was a French girl on her own, more than capable of holding her own. She was another world traveller down to her last pennies who blew with the breeze. She was the type of woman men fell instantly in love with. Love had made her life easier yet equally hard. Men never left her alone but she always tried to pick a man she could love as well as be loved by. She'd spent time in Africa and North America before drifting to the Caribbean and two years of yachts and sun. She'd tired of it, and with a little money had wandered south to Latin America. She was searching for the elusive something they were all seeking, the endless search for understanding through the experience of love and hate and everything in between that's emotional. She knew a lot about emotions, they were her one weapon of defence against the physical, logical males who always tried to capture her. She was like a wild flower that withered when picked, she was the fragile ice that melted on being held. She was a *femme fatale* who understood that she only lived once.

Over the crowds of people in the passageway, she eyed Rob in his sombrero, puffing contented, nonchalantly on an Inca cigarette. Rob had seen her and their eyes flashed a deep first introduction that went beyond saying 'hello'. Slowly during the journey she made her way towards him, her beautiful French face, her sun-filled hair gliding through the sweat and dirt of the Peruvian peasants babbling away in Quecha.

The train trundled on, and the hillside changed to dry grassland under starlight. The moon was in the last night of the last quarter and had not yet set over the mountains. The air was decidedly still and held a chill which did not deter the nocturne bats from their prey of moths and beetles. Over a small marshy pool hovered a pupa dragonfly in murderous operation.

As the train pulled into Anta, the French girl pushed through the carriage crowd to reach Rob and tripped into his arms. He caught her, and as she straightened, she mumbled that she would like him to travel back to Cuzco with her. Who could refuse such an offer from a *femme fatale?* Rob watched Charlie descend from the carriage. It was too late. He pulled the French girl into him and kissed her on the lips. "We'll meet again somewhere" he whispered. He was thinking of her spirit. He would find the same vivaciousness again in someone else's eyes and body, and commit. Now was not the time. He couldn't abandon the kid.

After a night in Anta's Central Hotel, Anta's only hotel, they took a ride in the back of a truck carrying sacks of grain to Abancay. It was no picnic party as they began the first leg of the journey to the coast. Abancay lay over a twenty thousand foot ridge of cordillera, connected by a road that bashed the life out of them as they were being thrown around in the back.

It couldn't have been more than eighty miles, but it took seven hours to climb to the top of the last barren fourteen thousand foot pass and descend into the green Abancay valley.

Charlie, gazing forward over the cab, saw the town lie hazily below encircled by mountains. His eye travelled over the peaks to the white snow caps a hundred miles away. From Abancay, valleys and ribbons of tortured road seemed to lead into the bellies of gigantic mountains, to be swallowed up in cliffs of scree and wastes of bracken.

Rob meanwhile held on tightly to the truck's tailboard, his hands almost numb at that altitude. He looked back over the pass towards Anta and Cuzco and saw nothing but jagged summits and Ice floes topped by pale cumulus, everything below fifteen thousand feet in black shadow. It didn't make him feel any warmer, but it held his gaze until the view disappeared when the truck took a switchback bend and left him facing Abancay and Charlie facing barren hillside.

They descended eternally, zigzagging violently, the driver needing every cog of brake strength his gear box could supply to prevent them heading over the edge and a one mile drop through space. The road wound down and down and didn't straighten out until twenty-five miles later in Abancay.

Rob and Charlie got out. They were shaken The driver was paid two hundred soles and they shook his hand, thankful it was over. Charlie, the driving enthusiast, stated that he'd never want to drive on roads like that. It was gambling with suicide making a living as a truckie in Peru. Rob retorted it was gambling with suicide being a tourist in the back doing it for fun.

But it seemed worth it. Abancay was a friendly town. The locals were in high spirits, it was Independence Day. Being a town cut off in the high mountains of Peru, there was a shortage of firecrackers, but no shortage of laughter and music. The red and white flags were out and everyone had on their best clothes for the occasion. The boys met the girls in the Plaza de Armes and flirted with them as the mothers stood in admiration of their daughters, and the fathers haggled with other fathers over whether he or she was a good enough match. The local police were drunk, as were half the town. Everyone was celebrating the national holiday with beer and chicha.

Rob and Charlie paid a dollar for a double room and ate *bistek*, *arroz* and *frites* at the nearest eathouse. It was a relaxing place, and as the only customers, the waiter boy took off the Spanish music and played the Beatles records 1962-66 and the albums 1967-70. Rob laughed and sang along with *Listen to the Blackbird in the Dead Night* and almost cried over *Yesterday*. Rob told Charlie that he'd be too young to remember *Can't Buy Me Love*, but Charlie was up in arms protesting he knew the songs as well as anyone. As proof, he commenced to sing *She Loves You* solo. The waiter boy applauded and Rob spluttered his coffee all over the table. He almost fell off his chair in an attempt to control his laughter. Charlie asked him what was so funny and Rob just laughed more. Eventually, calming down, Rob said it was the first time he had ever heard him singing and it had come as a shock.

"It couldn't have been that bad" Charlie asked. Rob replied. "No, just that I've never heard such a rendering of *She Loves You* before." "What do you mean?" Charlie asked. Rob replied that although Charlie said he knew all the songs, he had in fact just sung *I Want to Hold Your Hand*. "I did not," Charlie said in denial. "I sang *She Loves You*." "You didn't, you know" Rob said calmly. "Well, what do you expect? I was about five years old when it came out. How am I expected to remember some crappy old Beatles song? They all sound the same to me." "I bet you don't even know the names of the four Beatles" Rob quizzed. "There was Paul McCartney, John… somebody. Awwh, what does it matter? I bet you couldn't name the blokes that make up the Sex Pistols." "No, I suppose I couldn't" Rob answered, racking his brain hard. "There's a fair age gap between the Beatles and Punk. At least ten years"

"Well," Charlie beamed. "There you are. I was too young for the Beatles and you're too old to know any more about the Pistols than Johnny Rotten and Sid Vicious." "Guess we're even then" Rob admitted. "Let's pay the bill. You make me feel like an old man."

Outside, the stars were twinkling brightly but no one was looking at them. They were queuing up for the cinema. "What's on?" Charlie asked. "This Spanish has me confused." "*La Guerra de las Galaxies.* Star Wars" Rob translated. "'Star Wars!' Whoopee!" Charlie shouted, bouncing up and down. "Its just come out. We'll have to go and see that. What time does it start?" "Now" Rob answered. "C'mon, let's get our tickets" Charlie enthused.

And from a world of isolation in a remote town in the Peruvian mountains, Rob and Charlie paid thirty soles each (ten pence), and escaped to the Dark Star and the Universe of Darvada to be blown from the galaxies by Obi-Wan Kenobi, the Princess, Rick and a collection of robots, forgetful of their own existence and ignorant of the peasants a few miles out of town, living on goat's milk, huddled under a pile of llama skins keeping warm, as the cold of night penetrated their mud thatched-roof huts. The peasants who were unaware that the sky visible through the straw overhead bore more than just a flicker of light and represented more than just an indication of whether it was a cloudy night or produced anything more spectacular than a shooting star.

Rob and Charlie had been in South America three months and covered eight thousand miles. They had cashed their first traveller's cheque in Macapa on the 2nd June and Rob wondered where the money had gone in the last sixty days. Besides the two hundred pounds they had lost in the incidents of the Santa Fe bus and the Death Train, the other five hundred had evaporated. They were down to their last twenty pound traveller's cheque, had eight one-dollar bills and a handful of soles.

Rob wasn't overly worried. He had arrived in South Africa with four pounds in his pocket and bumlived three months in Johannesburg without working a day. It hadn't been the happiest time of his life, but he had survived and kept his mind intact. Being broke in Peru was a case of being broke while abroad, just like all the other times. And each time it got easier to handle. The first time had been a case of selling blood in a clinic in Athens, hitching bare-footed up to Istanbul, buying a bowlful of puzzle rings and selling them to pay his way back to Britain. Another had been on his return from India. He had run out of money in Kabul. But six weeks later he had been standing on the Dover Quay with a pound note in his pocket. That experience had taught him not to worry too much about not having any money. Things always worked-out.

Charlie was less optimistic. In St George, at the back of his mind he knew they had the lost traveller's cheques to cash. Now they were in such a beggarly financial state, it was playing constantly on his mind. On top of this he had caught a cold from the truck ride and his cold was running stronger by the time they reached Chalhuanca, a four hour truck journey from Abancay. It was another sleepy little town tucked away amongst the mountain ridges and they were forced to stay the night. The connecting trucks onward had already gone.

Rob paid the truck driver two hundred soles for the ride and when he insisted on being paid more, Rob gave him the pair of shades they had found with the backpack on the Inca Trail. He seemed happy.

With two hundred soles in ready cash left, they ordered two fifty soles *cubierto* meals in a gloomy little restaurant on the main street. Fortunately, the serving boy, the owner's son, asked them if they had any watches for sale. Rob looked at Charlie, Charlie looked at his wrist, and said no. His watch had been an eighteenth birthday present from his sister and he wasn't going to part with it so easily. Then Rob remembered the clock they'd picked up on the Trail. The boy's eyes lit up as he produced it, and after some close inspection and ratification of the deal by the boy's mother hovering in the background, they settled on four hundred soles for the clock. It wasn't much, but they were able to eat without worrying that it would be their last meal. They took a double room for two hundred soles in the hotel next door, and Charlie went straight to bed.

Rob meanwhile wanted to have a look around Chalhaunca and left Charlie to sweat it out in the room. There was a poster pasted up on a wall on the main street announcing a three-day Fiesta of bull fights, starting the following day. He watched as five or six bulls were chased through the main plaza on their way to the ring. It appeared that the locals were into the finer aspects of the Spanish legacy. Yet the majority of the population spoke the indigenous language, Quecha, and no Spanish. In Abancay he had learned the first thing to ask anyone was whether they spoke Castilian. Invariably the answer was no. Rob believed that most of the citizens were just too shy or too lazy to try and reply in Spanish. On the other hand, maybe his Spanish was bad. Before he had left England, he had taken a course at Newcastle Polytechnic and sat through endless tapes of *Getting to Know Spanish*. He had never been hot on languages, but his Spanish was improving, he now had the confidence to say more than just  where he was from, where he'd been and where he was going. He felt humour was important and developing it in another language was a difficult and lengthy process. But his Spanish was coming on, though it didn't help him much with Quecha. Charlie's Spanish wasn't so good, he was picking it up very slowly.

Rob walked up the hillside overlooking the town and saw the bull ring half way up a hill to his left and the bulls being amassed in a large compound. He felt relaxed and happy to have more than five minutes to himself. It was nice to leave Charlie behind for a while and take in the open spaces of the valley. If asked to describe a typical South American town, he thought he would choose Chalhuanca. The river winding below, the mountains clothed in fingered cactus; the red-tiled, white-walled shack-cum-houses leaking black smoke; the sounds of muffled staccato Latin music floating upwards; the town's dusty deserted streets; the guffs of laughter of men having a celebration drink; a bugler practising down at the army camp; flags limp, hanging from first storey windows; a little raggy kid shouting 'gringo' and an echo replying 'dago'. Yes, Chalhuanca was typically South American.

As he eyed the fingered cacti, his thoughts suddenly changed. He had read various Castaneda cult books in which the characters had dabbled with the powers of cactus. None of them ever explained which part of the cactus to eat, or if they did, he couldn't remember, but that didn't matter. Rob had since met someone who explained how to go about it without poisoning himself. The only thing he couldn't remember was whether it was the five fingered or seven fingered cactus that was the magic one. Come to think of it, the guy who told him wasn't very sure either. But he brushed the doubt aside and told himself he only lived once.

Chopping the tip of his middle finger off with his knife, and yelping as a needle poked hell out of his thumb, Rob sliced away at the cactus until he isolated the dark green flesh just under the skin. He looked wistfully at the green gunge and gazed at his beautiful, tranquil surroundings wondering if he was doing the right thing. Two horses grazed nearby, lifting their tethered heads to sniff the breeze and glance at Rob hunched over his cactus. Below, the local band began their revelry, their trumpets and horns drumming along while the natives in bowlers danced in circles together, keeping time with a large bottle of liquor passing around as they swayed down the street and out of sight.

The Fiesta continued and Rob ate his cactus in the hope of enlightenment. It was not pleasant and a short while later, he scrambled down the hillside and back into town. On the way back to the hotel, he bought Charlie six oranges for his cold. He was not any better, sniffing into a handkerchief reading John Fowles' *Magus*, which he had swapped *Decline and Fall* for in Cuzco. Rob warned him he'd damage his eyesight reading by the forty watt bulb in their windowless room, then threw him his oranges.

Charlie sniffed a thanks. "What have you been doing?" he asked. "Oh, nothing, went for a walk. I see they're having bull fights here tomorrow. Do you fancy staying to see them?" "No, I want to get out of his shit hole and on to Lima." "What's the hurry? We might not get the chance again. It's not every day they have bull fighting." "I don't care, we'll see some fighting somewhere else. I don't want to get stuck here" Charlie stressed. "Well, I don't know about seeing the fighting elsewhere, but if you feel that strongly, we'll move on. It's a pity, this place is a nice town."

Rob lay on his bed and Charlie continued to read, trying to forget about money. He was feeling homesick and missing all the things familiar to him. What he'd give for a hot bath or one of his mother's meals. He missed his stereo, though surprisingly not TV. He longed to sit in a pub and have a pint and talk to his friends about his adventures, and tell them what they were missing. He was tired of travelling and eating Latin food and sleeping outdoors or in dirty hotel rooms. Tired of putting clothes on and taking them off as the climate changed. Tired of talking in Spanish. Tired of Rob. All he wanted to do was go home. Chalhuanca was impossible. He'd have to get to Lima before he stood any chance of getting home. If things got bad he'd go to the Embassy and ask to be sent home. He couldn't see any alternatives except perhaps write to his parents to send money. He had written from La Paz, telling them he was getting low on cash, and told them to write back care of Poste Restante, Lima. Whether he'd given them enough time to reply or not was questionable. If there was no letter when they arrived in Lima, he had agreed with Rob just to keep going northwards. They were getting to the begging stage but it didn't seem to matter as long as they kept heading northwards and moving closer to home. Stopping for the bull fighting meant another day's delay and another day longer on the breadline, and Charlie didn't like that idea at all.

Meanwhile, Rob was wondering about his cactus. He felt his perception increased and his concentration improved but he put that down to high altitude. If it was real cactus he reckoned the effects would have been somewhat more clearly recognisable to him. Yet he couldn't say... no, he believed it to be a bum cactus, and he'd have to try some other time with the right type. The main difficulty he thought would be finding someone to show him the good from the bad, and he guessed there weren't too many heads of that kind floating around Peru. People had said Mexico was the place, though he'd heard of cactus munchers living around La Paz. "Damn" he scolded himself, why hadn't he climbed the hills around the Bolivian capital and tried it out himself. But too late! Never mind, maybe somewhere along the trail he'd hit it lucky. He was forever optimistic.

In the morning, Rob and Charlie were waiting patiently by a truck they had been told would be heading further up the valley and then over the pass that carried the road down to the coast. They were supposed to leave at noon, but it was now two o'clock. The town streets were busy with market sellers attracting custom from the hordes who came to see the bull fight, travelling from as far as a hundred miles to watch the famous Jorge Villafuerla and equally renowned Jose Eschevarria, two of Peru's greatest matadors. The Mayor, the matadors and the town dignitaries rode through the town chaperoned by a puffing band of musicians. The children followed them everywhere as they collected the multi-coloured capes from the doors of the local women. The Mayor, as was his right, was beset by capes draped over his shoulders, a sign of favouritism. It bolstered his importance. The good looks of Jorge and Jose helped them do well for capes as well.

Charlie was indifferent to the excitement and continually looked for the driver to get them on the road. Rob wasn't fussed. He went for a cup of coffee and found a shopkeeper who exchanged five dollars for eight hundred soles. Despite the Fiesta, business was business and smiles all around. He and the shopkeeper politely chatted as the Mayor and his entourage passed by for the umpteenth time. The band and an assortment of rags, hands and mouths on instruments, with feet and legs wobbling drunkenly in the dust, whirled past not far behind.

The shops began to close and the people filtered up the narrow alleyways towards the bull ring on the hillside. Rob and Charlie sat on the truck's tailboard watching the street empty and the sound of the band receding. Suddenly the driver appeared from nowhere. "We go see the rueda" he shouted behind bloodshot eyes swimming in local whisky, and that was that. They were going to see the bull fighting after all. Rob smiled and Charlie, resigned to his fate, decided to enjoy it. They jumped in, closed the tail-gate and the truck rattled its way along and up the narrow cobbled alleyways, at a steady five miles an hour. They had to stop. A bull had escaped and was rampaging in the street. A dozen cowhands lassoed the bull and dragged the stubborn animal up the hillside. The driver follow-ed, tooting his horn, bumping the bull in the rump with his truck until it finally broke into a run and stampeded the cowhands in all directions. The driver laughed his head off. Rob and Charlie joined in and shouted "Toro! Toro!" in the excitement.

The bull fighting had only just begun as they pulled up by the ringside. "Today warm up! Tomorrow ke'll!" the driver roared as someone handed him a container of *chichi*. "Today the boys! Tomorrow the men!" he blared, falling out of the cab to lie drunk in the dust. No one noticed. All eyes were fixed on the ring.

The introduction of each bull to the ring brought a roar. The town and the people from the hills and valleys were there to watch the young budding hopefuls chance a jig with the horny animals. Not one bull behaved the same as another beast. Some were sickly tame and inspired jeers for the picadors to take them out. Some were buckers, others downright ferocious. The one that caught the young toreador and tossed him into the air had horns of spirit. So too the toreador who got up, shook off the dust, and went back for more punishment. This time the bull just missed goring him as he was hurled to the ground. He placed his hands over his head to show he'd had enough and a picador distracted the toro's attention long enough for him to scramble out of the ring. He was a brave lad. Some would say foolish.

The weighing down of a very aggressive bull by tying a dead condor to his back was comical. The bull tried with unsuccessful gores to dislodge the enormous bird tied firmly across its spine. With a toreador waving his red cape, the band playing thumping music and the dead condor flapping its wings to the toro's careering, it was not surprising that the bull was confused and chased anything in sight.

Everyone was well oiled on chichi and beer. By the gate where the bulls entered, staggered a drunk old man who continuously taunted the bulls with his hat and frequently his sweater. It was his idea to pour beer down the bulls' throats before letting them into the ring. His nonchalance when the bulls came for him was suicidal. His belief, in his drunken condition, that that nothing could harm him was borne out by his charmed existence throughout the afternoon. He was a favourite with the crowd and a comical sight pushing the bulls' horns away with one foot and hand while holding his balance with his other foot and putting a bottle of whisky to his mouth. The crowd just cheered and cheered.

Meanwhile, the Mayor and the Town Council already drunk out of their heads sat under a makeshift canopy and were endlessly supplied with more booze and food all afternoon. The capes they had collected in their tour of the town hung suspended from a line above the Council's heads. Each cape in turn was taken and tied round a bull's neck before it entered the ring. But the Council members had drunk so much they couldn't tell one cape from another.

In the compound, although drunk, the cowhands were taking note of which bulls would be put into the

ring the following day (by the cape colours). They kept
the bulls moving, prodding and whipping them to stir
things up. The bulls engaged horns with their fellow
captives. Together they looked a mean bunch.
Meanwhile, in the ring, the toreadors awaited the
bulls. Two youngsters coaxed on by the professionals
Jose and Jorge did most of the passing. The
professionals only took to the ring to distract the
fiercest bulls when they were getting the upper hand
on the youngsters. It was a dangerous sport; Jorge
already had three fingers missing and he and Jose
were covered in body scars. There came a time when
everyone made mistakes.

The crowd were now also drunk out of their skulls
and uproarious with enjoyment. Oranges, bananas,
cakes, bread, meals of rice, potatoes or *estofado* were
on hand to fill the lulls. There was more than enough
to drink. The *chichi* was almost given away while
cardboard boxes of *Cuzquera* beer were guzzled like
water poured on sand.

As the day progressed, the enthusiasm lapsed as
the shadow grew on the hillside and the crowd began
to disperse. Bonfires grew up out of nowhere and the
mountains were aflame with light as the sun laid down
to rest in the west. The day had been fun but *manana*
the seriousness business began. The toreadors gave
way to the matadors.

Charlie envied them. He wanted to try his hand
with a cape. The excitement of watching was tre-
mendous enough without the knowledge that one slip
could mean the end. He was thinking only in fancy, the
men who went out in front of the bulls were fearless
individuals. They had his admiration after the day's
showing and they had only been playing. He felt it was
unfortunate they had to leave because they were low
in money. He longed to stay now and see the killings.

Many may think bull fighting another blood sport
to be condemned, but Charlie thought that any sport
were man challenged another beast to prove his
superiority showed they were still in touch with basic
survival. Should man be a total animal loving
intellectual race concerned with living in peace and
harmony with his fellow beasts? To Charlie it was
invalid for man to degenerate from being physically
superior to beasts to being just mentally superior.
Bulls weren't fair game for man? Yet these same bulls

killed matadors. The odds are stacked? If so, the bull wouldn't prove that man was not infallible. The bulls are bred just for killing? So what! If not they would have been on some old woman's plate for Sunday dinner a long time ago. Isn't it better man challenges other beasts than challenging himself to prove he's better than the next man? That's what he hated about football and international athletics. It only led to regional and nationalistic resentment by the followers. At a bull fight, there was no way the matador's supporters and the bulls' supporters were going to beat the shit out of one another. No one was on the bull's side. It made sense. But mercy existed, no one wanted to watch a sick bull be put in the ring with a fit matador. And for the purist who detested the sport as he lounged in his armchair as an eight stone weakling, thought Charlie, if he had his way and man degenerated far enough, perhaps some day he'd be fighting his dog to the death, to see who was the fittest.

Rob gazed at Charlie's intent face as they booked into the hotel for another night. "What are you thinking?" he asked. "Nothing, just bullshit" Charlie laughed. What else could he do? His cold was getting better and they hadn't reached a dog's life level yet.

The bonfires were still smouldering as Rob and Charlie pulled themselves from bed, dressed and brushed their teeth over an old horse trough in the hotel courtyard. Charlie pushed his way in front of a fat Peruvian woman heading for the one toilet, ignoring her utterances. "How dare he!" she cried, but Rob turned the other way with a grin while Charlie kept the old hag waiting ten minutes even though she hammered on the door. No manners, these Peruvians, he thought as he unhooked the catch and quickly sidestepped the red-faced woman rushing headlong into the john. No fortitude either, he reassured himself.

Rob was packed and waiting. His little bag bulged with the extra sleeping bag from the Trail. The sooner they sold it the better. The straps on his bag took an eternity to force through the buckles because of it. Charlie's rucksack was equally overloaded with the items they'd found. Once in Lima though, they'd unload the lot. That would be another few dollars coming their way.

Having dithered around, they missed the truck. The drunken driver had said he'd wait and take them as far as the pass. They'd agreed on a seven o'clock departure but it was now close on seven-thirty and he'd gone. Charlie's heart fluttered but luck was on their side. A pick-up truck was driving on to the next village up the valley towards Lima.

Breakfasting on some marmalade sandwiches, they squeezed into the back of the pick-up with half a dozen Indians and trucked out of Chalhuanca in a cloud of dust. The cactus grasslands faded and steep thousand foot cliffs rose on either side. The rock strewn road twisted its way into the growing wilderness, its crippled trees barely surviving in the sheltered hollows. The pick-up cut cleanly through the early morning air that chilled the face and threatened to lift hats from heads. The Indians grinned and Charlie realised how beautiful life could be once they were on the move again. Nothing seemed to matter when they kept moving. The present became everything, the cliffs and the cold air removed any thoughts of the past or future. There was nowhere else in the world he wanted to be at that moment but travelling through this wilderness. Yet the day before... well, he hadn't been his usual self, he confessed.

A small village loomed up ahead and as they ground to a halt, Rob spotted the truck that had left without them. "Ola! Ola!" he shouted as it started to move forward. "OLLLLAH!!" The driver saw them, stopped and roared "Ah, les Inglesi! Pronto, pronto, nos vamos!" Rob and Charlie, leaped out of the pick-up, grabbed their belongings and scrambled aboard the truck. "Yahoo!" the driver howled as he shifted into gear and headed for the pass.

Rob and Charlie found themselves sharing the back of the truck with a band of musicians who had been attracted to the bull fight. What a bunch! With their woollen hats and holey scarves draped over torn jackets covering stained trousers at half mast, patched elbows, ripped and drop-stitched darned sweaters which on one came down to his knees. Each in turn gripped hard on a bottle of *pisco* whisky, swaying with the truck and rolling eyes that never settled on anything else but the bottle as it came back their way. Each sagging jaw exposed black teeth, chewing greedily on coca leaves, green and lodged in their gums. Saliva dribbled from their lips to coat their itchy stubble in slime which they licked and savoured with a smile. Their instruments lay prostrate, as each took his turn to smear the tailboard in relief. Each forced a grimace from a drunken look which showed no signs of being here nor there, but revealed a joy for living with little cares.

Hotly disputed, the dregs of the bottle seeped out into hungry mouths that craved for more. The violinist weeping, the bull horn player comforting the harpist and the drummer crumpled in a corner in despair. The truck bumped on, the conductor's sober eye giving away to stupor while his sizzled consciousness followed his waving arm still giving rhythm to an imagined beat. The notes flowed forth, but only in his head, his baton lay hidden, covered by the drummer's spread-eagled legs. The band for all its finesse and musical tastes were without doubt the ugliest band in all Peru.

A condor, vulture eyed and eagle swift, kept vigilant watch over them. It veered westwards, skimming a violent precipice to conquer a ragged ridge that led him into the main valley. Rob followed its flight, in the distance a cluster of distant dots he knew to be alpaca. A shepherd's hut lay as a darkened patch to the east. The condor was content to hover and patrol its territory. It owned the sky and saw everything beneath it. It tossed its head backwards, then banked towards the highest mountains as if in a desire to conquer the highest peak.

"I wonder if anyone ever shoots condors?" Charlie asked. "Whatever for?" Rob replied. "I don't know, something to do I suppose." They watched as the great black bird receded into the distance.

The driver changed gear quickly and they were thrown about in the back of the truck. "What a way to travel" Charlie moaned. "If I ever come to Peru again, I'm flying." "Huh! You're just a softy" Rob jibed. "You should try riding a camel." "They're supposed to be alright" Charlie said. "Anything's better than this." "A camel isn't. I was on one in Afghanistan and kept falling off." "Probably because you were stoned all the time" Charlie chuckled. "You never want to hear a decent story, do you?" "No wonder, I'm sure you're bullshitting all the time. The story you told me about drongo birds was just too ridiculous to believe, especially when you tied it in with King Zog." "You've just no notion of how complex the world is, have you?"

Rob replied disparagingly. "The Indian Black Drongo was a bird I saw frequently perched on branches and telegraph poles in India. It had the habit of darting to catch insects and attacking crows and hawks. It was a mean bird."

"Who's this King Zog, then?" Charlie asked, his curiosity inflamed once more. "King Zog was the last monarch of Albania, deposed by the Communists in 1945. Now King Zog and his Drongo pet bird who loved him deeply was left behind when Zog was exiled. The new President was a Stalinist, and he kept the bird caged up as a sign of the times. But this President didn't last long, someone took his place. The new President was strict but allowed the old Drongo bird out of the cage now and then to see the visiting Russian dignitaries. Then one day the Drongo noticed that it was no longer Russians he was shown but narrow-eyed yellow skinned people. However, the bird remained locked up in his cage except on these occasions. Then in 1971, he was alternately shown to the Chinese one month and the Russians the next. This proved too much for the Drongo bird and the next time the President came to show him off, the bird refused to leave his cage. He'd had enough, he had finally given up all hope of ever seeing King Zog again. His heart gave out and he died."

"It's a sad story, but I don't know if it makes much sense to me!" Charlie said with a wave of a hand. "Are you sure you told it right?" "Charlie" Rob said slowly "I think you should forget all about politics and stick to shooting condors. Either that or get a new brain." "I think you're bullshitting again" Charlie concluded.

The band had been let off long before. The truck was filling up with alpaca and vicuna skins and Rob and Charlie were sitting on a pile which deadened the bumps in the road. The truck reached the fourteen thousand foot high pass summit and stopped at a collection of stone and thatched-roof huts. It was the end of the ride. The truck driver was going to load up his last batch of alpaca skins then turn back. They would have to find for another ride to take them to the coast.

Rob and Charlie looked around, and sighed. At fourteen thousand feet little grew, only the odd tuft of grass. It was the winter season, the land broke unevenly and rocky and carried the eye to peripheral cliffs of eroded limestone, weather-beaten and topped by hard volcanic rock pinnacles. These white protrusions fingered skywards, pointing to the nothingness that existed all around them. It was another end of the world, a furthest outpost as remote as any wave swept island in the Atlantic. The barrenness inspired nothing more than a desire to retreat indoors and sit over a raging fire, but there was nothing to burn, no trees, no peat, no organic substance to consume for heat. Pockets of snow and polished ice lay in the rivulets and hidden slopes. In the shade, the wind blew icy. Only the sun blazing through the rarefied atmosphere and on to their well wrapped backs prevented the misery of the harsh conditions from sapping their spirits.

In these mountains, the locals were partaking in a losing battle. The alpacas and vicuna had no choice, man and his other beasts had forced them to survive on the bare mountain tops. Yet the alpaca and vicuna were the only means for Peruvians to live in such a forbidding land. A few die-hard Indians held on to the ways of the past, tending their beasts. The road was their life line, they had come to depend on traders buying the skins of their animals. Kerosene, flour and green vegetables were cherished luxuries beyond a basic diet of alpaca meat and hard dry potatoes grown in a few inches of soil.

It was three in the afternoon and Rob sat on an oil drum still warm from the midday sun. Charlie discovered that one of the huts was a store and bought some cans of fish. It was the one item that seemed standard all over the world. Whether it was sardines, tuna fish or pilchards, cans with twenty years of dust were to be found in the smallest stores in the most outback places of the world. Charlie opened a can of tuna while Rob sliced some bread left over from the morning's breakfast.

The driver and the store owner produced a football and jibed Rob that Peru had beaten Scotland in the World Cup. Rob looked over and nodded that they would take up the challenge. "OK Charlie, hurry up and finish your sandwich, we're going to take these two blokes on and show them a thing or two." "Eh!" Charlie spluttered. "Where are we going to play football in this desolate rock pile?" The store owner pointed to a grassy patch, on which a herd of sixty alpacas chewed contentedly. "This is crazy" Charlie mumbled as he followed the other three. "Playing football at this altitude. We'll kill ourselves."

Rob and the driver jumped up and down waving their arms to clear the pitch of the alpacas, but they just stared in blankness. The driver dropped the ball and booted it into the herd. It had the desired effect. The pack scattered but one sprightly alpaca dribbled off with the ball before being relieved of it by another. The store owner tried to dispossess the fancy footed alpaca by throwing a large stone at him but he missed. Meanwhile, another alpaca took up the game and tossed the ball into the air with its head. "Stupid animals" Charlie muttered, watching from the road. Rob tried a headlong rush for the ball but only succeeded in chasing the alpacas and the ball a hundred yards further into the wilderness. The store owner held his head in exasperation. "Stupid" Charlie groused. "What a bunch of idiots."

The three chasers had a little conference. Watched on by the alpacas who still retained possession, the store owner went off to the left, the truck driver to the right and slowly circled round the herd. Rob stood patiently until the other two were in position. With a whistle from the store owner, all three ran as fast as they could into the pack. "Always preferred rugby myself" Charlie grunted.

While the other three were all legs and arms midst a ball of alpaca fur, Charlie spotted a vehicle coming from the direction of Chalhuanca. It was travelling at high speed, the cloud of dust it trailed was quite considerable. He kept watching as it approached and made it out to be a high-axled 4x4 pick-up. As it neared he saw it carried blue number plates. It wasn't Peruvian.

The other three meanwhile, had recovered the ball after a lengthy struggle. Rob, holding the ball, looked up to see where Charlie was, and saw him talking to someone through the wound down window of a Ford F6 truck. Charlie turned round and started beckoning with his arm. Rob knew what he meant, dropped the ball and began to run.

They had side-stepped into a different world. All the planes ran parallel and were rarely crossed except by mere chance. From the wastes of Peru, they entered the soft living of California. Hitch-hiking did that, it crossed all boundaries and became a means of dipping into life's sometimes sad but lucky barrel. Good fortune oft-time stood as a magic gamble of thumb and hope on the open road. Opportunity lent itself as a reward for having faith in life and people who were usually insulated from the other planes. A hitch-hiker could prove to be a drag, but he was also a human curiosity.

Colin Shark knew all that, he had wound his way across endless planes to be where he was now. He had been born on a plane that offered little more than a life of contemporary and partial illiteracy. Something had sparked his imagination and shown him the key to the planes. The first step had been the escaping of his childhood environment. He had been brought up in Greenock, ten miles from where Rob had spent his boyhood days, albeit twenty years later. Greenock had less to offer childhood than Glasgow, it was a drab parochial Scottish town, full of shipyards and a factory that refined sugar. All the houses were grey and grimy from the smoke belching from the aluminium casting and the tin plate industries. The River Clyde ran red with the waste from the chemical plant and in winter, scarves were drawn over mouths and noses to filter the smog. The people of Greenock were proud that it had been the birthplace of Robert Watt. Parents wanted their sons to be like Robert Watt, or at least marine engineers in the tradition befitting the town. Living in a draughty cold-tap, gas-lit tenement building was bearable if the future secured a continuation of engineering and jobs. No one openly encouraged art, it wasn't in the town's interest. Nor was the town ever expected to produce artists. Again, by tradition, Glasgow and the West of Scotland produced the engineers and scientists, and Edinburgh and the East the lawyers and artists. Glasgow and the West had the capital, while Edinburgh was the capital. In Greenock tradition was tradition and Colin didn't like it, and as tradition had it, the only alternative was to move away.

Having scorned Greenock's tradition, it left him with no specific skills with which to make a living. Job after job left him dissatisfied with work or his boss. He was milling around like a million others trapped eternally. He turned to writing and discovered another life. It was no easy road, but five novels later and in his middle-thirties, Hollywood liked his work and offered him a job as a screenwriter. This wasn't a key, it was a door. Yet during the time he was making sacrifices to secure his future, other tugs in life tried to hold him to the plane he was from. The breaking with tradition left him with a distant family, a divorced wife and a twenty-one year old daughter trying to catch up with him. In California she eventually did and went to live with him in LA.

Life in California for Colin after all these years was sunshine and wide open spaces and elbow room to cough, even though he was still trying to give up the cigarettes that got him there. Working on a film like any job was work, creative as it was. He needed breaks as much as anybody. On a hundred thousand dollars a year he could afford holidays. His daughter wanted to go with him when she found out he had decided to see his old country play in the World Cup finals in Argentina. He'd shipped the F6 truck, fully converted to sleep three in the back and one in the front, along with stereo cassette, books, chess set and other distractions of the usual paraphernalia, mechanics set of tools and spare parts; flown to Argentina and been reunited with his vehicle at Buenos Aires docks. The World Cup was a fiasco for Scotland, but a crazy drunken one of supporters competing with the BBC, press and camera crews over the women that were being supplied by the Argentinean authorities. He took no part in it. He just took photographs and as a writer, took plenty of notes.

With football over, Colin and his daughter Jenny began on the long drive northwards to the States. He had for years been planning to drive the length of the Pan American Highway. A branch ran from Buenos Aires to Santiago and from there they had joined the main road running north to south the length of the Americas. Meanwhile, Colin's girlfriend couldn't miss out on the adventure and flew into Santiago to join them. United, they were all ready to leave when they found a stray dog in a back alley. They decided he should come along too and they nicknamed him 'Duke'. They glided across the Atacama Desert to the music of Dolly Parton and David Bowie. Beyond Anta-fagasta and on to Arica with The Eagles and Elton

John. Into Peru and on to Cuzco to Billy Joel and the Almond Brothers. And by the time they'd picked up Rob and Charlie they were drifting along to Van Morrison and Fleetwood Mac's latest album *Rumours*.

"Where are you's boys going?" turning down the volume, Colin shouted into the back of the truck where Rob and Charlie lay lost in the music. "Eh!" Rob said, jolted. "Oh, the next town" he replied. "OK." Colin whistled with a big grin in his gruffy but friendly Greenock accent, then turned the music up again. "You should have told him we were going to Lima" Charlie nudged. "We'll tell him later" Rob replied, "let's enjoy the present." They fell silent to the Average White Band.

Night came rushing over the mountains and Rob and Charlie began to notice and feel every little bump in the road that threw them into the air and sent them crashing down again onto their spines. The road tortured its way along cliff ledges and semi-desert mountainside, ever descending, until the lights of Puquio lay spread beneath. The lights haunted their vision for a half-hour before they reached the town limits and into the dog barking half-light of a Peruvian evening. Children rushed to awe at the dust coated white dream of a vehicle with its cow guard and massive track wheels. The older folks seemed impressed by the blue and yellow Californian number plates. The locals' assumption was that they were American, extremely rich and therefore important. How to take advantage of it was far from anybody's mind except the only hotel owner. The rest of the town was out on a demonstration supporting the three-month old teachers' strike. The Plaza de Armes had become a political platform for the teachers' grievances over pay.

"Why should so much be spent on arms when we have no one to fight?" they chanted, waving their 'no pay – out we stay' placards, the town listening to the speeches while Rob, Charlie, Jenny, Colin and his beautiful long-legged sunshine girl, Mona, ate egg sandwiches at a Plaza eat-house. In Cuzco the teachers had been cleared out a number of times from the main Plaza by the army and tear gas. But the teachers persisted and knew they were on a winning crusade. Every time the soldiers were used to quell the protesters, the people threatened more earnestly to

bring down the government. Military leaning government or not, Peru struggled with an ailing democracy.
The teachers wanted more pay and out they'd stay 'til
they got it.

The five travellers didn't really want to know, they
were all tired. Colin, Mona and Jenny slept in a dark
hotel room with a blocked toilet, while Rob and Charlie
slept in the back of the truck as the newly hired night
watchmen.

Charlie took a physical liking to Jenny but he
couldn't stand her temperament. To him she was a
stuck up socialite, nose-in-the-air know nothing who
babbled through everything and was far more
homesick for the things she knew than he ever was.
She was good at dishing out the cigarettes but low on
the smiles. She was the sort of woman he could make
love to, but never like. They were worlds apart, but
only because of her father's money. She was just
another typist lost in the London merry-go-round
before she tracked down her old man and latched on,
and now that she had, she was acting out the role.
After all, to her Charlie was a broke, begging bum,
hitching a lift, who with his friend, was now suitably
slotted into their security plans for the truck while they
slept. She didn't want to know Charlie. Life in LA
tumbled so many men from the sky that by
comparison he was just a kid, and kids were never
fun.

"That Jenny's too fat on money!" Charlie told Rob
as they rolled along the next day. "I thought you
always fancied marrying a rich chick" Rob joked. "Not
like her. She's a snotty-arsed bitch. She'd be too lazy
to even give you a hand job." "All depends on what
you're into" Rob laughed. Charlie cursed, then buried
himself in the encyclopedia to escape. Meanwhile, up
front, Jenny was complaining to Colin and Mona. "I
don't know why we're taking them along, especially
that uncouth Charlie one" Jenny said to Colin. He
rubbed her on the head and said "Never mind, kid."

Little Duke was as mongrel a dog as they come.
His cross-breed status was in doubt. Yet for an alley
dog he seemed well trained. He knew how to watch his
Ps and Qs and let out a low whine when it was time.
What he thought of rolling the length of the Americas,
leaving the temperate nights of his native Chile and
experiencing the rigours of the road out of three

people's fancy, was gratitude. It was no hot deal, raking dustbins and hovering round the back of restaurants for the scraps. Especially the Chinese, the tasty morsel offered while the meat cleaver held hidden slyly behind a smiling Chink's back – old friends had often disappeared that way. He was joking of course. Romance was rarely more than a gang-bang and with his short legs it had narrowed the field. He had developed the survival habit of always looking over his shoulder and keeping on the move. The kennel wagon was always lurking somewhere and that was no joy. He'd been thrown in once and a notice stuck on his kennel door stating age, colour, sex, breed and the number of days to live. Luckily, it was Christmas time and some middle aged couple bailed him out and handed him over to their son. But he was a right horror. He twisted his tail, stuck pencils in his ears and tried to make him eat shit. Of course, he wasn't allowed to bite back in retaliation. One day though, it got too much and he let the little rat have it. There was an instant reaction. He was belted off the walls, smashed against the floor, then kicked out for good.

So it was back on the street, without as much as a collar. It was a sad, though at times happy, life of running in gangs, beating up cats, scratching the paint off new cars, knocking over morning milk bottles and playing dodgem with the trains down by the tracks. The nights could be cold though, huddled in a dark alleyway on a doorstep in retreat from the rain, or under a bench in a park shelter, hiding from the wind. Few humans stopped to say hello or throw some food. It was a fight with the birds for the morning bread or a race with the cats to scavenge the bins. Everything was free but everything had to be worked for. Life was like that in the alleys.

One cold Santiago day he was picked off the streets by two firm hands, bundled onto a lap, chauffeured around town, carried upstairs, bundled onto a bed, fed and allowed to sleep, then carried downstairs, cradled on another lap, chauffeured around town again, let out for a 'P', put on a lap, carried upstairs, had a needle pushed into him, carried downstairs again and left to crash out on another lap. He didn't know what was going on. The next he knew, he saw great big noisy walls, continually breaking up on yellow stuff that moved under his feet. He heard a strange call, looked up and saw a big white bird. He barked but it didn't seem scared. They sky was blue and wasn't blotted out by buildings. Then he was picked up again and cradled in a lap that he was now beginning to recognise by the blue jeans. He looked up and saw three human faces all looking down at him and smiling. A big hand patted him on the head and said, "Never mind, Duke, you'll learn to understand."

Rob was elsewhere lost in thought as they reached Nazca and joined the Pan American Highway once more. Mona passed a reefer to them in the back and told them they were cruising on by the Nazca Lines. There was no time to stop, the whole world was before them she said. Rob liked Mona, her long slender legs, dark brown eyes, thin sensitive lips just to be going on with. If all the chicks in California were like her, he was going there! Somewhere in between that long pause and Rob's next thought, whole pages of history whizzed past the window. It was a barren desert landscape with a white burning ball of fire overhead. The road stretched endlessly counting down the kilometres to Lima. Yet out there lay the Lines, the lines that Van Daniken says were drawn by God's Chariots. Out there lay a gigantic monkey and its association with flying saucers.

Out there could have lain an answer to the universe for all Rob cared, puffing heartily on the marijuana, thinking about the only thing left to think about when it came down to it. Girls! And music, and drugs, and drink, and cars, and food and everything else until you end up with the universe again. There didn't seem to be no beginning or end. Everything rolled on and he agreed there was no point in stopping to see the Lines. It would tell them nothing about the whole world before them and who knows if it would tell much about the past. What he knew to date was that the earth formed four thousand six hundred million years ago, had dinosaurs up to one hundred and thirty million years ago, man appeared a million years ago who only learned to write eight thousand years ago and how to fly seventy years ago and who still died at about that age. From those figures, Rob computed which things affected him and came up with girls, music and drugs.

Colin drove mile after mile. For him the sunrises

and sunsets were continuous. He had everything he needed; his girlfriend, his daughter, a dog, two hitch-hikers, dope, music, the truck and the open road before him. He drove and drove, which gave him time to think about it all. He didn't have to talk much, he didn't have to listen much, he just drove and the rest took care of itself. Money no longer seemed to bother him, he had it and that was that. His work was respected, so the social status followed on. He had the freedom to travel and divorce left him free to be with who he wished. He had LA as his adopted home and uncountable friends. He had it all. Yet in his mind something rankled. In every mind pushing forward, there is a desire for something which never seems fulfilled, an emptiness, a capacity that's never completely satisfied. Except in the most hermetic of men companionship throughout life keeps the mind questing for the ultimate companion, the love of one's life. His marriage had been his belief in love and its durability. In France, love meant a love of emotion. In Britain, love usually meant companionship.

Colin loved Mona, but she had lost her husband in a motorbike accident, and that stood as barrier in the development of their relationship. She wasn't over it yet and distant mists sometimes clouded her eyes. He was wise enough to keep things on an even keel. He didn't want to be the captain of a sinking ship. As he grew older, Colin's friendships with men grew stronger, and more and more he was drawn by their strength and intellectualism. But as a heterosexual, they couldn't supply the emotion. He realised he could never find the answer to his love in one person. He had broken the desire to hold anyone again by a marriage certificate. He could live with what some people saw as the ultimate fate, loneliness. To them loneliness meant widow, spinster or bachelor. Yet Colin had never been as alienated from life than during his marriage. It had taken him years to realise it. Now all he did was drive. At forty-thee years old, he should have been tucked up in bed in a Greenock tenement building with a hot water bottle on a cold winter's night, instead of driving, driving, driving into the sunrise – sunset of the Pan American Highway.

"God, we're back in South America" Charlie said as they booked into the Hotel Europa, Lima. "At the rate we got here, I thought we were heading for the moon." "If you realised" Rob said as they unlocked their room door "that travelling has nothing to do with your surroundings, you'd maybe see things clearer. Being in South America's like putting yourself on an island and isolating yourself from everything you know. It doesn't matter where you are, you could just as easily be on another planet or on a deserted Scottish island, or a cottage in the English countryside, or if you're lucky, sitting by your own fireside, you'd still come up with the same answers."

"How long is this story, Rob, I'm tired." "Unfortunately, Charlie, you and I don't have the patience to sit by our own firesides and work out the universe. Take Phil Jones, for example. He's never been out of England, and I'll go back and tell him stories about South America. And what will he say 'Sure, I understand, the same things happen here' and he'll tell me a story based on the same logic. And in the end we'll come to the conclusion that I have to travel in distance to find my answers, and all he has to do is sit by his fireside, rarely going out while travelling in space and time in his head. Each one of us covers the same distance but by different means, that's why being back in South America doesn't really matter."

"You know something" Charlie said, stretching out on his bed "you confuse me. In Argentina you were telling me to be more aware of what was going on around me and now you're saying it doesn't matter."

"All I'm saying" Rob yawned "is that you've got to be able to see everything at once. South America is stimulus, that is all. Sitting by a fire, the flames are a constant stimulus of change that keeps the mind tumbling. The same with travelling. After a while you notice that the tropics have certain common characteristics. As it's your first experience, your eye notices the different fruit, the colourful vegetation, the change of habit and custom of the people, the foreignness of life in general. Inevitably a desire for something familiar leads to pangs of homesickness. "I know what that feels like." "I know you do. But for me, the tropics have become so familiar I see the sameness in most countries, and it's not homesickness I feel. It's a realisation that I now do my travelling in my head, and could easily spend three months under a coconut tree as travelling ten thousand miles.

Travelling is a case of isolating oneself from everything. People use all different methods, from mediation which is a personal search, to organised religion which is a mass pilgrimage. The only thing with travelling is that the isolation becomes more and more elusive. The more I travel the more of a social beast I become though understanding of peoples, individually and collectively."

"Really? I haven't seen any evidence of that" Charlie interrupted.

Rob removed his filthy socks. "All I desire is isolation, to be allowed to escape from the world and become a spectator neither interested nor disinterested in what's going on around me. It appears as a double entity. A development of outward character while seeking an understanding of the inward character. You see my outward one, but is it the inner one? The outward one wants to travel, travel, travel in miles, but the inner wants to travel in thought. The outward is the teacher, the inner the learner. Perhaps it's a good thing. If I sat under a coconut tree cross-legged, after a day some dumb shit would come along and say, 'Heh, what are you doing?' Where would I begin to start to answer him and in the end I would have to remain silent. Next, I know there would be ten people wanting to know what I was doing, then a hundred. There would be no peace. I would have to move somewhere else and the travelling would have begun again."

Rob starts to take off his filthy jeans. "I saw men in India like that, sitting but left in peace. Of all the countries I've been, it's the only place where a man is allowed to leave his body on earth without someone trying to move it on. Phil in England was a lucky one. Time and time again, he found disused cottages in Northumberland and hid from the world. But people always came to ask him what he was doing, I amongst them. In these times he travelled, free of transport hassles, hotel worries, money problems, border difficulties and the world's rip-off artists. But even he wasn't free; he had to eat, make fires, cut the wood, draw water from the stream. His environment was ill-suited. Rob looks at the hole in the knees of his jeans. "Only the old men of the tropics come closest to the perfect journey. In India, they sit by roadsides or on hill slopes with a food bowl and a loin cloth. In Africa, they sit the same, in some spot safe from the lions. They were the wisest men in the world, but wanted nothing to do with it. In South America we haven't even met a real beggar. That puts it in perspective. Look at Lima, we see dope dealers and money changers. European ones too, French, Italian and in Cuzco, English in the cafes. It reminds me of my days in Delhi. In them I see myself and know of the type of sham world tinged with mistrust in which they live and work. To begin with it's exciting, but after a while the novelty wears off and they must content themselves with being small time crooks.

Rob takes his jeans to the bathroom sink. "Yet many people will think of it as the highlight of their travelling life. But to me that is no longer travelling, that is existing. We stole seven hundred pounds from Barclays and Thomas Cooks. We lost two hundred and spent the rest. We found the rucksack on the Trail and for all we know the two women might have been dead. That is about the extent of our dishonesty on this journey. The traveller's cheques initiated the whole trip and without them we probably wouldn't have got far. But with travelling I've developed a faith that goes beyond all money. Not once have we cheated anyone out of a cent on this trip, except at the Lost City when we climbed over the gate. Twice we've been ripped off, but we've maintained our trust in people. Whether they are Brazilian, Chileno or Peruvian it doesn't matter. We've trusted them. But the travelling would be so much easier if we could dispense with people and places and retreat so that even the palm tree can be taken away, the warm sand removed, the rolling waves forgotten and the blue sky replaced by nothing."

After two days in Lima, Colin had his pocket picked, Mona had her passport stolen, Jenny and Charlie saw *Saturday Night Fever,* and Rob dabbled with some cocaine. Colin slipped Rob a hundred dollar bill on hearing of the boys' poverty stricken situation. They had managed to sell the rucksack and sleeping bag for thirty-five dollars. But they spent their new wealth like men with no arms by adopting a philosophy of 'you only live once' which helped them spend it even faster. Charlie liked Lima and its hustle-bustle city life. Watching John Travolta squirm his way through a film as a nineteen year old trying to get on in life made him turn to Jenny and see himself in Travolta's shoes. Whether Jenny saw the parallels of his situation with Tony Manero, who was trying to stick a chick higher up the social ladder, was doubtful. She was too dumb, Charlie thought, she took everything in and gave nothing out. She was what he called a non-person. He could tell her his whole life story and she would go, "Oh yes," accompanied by a vacant look. Nothing ever came back out but "I don't like this film" or "What's the time."

After the movie, Charlie took her to a little café cum cake shop he'd found in a Lima side street. He sat her down, ordered a number of tarts and cream cakes that he thought would make her mouth water, and what did she say but "I don't like sweet things." "How about a beer then?" he asked. She jumped off her stool in disgust. "I only drink daiquiris" and he was following her out the door before he knew it. "Women" he muttered to himself. She insisted on getting a taxi back to her hotel, two blocks away. He'd taken her up to her room and that was it. They opened the door and there was Colin and Mona playing chess, and Rob snorting coke.

Rob and Charlie had been staying in a poorer part of town while Colin, Mona and Jenny enjoyed the luxury of one of Lima's best hotels. In gratitude of the lift, they'd scored some marijuana for them and decided to drop it off and inform them that they were heading for Ecuador the following day. As things worked out, Rob took on Colin at chess. When Charlie and Jenny went to the cinema, and while Mona snorted coke, they agreed that all five of them should drive to Ecuador together. They were shipping the truck out from Guayaguil and then flying to Panama City to meet it. Under friendly insistence, they couldn't refuse?

Life was moving too fast to catch up on what was going on. The images were flashing too quickly to dwell on for any length of time. They had been rescued from the heights of the Peruvian mountains and whisked along at an average of sixty miles an hour, instead of sixty miles a day. Every hour shortened the journey by a day, and made South America no more than a blur on the windscreen. From twenty pounds in their pockets, they now had seventy. Everything was figures and nothing was reality with the amount of grass they were smoking. The last thing of South America they could remember was the football game with the alpacas, and that didn't seem all that real at the time. So, as Lima disappeared out the back window and Fleetwood Mac carried them through the waves of happiness, there was nothing else to the world but four rolling wheels, sweet flowing music and marijuana. Their days of being dust bitten and broke were sheet joy.

Trujillo became just a passing place like another thousand points on the highway. The Plaza de Armes, the Cathedral, the people, it didn't matter, they had their substitutes or alter-egos in a million similar larger or smaller towns. Why did one woman wear a striped suit resembling pyjamas while another wore a plain shirt and woollen cardigan? Cities were contrasts, not of their buildings but of the people who built them. Nothing mattered whether another earthquake hit, it was inevitable something would destroy what already existed. For who cared if Trujillo disappeared in a flash of raging flame the following day? Who cared? In far away Jakarta, Trujillo was a word which had no conception to the non-Spanish speaker. Trujillo, where was Trujillo?

Trujillo disappeared out the back window, and Rob, high as a kite, didn't know where he was. Night was coming on and he didn't know. The stereo in his ears didn't help to clear his thoughts. The while lines in the road just kept coming through the windscreen and going out the rear window to fade in the distance. Where he was didn't matter any more. He was totally isolated in the darkness. He could only make out the others' shadows. Charlie fast asleep by his side. He couldn't hear anything but Van Morrison's wailing voice, and feel the miles rush by, beneath him, mile after mile.

Sometime after dawn, Pope Paul VI died. God rest his soul. Sometime near lunch the President of the United States was assassinated and sometime after dusk the world went to war, and all they heard was The Band and all they saw was while lines coming through the windscreen and going out the back window to disappear forever. Stopping in Puira for petrol and a bite to eat, they found out the Pope really had died. Charlie was the only Catholic and he didn't think much about religion. But at that moment he remembered the two Mormons in Paraguay and their talk of God's Kingdom. They were right, he hadn't found it in Argentina or Chile or Bolivia. But now he understood what they were talking about and because of that, he crossed himself for the Pope. He'd come a long way from sucking a mango in the wooden Cathedral in Georgetown. From being a punk going nowhere, he was emerging into society by trying to outgrow it. He was realising he had to drop in to drop out.

Thousands of thoughts were flowing through Charlie's head at that moment. Then suddenly his ears popped and he heard the church bells ringing dolefully, and the Peruvians brushing past dressed in black and heading for Mass. He watched, and a melancholy overtook his whole being and he wanted nothing more than to get back in the truck and play some Blondie or Elvis Costello or Ramones or Boomtown Rats, something to take him back to what he was before he ever came to South America. Previously, he had lived in a small world that he had rebelled against, but understood.

Now he understood nothing and was forcing himself to try and fit into a world that had no limits. He had crossed himself, he told himself bitterly. Before, the Pope had been a figurehead who stood for where the world had gone wrong. He was rich in the poor man's world. Like the Queen, like anyone who was richer than he was. They all exploited the workers. He was a worker and they would exploit him if he gave them the chance. He had seen no way out. Rebel, rebel had been the only answer. Smash everything. Kill everyone. Death, death, death had been the only end. The Sex Pistols had typified it all. Violence! Violence! Wipe out the inequality. The frustration had built up and up and just exploded. But it hadn't spilt out onto the streets, it was only the teenagers who had nothing to do but fight each other. And even then there had been the dole. There was no need to fight just absolutely none. It just gave his generation an identity, a forgotten age group with no jobs and the likelihood of never being more than a car washer or shop assistant, and all he could keep thinking was that he had got out of it, thank Christ, he had got out of it, and ended up crossing himself for the Pope.

What would his mates at home think? Yet they wouldn't be on the same level any more. When he got back he'd... he still didn't know what he wanted to do. One thing for certain, he wouldn't go back to the same style of life he'd had when he had left. Yet he couldn't see the changes, he knew he had changed but couldn't see the changes. The only way to find out was going back and comparing himself with his friends. 'I'm a moron, I'm a moron' went through his head. New Wave had certainly left its mark. When the dole had got him the job at the climbing shop and he'd hesitated, she'd said he better hurry up and make his mind up, plenty of others were waiting to take the job if he didn't want it. He had been a moron then. Now, he would tell her, let someone else slog their guts out for twenty-three pounds a week, he would never again.

How time changed things. He was in Peru now, he reminded himself, rolling along with the whole world in front of him. People would have to pay a million times twenty-three quid to be in his shoes at that moment. The Pope had died, but Charlie finally felt that he had been born.

The road to the Ecuadorian frontier was a pioneer's track, or a rally driver's nightmare of pot holes, rocks and the thickest red dust that choked the lungs. It reminded Rob of African roads and put him off any thoughts of returning there. For Colin it was all good fun. For the girls and the dog it was a bout of sneezing before the real coughing began.

The track led high into the mountains as they spiralled upwards to David Bowie's *Heroes* which obliterated the calling birds and the rattle-rumble of the tyres pounding along. Peru was being left behind in a cloud of distant memories first ignited by the high Andes and now extinguished by the same range of sentinels seemingly impervious to human comings and goings. Considering that Peru attracted most of South America's tourist traffic, Rob and Charlie had met too few to mention. Then again, they weren't dallying in any one place long enough to get beyond a nod and smile situation so common in life, especially travelling in the space bubble of the truck.

Rob was looking forward to reaching Guayaquil and returning to the use of local transport to get them back in touch with life beyond their vehicular cage. He felt that life was rushing by too fast. He wouldn't mind a grubby little hotel room for the night, and a quiet cup of coffee in a local café while he reflected over the day's happenings. That was the type of travelling he was used to, a thread of routine to keep him sane. Travelling at sixty miles an hour was beginning to drive him crazy. It wasn't that he didn't like high speed travelling, it was just that he liked to go at his own pace. In the truck he was experiencing no real external stimulus. Everything was happening inside his head. At the end of the day, there was nothing to reflect on. Nothing had happened except a continuous thought process that was driving him to distraction. He had tried reading a book, but the bumping of the truck, and the nauseating effect and disorientation that following after an hour of strained eyes, made it exhausting. Conversation with Charlie was impractical because of the noise of the wheels on the road and now with the dust there was no point even looking out the windows. It wasn't a case of not being able to live with himself, he was better at that than most, it was the physical discomfort and the comparative imprison- ment in the confines of the truck that was making him pine for freedom. He was under no compulsory sentence to be somewhere on a certain date. All he felt was that he was in a fireside situation without a fire to look at, or cross-legged under a palm tree with no sea to gaze out on.

Charlie rued the thought of returning to a life of uncertainty, of not knowing where to spend the night or which bus to catch or even how long to stay in one place. He'd given up all independence and accepted the limitations on his freedom the truck imposed. He didn't mind the people and the countryside slipping past, deep down he still had the desire to have the journey through South America over with. Much of the time, he was considering his experiences as something he must go through, but which he needn't necessarily enjoy. He admitted to himself though that he was beginning to drive himself insane with thought, and concluded that the sooner they stood on their own feet again, the less introverted they would become. Guayaquil and the less cushy life that lay beyond was just the return of the old malady – a fear of the unknown, and an uncertainty about the future.

## ECUADOR

"Get yourself to LA" Colin was saying to Rob and Charlie "and you can come and stay a while." All three were covered in oil and grease and dripping sweat as they replaced the wheel back on the axle. A shy mountain family had watched from their shack as the *gringos* had struggled in three hours of midday heat to determine what was causing the grating noise from the front right wheel. The family had sat in the shade of their verandah with a curiosity typical of their nature, but they had kept their distance. All *gringos* were best avoided. They had brought nothing but misery to South America. Before the discovery that bananas were so profitable, the *gringos* had little bothered with their small country. Now Ecuador was laughed at by all other Latins and referred to as Bananaland. An Ecuadorian could go nowhere without being continually abused with bad taste jokes about their bananas and their sexual connotations. Bananas had ruined the economy. All the best land had been turned over to plantations and had been bought by money-minded 'gringos' who drank all the profits.

A man in Ecuador could not longer by master of his own land, peasants' rights had sunk to the level of being employed by an imperialist foreigner who paid bananas and not even peanuts for his labours. The government tolerated it as they were the only Ecuadorians growing rich on banana profits. The 'gringos' didn't care as long as the banana boats left Guayaquil and ports along the coast with a full hold. Life on the plantations was of little concern to the buyers and distributors, who stuck blue labels testifying they were Ecuadorian bananas, whether they had come from Ecuador or Costa Rica or wherever. Everyone knew Ecuadorian bananas were the best, but in Ecuador no one was proud of that fact. They detested the memory of bananas. Bananas meant total dependence on 'gringo' money. If the foreigners wanted, they could bring Ecuador to its knees in a matter of weeks by curtailing the banana trade. The bananas would lie and rot on the wharves and piers and no one would be paid a cent for the work of growing and cutting them down. The 'gringos' continually reassured the plantation workers not to worry, that they would never desert them. But 'gringos' were as slippery and as dangerous as eels, and their eyes always laughed in mockery when they talked of their 'banana manners'.

Ecuador had rid itself of the Spanish yoke early in the Latin American revolution, but had fallen to the 'gringos' without even a fight. And now with the exploration of oil, it was the foreigners who made all the profits again. Ecuador was little more than a colony with a facsimile government dancing like puppets to amuse the children, while the marionettes produced the voices and instigated all the actions with a nimble twitch of strings. 'Gringos' wanted their bananas, but an Ecuadorian didn't have to help any more than grow the damned things and chuck them into a bottomless ship's hold. 'Gringos' needed no assistance. This, the shy Ecuadorian family knew, watching quietly as Colin tightened up the nuts on the wheel and released the jack.

"Needs new bearings" they all agreed as they woke up Mona and Jenny asleep with the heat. Little Duke was panting. The Ecuadorian family watched them start up, and shatter the mountain silence, before receding along the bumpy road to Guayaquil.

It was one of those bright tropical days where the birds sang and the city traffic thundered below. The locals were off to work while Rob and Charlie were dragging themselves from their hotel beds. They had agreed to help Colin out, to take the truck to the Ford dealer for a new bearing and have the brakes aligned. It was pulling so badly to the left that a touch on the brakes sent it veering across to the other side of the road. And in Guayaquil where everyone was Emerson Fittipaldi or had the driving mentality of a seventeen year old kid out for his first joy ride, such a defect could be fatal.

Once dressed, they crossed the street and entered a low budget café for a coffee pick-me-up and an early morning snack. With the usual precaution, they settled on the price with the fat woman owner before they sat down. A coffee and a potato cake would be six sucres each, mused Charlie, not a bad deal; next door was ten.

They sipped their coffee and munched happily on their potato cake, gazing idly out into the street at the passing neatly groomed colourfully dressed office girls gripping mauve shaded folders under their arms while somewhere in a spacious office on the third floor of an edificio, their bosses sat with their feet up on their desks reading the morning newspaper and sipping glasses of imitation Grant's Black Label. Guayaquil was an edgy city, enjoyment of it seemed tempered by tinges of hate. The people seemed constantly on the defensive and certainly unwilling to open their hearts to a 'gringo'. For an equatorial city, the people worked too hard and appeared ready to lunge with knives at one another when competition became too severe. They were hungry, discontented people out for themselves and inconsiderate of anyone else out for the same thing. Not since Georgetown had Rob and Charlie seen any city with as mean a streak as Guayaquil. Ambition in each striving individual to be rich when he spotted his neighbour driving a brand new Ford was uncomfortable to be around. Rob and Charlie, merely for being white Europeans, were considered rich. How could they explain while driving around in the truck or walking the streets with their self-assuring arrogance that they had only forty dollars in the world between them and that that was borrowed. No, there was no way. So the inhabitants of Guayaquil prepared to rip them off.

They drained their coffees. Charlie asked the fat woman for the bill, preparing to hand over twelve sucres. Meanwhile the woman had been doing her own addition. "Twenty-six sucres" she said. Rob and Charlie laughed. Charlie handed her twelve sucres. The woman grabbed him by his shirt and began screaming that she wanted more. Rob told Charlie to ignore her and walk away, but the fat woman broke into hysterical screeching that stopped people short in the street. She was holding on tighter than ever to Charlie's shirt as if her life depended on it. Charlie was worried that the fat woman was going to rip his shirt. Her screaming wasn't doing his brain any good either. With a struggle he reached into his jeans and offered the fat woman a further twelve sucres. By now she was too far gone in her own hysteria to accept, and the money tumbled to the floor. Rob suddenly felt that trouble was brewing. A crowd had gathered, and everyone stared as the woman cried her heart out as Charlie stood trapped and flat-footed, trying to disengage the woman's hands from his shirt. A policeman with a sword hanging from his belt appeared. The policemen wore swords in Guayaquil.

Before the policeman could ask anything, Rob began explaining the situation in his broken Spanish. He'd learned early in life to get his side of the story in first. He pointed to the fat woman, pointed to Charlie, pointed to the money on the ground, pointed to the crowd, then pointed to the policeman on concluding his story. The policeman satisfied, told the fat café owner to let go of Charlie and signalled both of them to clear off. Charlie let out a sigh of relief.

It was late afternoon by the time the repairs to the truck were completed. Rob and Charlie returned to check out of their hotel and collect their gear before returning the truck to Colin. They drove round the area a couple of times before they found a parking spot, a few blocks away. They casually strolled along Calle Sucre and climbed the stairs into their hotel. The receptionist shrieked in alarm and a dozen guests started quivering and babbling warnings in Spanish. Rob asked what was going on. "Ah, Signors, Signors. Zee husband ees looking for you with a knife. Danger! Mucho peligroso. Beware!" the receptionist shouted, jumping up and down. "E will kill you."

Rob and Charlie gathered the gist of the receptionist's warnings. It was a ridiculous example of Latin American pride and honour. The fat woman owner of the café opposite the hotel, embarrassed by her own degrading display of hysteria that morning, was attempting to cover up her embarrassment by fabricating a story of physical brutality administered on her by Charlie. This is what she told her husband, who in an environment of simmering hatred was goaded to take action to salvage her self respect, and his honour. Two wrongs make a right is law in some domestic situations. The husband's loyalty to his wife put him in a position where he took his wife's word as he was a bad judge of character. He was a bull ready to lunge at anything red, and red was all he saw.

"I'll go bring the truck round to the front" Charlie said. "OK" Rob replied. "I'll pack the bags. But be careful. Park right outside and I'll bring everything down." It was wise to get out of there before any blood was spilt. "And if anyone comes anywhere near you" Rob shouted as Charlie descended the stairs "run for your life." Rob rushed to their hotel room window and to his horror looked down on the street to see the fat woman wielding a whip. Other masculine types were close at hand. Rob shouted to warn Charlie but Charlie was already halfway up the street, the vigilante party in hot pursuit, knives at the ready.

Rob crashed his way to the hotel phone to try and call the police, while the other guests reminded him that they had warned him that the husband was waiting downstairs to get them. But he wouldn't listen. He couldn't wait all day to let the madman cool down.

Meanwhile Charlie had shaken off pursuit and was skirting down a side street, taking as indirect way as possible to the truck. He was more worried about a reprisal on Colin's truck than on himself or Rob, though deep down he was praying they'd both avoid physical harm as well. For all he knew, Rob by now was being besieged in the hotel, fighting for his life. But he knew Rob. If he got the truck, for sure Rob would escape with the baggage. Then all of a sudden, out of the afternoon shadows, lunged the maddened husband who took a swing and struck Charlie in the eye with his fist. More shocked at the unexpectedness than by the blow, Charlie saw half dozen heavies backing the husband up, decided not to stand his ground, took to his heels and sailed straight into a cop. Charlie was stopping for no one, turned and legged it and now well in front wasn't unduly worried. Then, wriggling between two parked cars, he caught his Levis on the bumpers. The chase was all over, the cop laid hold of him, took his passport, and escorted him back to the hotel, fending off the enraged husband and his vigilante party. Rob, who had dropped the phone at the sound of the coming commotion, watched from the window as Charlie, the cop, the vigilantes and a mob of about fifty people stopped the traffic on Calle Sucre and headed for the hotel.

What followed for the next half hour was a gnashing of teeth passed between the husband, the cops (there were three by this time), Charlie and Rob, until no one knew what was going on. Rob's Spanish was sufficiently good to demonstrate the events of the morning, and his re-enacting of the fat woman's sobbing and frustration was done so well one of the cops pulled out his sword and threatened to strike. Rob then offered the husband the additional two sucres to make the total twenty six, but the husband flew into a rage and this time the cop showed him the sword. The husband, calming down, then attempted to bribe the cops to take Rob and Charlie down to the station and charge them with assault on his wife.

Rob, straining his ears to understand their gabbling in Spanish, could see the cops contemplating his proposition. "Money's a ridiculous way to settle this" he shouted in Spanish, for he could see himself and Charlie being locked up on a trumped up charge. "We've been all round South America and this is the first time we've come across any trouble." The cops listened, put their heads together and the word deportation was brandished around. They dropped that idea when they finally believed Rob that they hadn't gotten into trouble before.

However, the blood thirsty husband, out for his pound of flesh, was thrusting money into one of the cop's hands. The policemen, presented with this new approach, put their heads together again and had another little talk. They decided everyone was to go out into the street. Rob and Charlie picked up their belongings and were escorted down the stairs and out of the hotel. Outside in the glaring sun, the husband offered the cops more money if they arrested the Gringos. The cops started moving Rob and Charlie up the street to diffuse the situation. The one who had taken Charlie's passport was on the point of handing to him back when the husband hailed down a taxi, paid the driver, and insisted they take Rob and Charlie across town to the police station. Their hearts sank as they were bundled into the cab, one cop in the back, another in the front. A swarm of inquisitive people surrounded the taxi demanding to know something of the high drama which had gone before. Rob meanwhile, kept reiterating "Hacemos nada, hacemos nada" (we've done nothing) in true Hollywood style while the cops sat with downcast eyes. The policeman in the back belted a clutching hand with his baton, and the taxi took off for the police station.

The Guayaquil 2$^{nd}$ Command Police Station was a grim looking place with thirty foot high walls and turrets. On the journey across town, the cops kept reassuring them there would be no problems, while Rob attempted to find out how much it would cost to bribe them. They kept replying "No problem, no problem." On seeing the police station, Rob wasn't so sure. But once they were escorted inside, to the turn of a few heads, including the inquisitive machine gun toting guards, they relaxed and waited in line to tell their story.

The facts were read out to the captain on duty who sat with bemused eyes behind a high raised desk. Pointing to Charlie, the cops said that a man had hit Charlie in the eye, to which Charlie pointed to the red sore, in confirmation. "Did he hit him back?" the Captain asked the policeman. "No" the cop replied. "Why not?" the Captain asked. "Because he's a nice boy" Rob butted in. The Captain told the policeman to read on, then before he could continue, asked why the man hit Charlie in the first place. "Because he assaulted his wife" the cop replied. At this point, Rob was called upon to demonstrate again the happenings of the morning. "The woman, a big fat woman at that," the Captain suppressed a laugh at Rob's Spanish "grabbed my friend by the arms and shook him, screaming that she was being beaten up. My friend, my good friend, stood there motionless while the woman went into hysterics. Twenty six sucres for two coffees and two buns, come on, I ask you?" The Captain turned to the two cops and laughed, told them they had brought in the wrong people. They should have brought in the husband and wife for extortion! The cops wandered off, while Rob and Charlie recounted their other South American adventures to the Captain.

They returned the truck and didn't hang around in Guayaquil much longer. They said their farewells to Colin, Monica and Jenny who were flying to Panama, having arranged for their truck to be shipped there. Rob and Charlie spent the following night in a hotel room in Riobamba, looking up at the ceiling, at the hole in the plaster roughly the shape of Ecuador. "That proves Ecuador's a hole" Charlie commented, thinking back on the previous day's events. "It's good to be on the road again."

Rob smiled at Charlie's resigned fatalism thinking Charlie was no longer the same young kid he started out with. The fight in Guayaquil had been of a different nature from the one in Brasilia. Charlie had come out of the latest one with some dignity. Yet, how time flew, Brasilia seemed so long ago. Was it only two months since they had left there in the middle of the night? It was as if they were starting afresh all over again. The memories of the previous three and a half months felt like a lifetime. Argentina and Chile were hazy beyond recall. Bolivia seemed years before. He had even forgotten all about Paraguay. In a way it was a relief to have them all behind him. The road in front was all that seemed to matter. The unknown road without any end.

The sun lit up the volcanic crater of Chimborazo and morning flooded into their hotel room. Charlie wiped the sleep from his eyes and looked up at the hole in the ceiling again. Ecuador was not a hole. In the mountains, it was a land of green pastures resembling the soft slopes of the Alps. Neat little fences encased the cattle in fields and added a finished touch to the landscape which was missing elsewhere in South America. Trim little roads swept through valleys and crossed rivers as delicate little bridges. Shacks turned to farm cottages and fields of wheat led on to cabbage patches and furrows of potatoes and carrots.

It was some of the richest farming land in the continent and the cool wet temperatures produced crops in abundance. The land lay less than one degree south of the equator. It was such a contrast to when they crossed the equator on the 'Ely'. From where they were now in Riobamba, a hundred miles away rose rivers that flowed the three thousand miles to the mouth of the Amazon. In between lay the untamed wilderness – savage and barbaric settlements of uncivilised tribes who lived harmoniously and knew nothing of the approaching jungle clearing operations that would herald the beginnings of progress and the end of solitude. The wilderness where man's big silver birds trailed a rainbow across the tree tops of an eternal plain of jade. Where rumours of cannibalistic tribes and pre-historic animals who looked upward from a perch of greenwood and shirked in fear. Where an undergrowth of florid orchids and vivid primeval plants thrived jointly to defeat the insects and reptiles struggling with each other. The wilderness in which man stood little chance without destroying it and transforming it into a fertile plain. For he had begun. The tiny isolated and forgotten settlements like Saint George would grow larger. The one armed crocodile hunters and Captain Brazil would multiply. The great roads driven by Narcotico Mercedes would became more numerous. The jungle boys like Corruba would grow more civilised. The wilderness increasingly cleared away for man's own ends.

Progress? The wilderness was a threat, it was the unknown, and by challenging the unknown, the known became more certain. The known was retained by faith, but faith was lost by the realisation of greed, and greed just led back to destroying of the wilderness further, with no thought as to why. The cycle of wilderness to a cultivation of lands as pretty and as productive as the Ecuadorian mountain slops – which Rob and Charlie rolled by on their way to Quito – showed that perhaps one day the history books would be unable to tell of the great Amazon wilderness that once existed, and that was fast disappearing while they were there.

Quito was a pleasant city full of narrow twisting cobbled streets lined with stalls selling all manner of things. The church in Plaza de Sucre rose attractively, its white washed walls, small square windows, and clock bell tower crowned in gold was one of the oldest in South America, it blended picturesquely with the other old buildings that constituted the traditional centre of the city.

Rob and Charlie were passing under the statue of Marchal Sucre on their way to the cinema. There wasn't much else to do in Quito. The food was reasonable, the weather nippy in the shade, but dry. After they had visited the market and half a dozen churches and sucked on innumerable ice creams to pass the time, they had gone back to their hotel, the Zulia. It was reasonably clean, but it had light blue walls which flaked. It reminded Rob of Indian hotel rooms. Without fail they had light blue walls that flaked. But in the Zulia beds were wide, though as usual lacked the extra few inches in length which made the difference between comfortable and luxurious. "Cold feet" Charlie would say in a dream as his pushed through the blankets and stuck out the bottom of the bed, "was not uncommon in South America if you are taller than five foot eight."

They were wrapped up in their Paraguayan jackets as they paid their ten sucres to see *Close Encounter of the Third Kind*. Their other clothes were a wretched assortment of ragged tee-shirts and disintegrating jeans. Rob's jeans were still hanging off him after a patching session that afternoon in which he mended five holes and took three hours to do so. The instep of his right foot showed a darned pair of socks where his monkey boot had split. Charlie had his alpaca sweater from Cocabamba market hiding the rip down the back of his red and white striped tee-shirt, but felt uneasy over his toes protruding from his clapped out tennis shoes. The dust of the Pampas, the Atacama Desert and the wilds of Peru still clung to their jackets and neither of them had shaved for a week. Rob covered his greasy hair with his sombrero and Charlie hid the dirt under his nails by stuffing his hands in his pockets. Neither of them felt like a million dollars. They were on the verge of being broke. The usher took their tickets with a second glance and Rob and Charlie sat down to watch Richard Dreyfuss drag his heavy body through the movie, while trying to act dumb.

They crossed the equator and arrived in Tulcan by the local bus from Quito. It was an overcast day and they shared a taxi to the Columbian frontier with a Venezuelan and Argentino. Between them they had about enough money to get them to Bogotá.

## COLUMBIA

Having cleared Ecuadorian formalities, the taxi crawled across a concrete bridge that acted as the frontier and stopped outside the Colombian immigration office. It was a busy crossing point and the Colombian officials seemed oblivious to that fact. If the world was going to end, Columbia would be the last place for it to happen.

Rob's turn came to hand over their passports. The immigration officer looked at him, glared at the gold earring, gazed at his patched jeans and asked him how much money he had. "Four hundred dollars," Rob stated immediately. The immigration officer was just about to ask if he could see the money, when a colleague interrupted to ask his advice on something. The immigration officer babbled something in Spanish and turned back to Rob, having forgotten where he was. "Ah yes, onward ticket! Out of Columbia" he asked.

Rob produced an air ticket worth twenty dollars. He had bought it in Quito from Braniff Airways to replace the Air France MCO stolen with his passport that had acted as his onward ticket for some of the other countries. As usual the sight of an air ticket, irrespective of value, proved sufficient. "How many days you stay?" the officer asked. "Thirty" Rob answered calmly. "How mucho money you say you have?" he asked again. Rob smiled. "Four hundred" he replied. The immigration officer looked at the gold earring again, stamped his passport and wrote 'Valid for Thirty Days.'

Rob thanked him in a courteous manner, then waited outside the office for Charlie who joined him a minute later. "Thirty days!" Charlie beamed. "Just luck" Rob smiled. "The Venezuelan bloke in front if me had an onward ticket, five hundred dollars, lives in the next country, and they told him to go back to Quito and fly to Caracas. It's a crazy world." "I know" Charlie said as they climbed in the back of the taxi. "This is our eleventh country in South America and we haven't had one hassle at the borders." "Thank God it's the last one" Rob replied. "I wouldn't like to tempt fate too much. This might be the last one in South America, but we've still got to get into Panama next." "Panama!" Charlie despaired as the taxi moved off.

"Where in hell does this journey end?"

Rob looked at him and laughed. "Where did it begin?"

The places Charlie hated most in South America were the little shit hole villages and towns on the borders and others like Chalhuanca. Inwardly he had a fear of being trapped in one of them for the rest of his life, and frequently bubbled under in despair. St George had been like that. Other places such as Brasilia and Guayaquil held bad memories because he got into trouble. Sao Paulo because had a dose of the shits. Oruro because of the money situation. Chalhuanca because it was in the middle of nowhere. Port of Spain because he was anxious to see more. Georgetown because it was his first brush with hostile blacks. Yet on the other hand he had enjoyed the rich life in Macapa, the beauty of Mendoza, the quiet of Vina, the solitude of Copacabana, the quaintness of Cuzco and the hot springs of Aguas, not to mention Cayenne, Rio, Buenos Aires, Asuncion, La Pa, Lima and the pleasant boredom of Quito.

But Columbia was going to be the biggest drag of them all. It was no reflection on the people. They were less straight-jacketed than in most countries in the continent, they were human and reacted similarly to their British counterparts. The culture had developed from different roots, yet the similarities of temperament were not as diverse as Charlie would have expected. What worried him, and which had been worrying him ever since the Death Train, was money. Yet there they were, Rob and he, sitting on a hillside overlooking the town of Ipiales, smoking marijuana, watching the hands of the numerous clock towers tick round, as they waited patiently for the departure of their bus to Pasto. Further up the hillside a solitary figure plied his kite in the wind, which wove endlessly over the town in gay abandon and with a 'joie de vivre' that took Charlie's heart out of the depths of his butterfly stomach and brought words to his mouth. "Nice day, eh!" he said to Rob. "Absolutely beautiful" Rob answered, not very responsive to his attempt at conversation.

Charlie turned inward again and thought it was a long time since he had heard anyone sing. The coca leaf seller in Cochabamba market had been the last besides their sing-along with the Beatles. Where had all the song singers gone, the Jose Gruesoms, the Legionnaires, the Mormons, the William Smiths, the Captain Brazils, the Narcotico Mercedes of the world. Even the singing waiter was better than no one. Everything had become so serious, but why? Perhaps people were still singing, it was just that his ears had closed and he no longer heard them. Even the birds held no tunes, he had seen none for such a long time. The humming bird on the Inca Trail seemed like the last, for the Condor had represented something more sinister than a feathered animal. Likewise with the dog, with whom he'd shared the night, it was more than just a stray. And the dolphin on the Amazon. And why had he been able to laugh at the alpacas and the football?

Money! It was money. Thoughts of money were clouding his brain so much that the sun shone and he felt cold. He had been wrapped in warmth when they began to cash the traveller's cheques, but each day the monetary clothing grew scanter and the cold had penetrated to his soul. The coldness grew from fear of being penniless so far from home, of being in the world with nothing but the clothes he stood in. He feared life without money more than loneliness. Yet his fears as yet seemed groundless, the point of poverty had not been reached. They had enough to travel to Bogotá, and he had a camera worth a hundred dollars. It had hardly been used due to lack of inspiration and a refusal to take snapshots just to show to friends back home. It had been a present from his parents and any thought of parting with it were out of the question. If there was no way of raising money to carry them on beyond Bogotá, they should call it a day and be repatriated. There was no point in prolonging a journey that was beginning to go on forever. Selling his camera would only be a short term answer. Inwardly, he'd had about enough, not with the journey but living with the fear of life without money. When the money ran out, so would his resolve, and the kite that flew over the town of Ipiales appeared as nothing more to him than paper and string.

Rob sat motionless, eyes fixed on the kite somersaulting in the air, lost in a maze of possibilities and distractions that made him so secretive to Charlie. Whatever the outcome of life, he was the ultimate in optimism and rarely defeatist. His determination stemmed from his experiences since leaving home, and the countless countries he had visited over the years. Each country had been another step, and an index of the past. Each country was a beginning and end that made him feel he was progressing through life. Thankfully, the direction didn't crystallise as something he could be tagged by. His lifestyle defied all definition and typified the free spirit of the undestined. To a twenty-four year old, the wanderlust had soaked his bones in adventure and experience, that was of no use to any society, only to himself. He had learned no skills over the years, but those that verged on the criminal. There was no place for him, he had given up his background and fitted in nowhere else.

The journey to South America, he had told himself, would be his last. But as he thought more and more about it, there was nothing else to take the place of wandering. He had hoped something would work itself out and he would see reason for settling down. But the age old wife and kids and house and car and everything else that went with it, was the only end to everything he had learned. There had to be more to life than a job and promotion. By taking to the road he had burnt all the ladders of his early twenties when footholds in careers were dug, and all the wisest women were looking for someone who would stay and make something of a relationship. He had only his experiences. He had filled his head while others had filled their living rooms with stereos and wall to wall carpets. At twenty-four he wasn't an old man, he felt he hadn't experienced anything, yet he remained optimistic. He was broke again and sat pondering the aerodynamics of the kite. He had never possessed vast amounts of money and held no ideas of what he would do if he did, except travel around the world. There seemed no cure to his lust, bar death. Money was most people's God, but lack of money Rob found, released him of any false hopes. Others dreamt of winning the pools or inheriting a fortune or contented themselves to allow their life insurance mature or reap the high pay rewards after thirty years service with a company. They waited to live. They waited to dream of journeys to safari parks in Africa or of romantic second honeymoons in Rio. Or saved to buy a yacht or private plane, or even a country villa to retreat to. But by the time the dreams materialised, death was knocking on the door. Dreams of money led only to false hopes and misdirection of thought.

Rob was not content to wait and build for the future with a job he compromised his happiness with. He saw the trap repeated through eternity. He wasn't born into the ruling classes and therefore had nothing to preserve, no morals, no obligations, no inheritance to maintain. He was one of the lucky few who saw life as short and aware that death was always around the corner. He saw complacency as the end of the free spirit, compromise as the beginning of the end of expectancy. Repatriation was the first surrender. Next came the inability to pay off the debt, while they had his passport. Then the complications of staying in one place too long and the developing of ties, and plans for the future and misdirected dreams of buying a house and having kids; while freedom drove him to a frosty winter's window to pine for the days of uncomplicated living day to day, before his passport rotted in a government office. One day he would be forced to pack his bags in nostalgia and regret all the time he'd lost in misdirected time.

To be free, as free as the kite with its string cut, to be free to fly over towns and cities and sail the clouds to the next country across the next sea. Onward, onward, free to blow with the wind forever. Forever free, loose of all strings that shackle life from birth to death. Each country enhanced a growing feeling of freedom in which money mattered less and less, in which each sunrise increased his optimism and renewed his faith in life as an uncharted course through time. For Rob knew he only lived once, and time was so short. The church clocks proved it. Tick went the clocks in Ipiales, tick... tick... tick... tick,,, tick, tick, tick, tick as they waited for their bus and watched the kite crash to the ground... tick...tick... tick... tick... tick...

In Pasto, someone took pity on Charlie and his toes and gifted him with a size eleven pair of tennis shoes. With a degree of relief and a touch of nostalgia, he threw the pair that had lasted eleven thousand miles into a gutter. They lay there as they boarded a bus for Cali, but a short while after, they were on the feet of a tall, skinny Colombian teenager who thought they were really hip and where feet were really at!

Cali was a modern city reminiscent of Brazil. The shops sold everything, the snack bars were full of cheap delights, and the pretty girls wriggled their bottoms as they passed on by. Tired, they found a room at the Hotel Vigo and agreed it was the best of the trip. They had their own private bathroom, side lamp and excessive space to use as they pleased. For three and a half dollars it wasn't bad. Taking a liberty, for the first time since Asuncion, they washed their jeans and scrubbed thoroughly all the dust of the last six thousand miles out of their other clothes. It was a beautiful feeling to be once again clothed in decent vestments (disregarding the rips and tears) rather than greasy rags hanging off them. That sort of thing didn't satisfy themselves, never mind common social convention. Yet Rob was convinced it would have been much more comfortable wearing nothing.

The following day on the way to the bus station, they were involved in an incident. Rob caught a Colombian attempting to sneak a hand into his shoulder bag. He grabbed him by the wrist and stopped six inches short of punching him in the face, to which the Colombian jumped back in fright and feigned drawing a knife. Everyone in the street turned to stare as the Colombian hotly denied attempted robbery. Rob, thankful he had caught the Colombian in action, motioned Charlie to carry on walking and mockingly told the Colombian that he was just an amateur. Letting the Colombian go, he followed Charlie up the street and made a comment to a passing policeman about law and order. He left the dumbfounded policeman in his wake and they continued on to the bus station.

The overnight bus wound up and down the Andes, leaving them tired and shattered. They arrived in Bogotá on a wet day, not unlike a summer's day in London. The hills rose close by the modern apartment blocks obscuring old church towers from the horizon. Being a Sunday, the city slept more than usual, the traffic sloshing along rather than screeching as it would on a week day. Although it rained, the tropical sun could still be felt through the racing cloud, the steam visibly rising off the roof tops. It was eleven fifty on a Sunday morning and Bogotá could have been anywhere in Europe, if not England itself.

Down on its streets roamed the dope dealers and

the corrupted cops looking for bribes. Chisellers hung on corners planning robberies, rip-offs, armed attacks or devious set-ups to outwit the unwary. Gangs of ten year old kids hunted to steal from tourists. Crime was rife and anything was legal on the streets of Bogotá. Pedestrians lived by staying alert and by their ability to run if things got tight. The city's streets were no-go areas at night, where even the prostitutes stayed indoors. Columbia was a nation that lived with fear. No one hitch-hiked, and no buses stopped between towns to pick up passengers. Daily murders and hold-ups on the country roads underlined the dangers. The narcotic syndicates ran Columbia from palatial mansions, while the impotent government representatives changed faces every four years, but changed very little else in their struggle for power and their lack of under-standing of what to do with it. Bogotá as the capital highlighted all the malcontent.

However, the country was doing will with its coffee and oil exports. The elections were over and the streets were less violent than usual as Rob and Charlie strolled down Carrera Septimus. Both stopped to laugh at a nine foot clown on stilts advertising meals at a local restaurant. In Quito, someone had given them an address of an English man living in Bogotá and had suggested if they got stuck to go and see him. He lived on Carrera Septimus. The found the flat, rang the bell and introduced themselves to a speechless twenty-six year old Walt Whittler, who out of politeness invited them in. He was wary of the two strangers, but after an hour he was convinced they were harmless and broke.

Walt was the proverbial inoffensive nice guy. He was another of these English teachers working abroad, and not exactly being paid the earth for doing so. But the choice was him and it was an escape from the humdrum, no chance of promotion prospects of a teaching post at a comprehensive school in the East End of London. The allure of a far fetched land was force enough for him to abandon the security of fish and chips, for rice and chicken, and tea for coffee. The additional handicap of being tone deaf to Spanish and dumb to its pronunciation was nothing. As long as he escaped the dunderheadedness of his punk rocker pupils or the semi-hippy mentality of treating them with love that his colleagues in the staff room insisted was the only way to make the punks respond to the usefulness of algebra in every day life. The loss of social contact, pub life and reading the Sunday newspapers in bed was compensated by pleasure trips to surrounding local beauty spots or neighbouring more exotic South American countries. His life had become one of self imposed isolation, where the self was the entertainer, the confidant, the introverted snob of colonial tastes in reading, music and worldly affairs viewed from the safe distance of a luxurious flat he could never afford back home. For home was still always England and although the humdrum no chance of promotion prospects of a teaching post in a comprehensive school in the East End had been the ultimate in laboured slavery, he had been at least only miserable forty hours a week and happy the other one hundred and twenty-eight. Out in Columbia time was passed, and passed in mediocrity, until the two year contract elapsed and freed him from his self imposed exile, where the dreams of mince pies and pints of beer were re-established in the gaiety of an East End pub, amidst a room of happy English drunks.

As Walt was a nice guy, he let Rob and Charlie sleep on his floor for two nights, let them listen to his Cat Stevens, Mike Harding and Fairport Convention tapes and made sure they had enough money to get themselves to Medellin.   And as he was a nice guy, Walt didn't care after that.

"I hope this guy shows up, he's our last hope" Rob sighed. "How much money have we left?" Charlie asked, pissed off, his face creased by dejection and self-pity caused by the sorry state of their financial affairs. "Twenty pesos" Rob countered. "That's about enough for a loaf of bread, three avocados and two bananas." "Jesus!  How are we going to get out of this place?" snapped Charlie. "Och, stop moaning. We'll survive." Rob motioned Charlie to take a seat on a bench beneath a tree. "Wait here and I'll go and buy breakfast." Just as Rob turned his back, Charlie said "I'm going to get repatriated." Rob laughed. "Wait there.  I'll be back soon."

In all seriousness, he always took Charlie's sudden flight of fancy as indications of youth and not of his rationale. But when he returned with the loaf and fruit he realised Charlie meant every word. "You're joking"

Rob blurted, lost for words, the shock even greater than the speechless stupor he had undergone when Colin had given them a hundred dollars. "No, I've had enough. I'll go the Consulate here and have them send me home." "Why?" Rob enquired. "Why do you want to quit now, after we've done the whole of South America together? We're so close to Panama. If you give up now, you're a fool. Why now, why Medellin?" "Why not? It's not the first time I've thought of going back," Charlie admitted. "When were the other times then? You never told me before. Its straight out of the blue. I just don't understand."

"I thought about it in Chalhuanca, when we were waiting for the truck, but you were too much into experimenting with cactus and engrossed in the bull fighting to notice I was pissed off. Anyway, there was nothing I could do in Chalhuanca. This time, I thought about for the whole fifteen hour bus journey from Bogotá, last night, and decided it was the best thing to do." "The best thing! It's the worst thing you could do" Rob was angry. "It's not a simple case of going along to the British Consulate and saying 'Please help me, I'm a poor lost boy, could you put me on the first plane to home?' Fuck no. They keep you hanging around while they check up with the Embassy in Bogotá, who get in touch with London, who finally make a decision. Meanwhile you've got to fend for yourself in a shit hole of a city with no money. And even if they ever get round to sending you back, the confiscate your passport until you pay them back for your flight. And then you might as well say goodbye to travelling for years if not for good. Because, if every time you ran out of money you got yourself repatriated, you would be better staying at home. If you're not big enough to go out in the world, don't go."

Just then bouncing down the street came the man they had been waiting for. He was an Americanised twenty-eight year old Colombian who had spent much of the last twelve years travelling the Americas and Europe. Dressed in blue boiler suit and yellow tee-shirt, his curly sun-bleached hair haloed a beaming smile and a pair of blue sparkling eyes. He bore down on the pair's conversation with a chuckle. "Sorry I've been so long, man! Them guys at the immigration office kept me hanging on. In the end I had to pay them fifteen dollars to get my exit stamp. Columbia's so screwed up, the only way to get permission to leave my own country is to pay them off. If you don't have money, you don't get out of Columbia ever."

Rob and Charlie had run into Jorgie Pardo at the local immigration office while seeking their own exit stamp. They were told to obtain theirs at Turbo on their way out of the country. Meanwhile, Charlie's despondent looks had attracted Jorgie's attention. With Charlie blurting out their plight of being penniless, Jorgie told them to meet him later, as he had to hang on to sort out his own business. Rob and Charlie, with no one else to turn to, waited just down the street until he appeared. "OK, let's go," Jorgie commanded, starting to move off. "No, Rob's coming," Charlie uttered. "But I'm going to find the Consulate." "Don't be daft, man" Rob said, concerned. "Come with us now, you can find it later." Deep down he felt that he had to keep Charlie away from the Consulate long enough so he could talk him out of it.

Charlie shrugged his shoulders, and thought that perhaps as it was getting late in the day, it would be better to seek the Consulate out the following morning. He gave Rob a defeated nod, picked up his backpack and followed on. "Where are going?" Rob asked Jorgie. "To where I work" he replied with a smile. "You'll see when we get there."

They took a bus across Medellin, along Carrera Forty-Five which rose steeply out of the centre of town and afforded a view of Columbia's third biggest city sprawling below. Its two million inhabitants were within half hour's walking distance of the green hills that cradled Medellin in the Magdellen Valley. Along the slopes, stood the barrio area, row upon row of houses, lacking the red roofs and chimneys which characteristically distinguish the back to back terraced houses of industrialised Northern England. But the barrios could easily have been England in the fifties.

They were let off at the junction with Calle 80. They walked a block, all the while Jorgie saying hello to friends, occasionally stopping to shake a hand. He was a popular man, his looks a winner with the women who stopped to drool as he said hello. He was a walking tidal wave, his smile mastered all the little ripples that were reflected back in his direction. Rob and Charlie felt that they were in good hands. After all, they had nothing to lose with only two pesos left between them.

They came to Jorgie's place of work, a single storey barrio house onto which he was building a second floor. He was the local building contractor, a family business passed down through the generations, specialising in adding on second storeys. This was Jorgie's sixty-fourth addition. Rob and Charlie were introduced to the two wide-eyed daughters of the house owner who appeared to be out for the day. It was obvious the two daughters were head over heel in love with Jorgie and he, married to a Brazilian girl from Rio, played on his exalted position by maintaining their love for him by keeping his distance.

The daughters made Rob and Charlie a *sancocho* soup while Jorgie went off to supervise his two workers busily constructing the roof of the second storey. He returned and took Rob and Charlie upstairs to watch the work in progress. To help things along, Jorgie rolled a twister which did the rounds of guests and workers and elevated the whole scene. Rob fell into conversation with Jorgie about travelling while Charlie slinked off to talk with the wide-eyed daughters before finally falling back to brooding on his repatriation. Later, everyone re-grouped below, while Charlie flicked through the telephone directory for the Consulate's address.

"Why does he want to go home?" Jorgie asked. "I don't know" Rob frowned, with outstretched hands. "He doesn't know either." Charlie continued to flick, trying to ignore the conversation being held in front of him. "He doesn't look ill to me" Jorgie stated. "If someone has caught a dangerous disease that is justification to go home. Are you listening, Charlie?" Charlie looked up, a sheepish look on his face, impervious to anything that was likely to be said to him. "You don't look as though you're dying of hunger either, you even look overweight. Hunger would be reason to be repatriated. You're not lonely, Rob's always close at hand. The only other reason I can think of is that you aren't man to face up to the situation you now find yourself in. Rob's carrying on no matter what, he's not giving up as soon as the going's rough. Let me tell you something now, if you got repatriated from here, you could never look Rob in the eye again and far more worse, you will never be able to trust yourself again, in any situation where you don't have money in your pocket, food to eat or someone to hold your hand. You're a mommy's boy and you might as well go home to mommy now."

Everyone focused in on Charlie, Jorgie, Rob, the two wide-eyed daughters and Jorgie's two workers. Even across the language barrier, everyone knew what was being said. Charlie didn't dare look up from the telephone directory which was now only a blur of words before him. "But" Jorgie continued "I like your friend. I don't even know why he stands by you when you're on the point of deserting him. You travelled around all of South America with him while the going was good, and now because you can't take any more you say 'to hell with my friend, I don't care what happens to him, I'm going home'." Jorgie paused. "When you started on this journey together it was like signing a marriage contract, for better for worse. But now you want divorce without even saying a word to Rob. The first he heard of it was this morning. Can you imagine his shock? If you think about it, you are the only one who has anything of value left. You have a good watch and an expensive camera and instead of selling those you'd rather spend much more on a flight back and be relieved at being home. Meanwhile, what happens to Rob?"

Charlie would still not raise his head, but Jorgie's words were beginning to sink in. Rob could only sit and listen, he no longer had the words to convince Charlie he was doing wrong. He was too much involved to decide clearly.

"Listen Charlie" Jorgie again. "Panama is the doorway to the world. Once in Panama you can go anywhere you want, Australia, America, Europe. From Panama things can only get better. You've come so far. To give up now with Panama so close is folly in itself. Think of yourself now. What story would you rather tell your friends at home? One, that you ran out of money in Columbia, got homesick, so got repatriated. Or two, you had run out of money in Columbia, begged and borrowed you way to Panama and taken the options of a ship to any port in the world. For in Panama you have options. Here in Medellin, you either desert your friend and fly disgraced in his eyes, back to your mother or you're going to pick yourself up, forget you ever thought about quitting, and get back on the road."

Jorgie finished, and everyone watched as Charlie thought out his decision. "You'd better hurry up and decide" Jorgie added. "To get some money you'll have to go to a pawn shop and they close at seven. It's five o'clock now."

Charlie spoke for the first time in an hour. "Where's the nearest pawn shop?" he asked meekly. "In the city" Jorgie stated with a smile. Rob let out a sigh of relief. "Let's go then, we haven't much time if you want to be on tonight's bus to Turbo."

They said their goodbyes to the wide-eyed daughters and all three of them and one of Jorgie's workmen Pablo, caught a bus into the city. They hunted out the company running a bus service to Turbo. One left at ten that evening and for two would cost four hundred and forty pesos. By now it was getting on for six-thirty. They set off in search of a pawn shop and eventually Jorgie chose one. He had a few words with the owner.

They all sat down. "OK" Jorgie said "get out anything that's valuable and make a pile." First out were the jackets they bought in Paraguay, they had little use for them now they were back in the tropical heat. Then their hats. The dominoes. Rob's agate heart he bought in Cristalina. Jorgie shook his head. "It's not enough" directing his look to Charlie's wrist. "What's up with you?" he asked.

"I'm not selling my watch. It was a birthday present" he replied. Rob gave Charlie a glaring stare. "It's your watch or we don't go." Charlie's watch joined the rest. Still it was not enough. Rob started to take his earring out but Jorgie told him there was no need. Charlie was the one holding out. Rob understood. It all rested on Charlie's camera.

Rob sat down, knowing he was no longer a part of the auction. Whether they caught the bus to Turbo or not depended on Charlie's willingness to part with his camera. "What about the camera, Charlie?" Jorgie prompted him. "No, I'm not selling the camera. That's that. If what we've put down is not worth four hundred and forty pesos then forget it. I'm going to the Consulate tomorrow. I'm not selling this camera."

Charlie began to pack up his belongings while Rob realised that Charlie thought his camera was worth more than he was as a friend. From there on in, Rob wanted only to teach Charlie a lesson. If materialistic things meant more to him than getting out of Medellin, then he deserved a lesson. Jorgie pointed to Rob and said to Charlie, "What about him? You go to the Consulate, but you do that and you've lost a friend for good."

Charlie, now completely lost, looked to Rob for advice but Rob could only look the other way. The decision was his. If Charlie couldn't see the answer, Rob didn't want to know him. "Alright, alright" Charlie almost screamed. "I'll sell it, but for no less than a hundred dollars. That's what it's worth." "You'll be lucky of you get thirty" Rob stated flatly, not giving a damn. As long as the camera was worth four hundred and forty pesos, for that was all it was worth to him. In Charlie's rucksack it wasn't worth a penny to anybody but Charlie.

The pawn shop owner and Jorgie had a quick talk and both disappeared out the back with the camera. Charlie, Rob and Pablo waited in silence. Five minutes, ten minutes, fifteen. Jorgie returned. "OK, he'll give you eighty dollars. Let's go and get the money." They left the shop and right away Rob guessed what was going on, but he no longer gave a damn. They walked three blocks, went into a bar and had a beer while Jorgie went off to collect the money for the camera. Charlie's suspicions began to grow, but Rob's had already calculated that this was going to teach Charlie a lesson.

Five, ten, fifteen minutes again passed as Pablo shifted uncomfortably in his chair. Rob watched for the slightest hint of the workman edging to leave. The seconds ticked like hours as Pablo waited for his moment to run. Then, in the through the door came Jorgie. "OK, here's two tickets to Turbo, on tonight's bus." He put them down on the table. Then he counted out the pesos. "A hundred forty, sixty, eight, eighty-five, ninety. OK, that's it. Here Rob, you take it."

Rob took the tickets and the money, relieved they had a way out of Medellin. Charlie immediately broke into shouts that he wanted his camera back. Jorgie agreed to oblige and they got up to leave. As they reached the door, Jorgie told Rob to hang back, that they were about to run off and leave Charlie stranded in the street. Rob agreed and hung back. Jorgie was about to be rewarded for his day's work by getting

Charlie's camera for a mere seventeen dollars. Charlie was being saved the disgrace and humiliation of being repatriated because he wasn't man enough to carry on. Rob, earlier that morning, had suggested they sell the camera so they would have enough money to travel on to Panama. Charlie's reluctance had now led him to be ripped off. Rob thought it fair. He' seen it coming, but they had two bus tickets for Turbo. From there they would only have a short sea journey to Colon in Panama. They were almost out of South America. And in one piece, despite Charlie's sulking with his desire to go home. For what was the loss of a few belongings if it saved their friendship.

Charlie was seeing red like a bull in front of a matador's cape. He was enraged with Jorgie for tricking him. He wanted his camera back. Seventeen dollars! He had been robbed. He shouldn't have agreed to sell it, all he wanted was an end to this hellish South American nightmare. Now he wasn't getting to go home. He had nothing. Nothing but Jorgie's back in his eyes as they stepped into the dark of the Medellin street.

Jorgie nodded to Pablo. They both broke into a run but Charlie caught Jorgie by an arm and swung him round. Everything exploded as they struggled and Charlie threw a punch which glanced off Jorgie's jaw. Pablo tried to pull Charlie off Jorgie, but to no avail. Charlie was blind with rage and knocked Jorgie to the ground.

Rob caught up with them. "Charlie! Man! Leave him alone!" he shouted as Charlie kicked Jorgie again and again. Charlie heard Rob's voice, but it took him a while to recognise it. He turned to face Rob and to his horror watched as Pablo lunged forward wielding a flick knife. Oh God, no. "Rob, Look out!" Charlie screamed. It was too late, Pablo was already withdrawing the knife from Rob's back. Pablo backed off and left Rob suspended in time, left him hanging in the air.

Jorgie scrambled to his feet as Rob slumped, then collapsed into the gutter. Jorgie and Pablo backed off into the dark, disappeared. Hunched over Rob as he bled to death in the dark of Medellin, Charlie had the fleetest recall of finding emeralds washed down from the mountains and lying in the gravel beds of all the rivers and lakes in South America.

"I've had the lesson, Charlie" Rob whispered into Charlie's ear. "Sorry for not looking out for you better." "What am I going to do?" Charlie uttered in despair. Rob smiled. "The thing about life is that once you've found the way to somewhere, you always know the way back."

Charlie held Rob in his arms, and cried.

Robbie Moffat was born in Glasgow, Scotland. As well as being a novelist he is a poet and a film maker. He began writing in his late teens and continues to write at the time of this publication. He currently lives in Buckinghamshire, England.

Other PALM TREE BOOKS by Robbie Moffat

NOVELS / NOVELLAS
Lost In The Landscape
The Lost Summer
The Desert
Christine and Her Teachest
The Loving
The Loving Child
The Loving Few
The Loving Many
Helmut Razor
The Great Getaway
Love The One You're With
POETRY
Complete Poetic Works
Rage Against The Light
The Wanderer
Universal Being
Frog
Sweet Surrender
BIOGRAPHY
Glasgow Boy

SCREENPLAYS
Hawk and the Dove
Seven Crosses
and many more

Please go online to find out more about the author

www.ingramcontent.com/pod-product-compliance
Lightning Source LLC
Chambersburg PA
CBHW060054150626
46556CB00017BA/660